"Believable characters trapped in a nightmare scenario—*Remains of the Dead* is a breathless, high-octane zombie thriller. [McKinnon has] written another great book here..."

—David Moody, author of *Hater* and *Dog Blood*

"Absolutely superb. This may be one of the scariest zombie books I've ever read. *Remains of the Dead* is tough as nails, defiant to the end, and the kind of book that reminds post-apocalyptic fans why we love the genre so. You've got to treat yourself to this book."

—Joe McKinney, author of *Dead City* and *Quarantined*

"McKinnon's strong writing, enthusiasm for head-busting action, and military know-how give the tale a you-are-there jolt of realism. Sure to please fans of *The Walking Dead*."

—Walter Greatshell, author of the *Xombies* series

"Yet another great zombie story with a Euro vibe. McKinnon illuminates the dark horror of the zombie apocalypse with the eloquence of the masters of UK literature."

—Bowie Ibarra, author of the *Down the Road* series

"Turns the intensity up a notch... The constant race against the undead, the desperate measures taken to survive at every turn, and the solid character development make this tale both a fun and invigorating read in the zombie genre."

—Patrick D'Orazio, author of *Comes the Dark*

"Hits dry land with an all-out sprint. Action-packed is not the word. This time it's war baby!"

—Remy Porter, author of *Dead Beat*

Also by Iain McKinnon

Domain of the Dead (Permuted Press)

IAIN MCKINNON

Acknowledgements
To Dave for being a mentor and inspiration.
To Audrey for wading through the raw nightmare.
To Emma for her reassurance.
To Don for his good nature when I pester him.
To Mum and Dad for your help, support and love.
To Alison for the love and tolerance.
To Brennus for filling my heart with joy.

A special thanks to all my friends on Facebook for your encouragement: Nick, Lyle, Richard, Keri, Paul, Mart, Aaron, Kevin, David, Kelly, Rachel, Cath, Matt and all the rest.

The soundtrack to writing this novel: Ink Dot Boy, How To Destroy Angels, and The Sisters Of Mercy.

A PERMUTED PRESS book
published by arrangement with the author
ISBN-13: 9781618680044
ISBN-10: 1618680048

Cover art by Craig Patton.

FOREWORD

If you're reading this, you probably get the whole zombie thing. You understand why legions of fans love them so, and how the genre manages to produce a glut of new books and movies and comics every month without its fan base going into terminal burn out. Others have already noted that there is a parallel between zombie fandom's ability to devour an ever-growing amount of new material and the insatiable appetites of the zombie itself, so I won't go over that ground here. Most fans shrug their shoulders at such commentary anyway. Suffice it to say that if you're a zombie fan, you don't need an explanation. You just need more cool zombie shit.

Fair enough.

But what of those people who are still mystified by the zombie phenomenon's growing popularity? What can we say to people who look at the zombie craze, shake their heads in disgust, and say, in all honesty, they see no redeeming value there whatsoever?

Well, first off, I'm not out to convert anyone. Some people just don't get it, don't care to, and won't be bothered by any reasonable explanation of the zombie genre and what it's saying about our lives and how we live them. More power to them. They are welcome to their opinion and I hope they have a nice day.

But there are quite a few people out there who are legitimately curious. They have watched the amazing proliferation of zombie-related material shambling into our lives and wondered if there's something of value there. Perhaps, if they're especially sensitive to social trends, they've even noticed that zombies have gone beyond the commercial success of *The Walking Dead*, *World War Z* and *Pride and Prejudice and Zombies* to infect our very language as well. They have successfully crossed over from mere pop culture references to accepted mainstream groupspeak. For example, following World War II we described people in shock as having the "2000 yard stare," after the Tom Lea painting of a Marine from the Battle of Peleliu. But today, we're just as likely to say "that person looks like a zombie," or "has that zombie look in his eyes." Going further, we see well respected professional economists such as Jeremy Grantham writing articles with titles like "Night of the Living Fed." Professional forensic accountants, testifying before the Supreme Court and Senate select committees, speak of zombie businesses. Computer experts freely use terms like zombie terminals and zombie programs. And on and on.

So what does all this mean? What's the point? Well, at a minimum, I think it suggests that once a concept becomes so integral to a society that it pervades the very language that society speaks, we are no longer free to dismiss that concept's significance. And with the zombie, we now seem to be talking about something more than yet another horror fiction trope. We are watching the apotheosis of a B movie icon into a full fledged member of our modern day mythology.

That's a grand claim, I know, but consider the shift in thinking behind the zombie's recent elevation. Horror fiction has a long standing tradition of using monsters as metaphor. *Frankenstein*'s creature played to our fear of science without a sense of moral responsibility. *Dracula* was, for the Victorians, an intensely sexual book, and an uncomfortable indictment of their cultural sensibilities. The space invaders of the 50s and 60s were thinly veiled Communists. Godzilla was the bastard stepchild of the bomb. Kurt Barlow was Stephen King's personification of the disease killing America's small towns. In each case, the monster was not only interesting, but stood for something.

The zombie too has been used as a metaphor. In fact, zombie writers have embraced this concept with gusto. George Romero used the zombie to criticize everything from racism to rampant consumerism. Max Brooks used *World War Z* as an amazingly subtle critique of world politics. Seth Grahame-Smith even managed to sneak in a little literary criticism with *Pride and Prejudice and Zombies*. The list goes on, but I think the point is made. The zombie as metaphor is simply part of a long literary tradition of making monsters matter.

Likewise, the zombie is nothing new in terms of what it is, which is basically your run of the mill revenant. It is a dead thing that has come back to pester the living, same as every ghost that's come before it, same as *Dracula* and his imitators, same as *Frankenstein*'s creature. All of which begs the question: if the zombie is just business as usual, how can I say it is something so completely new?

The answer lies in the zombie's plurality. All of the monsters named above are distinctive because they are singular. There is just one of them. They are monstrous because they are so different from the humans they torment, and yet we can humanize them because they have distinctive personalities.

Not so the zombie. The zombie, as many writers have pointed out (myself included), is a blank slate upon which nearly any fear or social commentary can be projected.

And of course, there's the fact that you never get just one zombie. You get wave upon relentless wave of them. Yes, they are plodding and stupid, but they are endowed with a single-mindedness that is as frightening as it is total. The individual zombie is nothing special. Detestable, yes. Frightening, certainly. One might safely say that a walking corpse is profound without being accused of waxing hyperbolic. But a single zombie is not an insurmountable obstacle. Even those who have never seen a zombie movie, or read a Max Brook book, know how to dispatch it. Destroy the brain with a gunshot or blunt object and the deed is done. Simple as that. Repeat as many times as necessary, or until you and your small band of survivors are all dead.

This leads, naturally enough, to the most common criticism of zombie fiction. Detractors accuse the genre, perhaps rightly, of being somewhat static. There is little content, they say, beyond the tidal motion of zombie violence, where the dead advance, are repelled, advance again, get repelled again, and so on until the reader grows numb and the continuing survival of the characters pointless. Why is this popular, they ask.

I would argue that this tidal motion, its endless repetition, is exactly what gives the genre its vitality.

Let me explain.

Modern life has a tediousness to it that is almost tragic. We go to work on Monday and begin the soul-sucking process of wading through an endless stream of bullshit emails. We move an endless amount of paperwork from pile A to pile B, then back again. We fill out forms that lead to more forms. Work takes on a painful sort of circularity, like dogs at the racetrack sprinting after fake rabbits. Those of you working retail know this pain at the molecular level.

Given the seeming pointlessness of it all, is it any wonder that the human spirit seeks to rebel? Is it any wonder that our creative minds seek to put a face on so much circularity, and annihilate it?

That's where books like the one you hold in your hands come in. With *Remains of the Dead*, Iain McKinnon has harnessed the caged rage of the modern worker, and given him back his defiant roar. The war he describes is of course one of attrition. Zombies attack and people die. And this happens again and again.

But this is hardly sloppy storytelling. Quite the reverse, actually. This is your life, your job, he's describing—only with zombies.

So turn the page and get mad for a while. Fight back, if only against the meat puppets of the mind.

And be glad you had this chance to vent.

Joe McKinney
San Antonio, Texas
August 31, 2011

"The heavens roared as with thunder and from the earth came the sound of moans. Storm clouds blackened the heavens and the world was shrouded in the stillness of death. Lightning cracked across the skies and flames flared up from the ground. From the bloated clouds there came rain, and the rain washed all life before it. When the flashes in the sky had died and the flames had withered all that remained was as ash."

—*Epic of Gilgamesh*

CHAPTER ONE
ALL THE TOWNS' FOLK

Dejected by the dead world beneath him, Cahz closed his eyes and listened to the throb of the helicopter's engine. The constant heavy beating of the blades and the drone of the turbine encased him in noise. He cradled the solid metal body of his carbine, its hard surface reassuring to his touch. The weapon sat in an unorthodox position, butt hooked over his forearm with the muzzle pointing at his feet. With every rock or turn the chopper made, the stock jostled against the helmet sitting in his lap, making a low clunking noise.

It was a sound almost lost to the din of the cabin, but Cahz felt it and loathed it, like the incessant dripping of a leaky tap, coercing his silent rage to a crescendo. With his eyes closed he focused on his physical state. His backside was numb, his legs were aching for a stretch, and there was a sharp pain in his shoulder from a strap on his body armour that was biting into his flesh. But it was the most comfortable arrangement he could muster.

The view from the chopper proved to be no distraction. Out of the window the corpse of one more unimportant city lay before him, ragged and dirtied by violence, neglect and nature flaking away the remnants of civilization. They were cities populated by the walking dead—the men, women and children who had found no rest in their demise. The wretched creatures were tortured by a malodorous and corrupt immortality that robbed them of their vital spark and imposed a ravenous hunger. They were forever-shambling husks in a perpetual hunt for living flesh.

Cahz opened his eyes, desperate to lose the nagging dread of coming in country. He purposefully kept his gaze inside the cabin and focused his attention on the minutia.

To his right was an invisible demarcation line—a few extra inches of space he would not cross. That area belonged to Idris, the pilot. Cahz didn't like to engage him in conversation or intrude on his side of the cabin. It wasn't a festering hostility that made Cahz standoffish. It was fear. Not fear of the man; Idris was a nice enough guy, a bit reserved and quiet, but there was nothing menacing about him. Cahz was fearful of something going wrong.

It was the fear that he might initiate some distraction that would cause them to crash, were he to nudge Idris' elbow at the vital point in a manoeuvre or break his concentration at a crucial moment. It wasn't that Cahz feared dying. After all, these days there were worse things than death.

He looked around the cabin trying to distract himself from the discomfort and noise.

The chopper they flew in hadn't been designed to ferry troops but it served well enough in its current roll. She was small, not so much compact as cramped, but she had good fuel economy and an excellent range. All things considered not a bad run about. Cahz very much doubted any new helicopters had come off any production lines for some years now. This was the third chopper sequestered to them in as many years. The first broke down and was dismantled for parts; he assumed because the vital part that was broken no longer had a replacement. The second chopper no one knew what happened to it or its crew. It flew out one bright morning on a specimen run and never returned. No distress call, no wreckage, nothing. She just vanished.

Maybe it's still down there in that grey landscape, Cahz thought. The land, for all its greenery, looked washed out and dreary. It was a depressing sight.

Thirty minutes ago he'd been briefly occupied by the sunrise—a palette of vivid golds, azure blues and iridescent pinks as the lingering period of murky twilight was forced back. It was beautiful; a rare splash of colour to this dead world.

However, the brilliant orange glow had quickly been obscured by a flock of dark rain laden clouds. With that the world had taken on the depressing insipid hues that shrouded the dead below. And as it did the claustrophobic oppression had returned.

Cahz had been a soldier all his adult life. He'd lost count of the number of flights over hostile territory—flights far more dangerous than this. The enemy below didn't fire ground-to-air missiles, they didn't drive a car packed full of explosives into your base, and they didn't leave indiscriminate booby traps. He'd served much of his time in uniform fighting insurgents, being shot at and bombed. But this world was a long way from those tours. In the old world people had tried to kill him, people had tried to help him and some people couldn't have cared less about him. But there were always people. The villages or towns or cities may have been battle damaged, but without fail life would return. The traders would reopen the market, the housewife would brush out the dirt and shattered glass and the kids would play in the street.

Not now. The city below was scarred from the damage inflicted during the chaos of collapse. But the wounds to the cityscape hadn't been healed by man. Instead nature had started the long task of breaking the concrete down and reclaiming the land, soothing the harsh grey back to a verdant green.

Unable to escape the dismay overwhelming his consciousness, Cahz purposefully switched back to his military mindset, preoccupying himself with the practical aspects of his mission.

He toggled his radio. "Angel, what's your situation?"

"Secure and in position," Angel answered in her thick Russian accent. "I have eyes on Bate and field of fire is good."

"Bates, how's your position?" Cahz asked.

Bates' voice crackled over the short range radio, "A-okay. Area is clear. Capture net is set. Activity is high but I'm ready when you are."

Cahz re-examined the terrain below. Raggedy figures shambled their way towards his man on the ground.

There were more than he'd expected. Normally their quarry was thinly spread out from their aimless wanderings, but here they looked more concentrated.

Still, it might make things go quicker, Cahz thought as he cast his gaze out at the dead city.

He craned round, trying to take in as much of the terrain as possible when he caught the eye of the last member of his team. Cannon was a giant of a man and had to cock his head slightly to fit in the cabin. His broad muscular chest wouldn't have looked out of place on a power lifter. And now he was wedged into the back of the tiny chopper.

At least I get to ride shotgun, Cahz reminded himself.

Even though the other two team members were on the ground,

Cannon filled the back seats. His only relief was the half hour or so when they set up and executed the collection. As soon as Bates and Angel were back in the cabin Cannon spent his time crushed up against the door.

The whole nine hours or so the round trip took, Cannon and Idris wouldn't leave their seats.

"Your biggest risk," Bates had once joked, "is getting deep vein thrombosis from sitting on your ass."

Cannon had quipped back, "And your biggest risk is me."

"I don't know why you insist on coming along," Cahz had commented long ago. "Let French or one of the Marines come in country."

Cannon had pouted ever so slightly in disdain, "And who'd look after your ass?"

That was all the dissuasion there would be. Cannon just sat there quietly waiting for his commander to take the lead.

It always amazed Cahz that even in this shattered world the logistics corps had produced body armour large enough to fit his frame. It had proven impossible to supply one small part for a helicopter and yet extra-extra large tactical vests were common fare.

"How's it look to you?" Cahz asked.

"Looks risky boss," Cannon said, "but that's what they pay us for."

Cahz gave a chortle. "When did you last get paid? You got a Cayman Island account I don't know about?"

Cannon gave a wry smile.

"Quicker we get this done the quicker we go home," Cahz said, turning back round. He shifted the carbine and fidgeted to get back into a semi-comfortable position before pulling his mission map from a pouch on his body armour.

He stared at the map. The paper was crisp and new but it might as well be a century's old piece of parchment. It may have been printed only six or seven years ago but the land below bore little resemblance. The sweeping roads were broken and incomplete, the sprawling cities crumbling to rubble and the place names lost to human awareness.

The city below looked anything but familiar underneath the grime and feral vegetation—a terrain more hostile and more deadly than any map could indicate.

After the loss of a chopper and its crew the ship's captain had argued for reducing the complement on specimen runs. The captain had wanted to reduce risk exposure. In theory a collection crew could consist of just two men. The pilot was a given but the capture net only needed one man to set it. Maybe the team size would have been cut if it hadn't been for Cahz's arguments. The extra manpower was an insurance policy in case of the unexpected. If anything did go wrong out here Cahz knew the only chance for survival was to work as a team.

Like the map the mission plan was not the reality. On paper things weren't as messy.

Cahz toggled his radio again. "Okay people, let's make this clean and quick. Bates, call them in."

He let his thumb slip off the send button and looked out over the crumbling city.

Things were certainly a mess out here.

***

"Get up, Ali!"

Ali was wrenched out of his sleep. He swallowed deep in his parched throat, trying to move the sticky mucus from his mouth.

People were shouting and rushing around. Doors slamming and lights blazing.

The warehouse was alive with the sounds of panic.

Ali opened his eyes but the bright lights made him blink and turn away.

More tentatively Ali peaked out from behind his eyelids, hand against his brow fending off the worst of the light. The hollering in the warehouse pressed in and he felt the panic gash a hole through his grogginess.

The main lights were on and Ali knew that was significant. The trickle of power the survivors got from their rooftop solar cells wasn't enough to feed the lights. Power must be getting drawn from the batteries. He knew that electricity was precious. To use it for the lights meant there'd be no power left for the microwave oven or the hot plate or any of the other atavistic appliances they relied upon.

He unzipped his sleeping bag and tussled with its embrace to get his feet free. As he kicked it loose he glanced around. His fellow inmates were bounding to their feet. They shouted and clamoured but Ali couldn't hear the tell-tale moans or see any shambling figures.

"Where?!" Ali barked out, pulling himself upright.

"On the roof!" Ryan, dressed in just his underwear, called back as he disappeared towards the stairwell.

Ali was standing now, alert and solid. Straight backed, adrenaline coursing through him, scanning the room for danger. Ali was a big man but he wasn't a youth like Ryan. His body wasn't as taut as the younger man's but he was still powerful. He knew that even after months of emaciation he could still put up a fight against the ghouls.

Ali looked at the stair door as it swung shut and mumbled to himself, "How could they be on the roof?"

If the zombies outside ever broke through he'd anticipated one of the fire doors or the main entrance would be the source. The roof didn't make sense. How could zombies get up there?

With a flicker of insight Ali surmised the roof must be where his fellow survivors were retreating. Glancing round, there was no immediate threat. He looked down at his bare feet. He had been sleeping in a vest and threadbare underpants. He knew his long black beard would be wild and unruly, his hair just as untamed. He knew he looked a sight. Hastily, Ali pulled his jeans on and slipped his feet into his shoes.

"Where are they coming from?" George asked no one in particular as he bumbled through the door.

"Don't know," Elspeth admitted, scurrying after him, cradling a baby in her arms.

The warehouse was strangely still. He was the last of the group to leave for the roof and now he stood alone in the threatening silence. As he pulled his thick and well worn shirt on, Ali listened for the moans of the zombies drawing closer. All he could hear were the footfalls in the stairwell and beyond that...

Ail focused carefully and tuned in. There it was like an unending incantation. The incessant droning of a thousand coarse voices conveyed in the air as background noise.

The whole situation confused him. There were no hordes of undead pressing into the warehouse, yet his companions had run off to the roof.

Still no less confused, Ali left his bedside and made his way up. He was perplexed by what was going on but no longer fearful of imminent attack.

His head pounded. He wasn't sure if it was the startled wakening or the lack of coffee. His knees creaked almost as loudly as the heavy fire door he barged open to access the stairs. His big frame, greatly reduced by the starvation rations, had taken its toll on his joints. There had been a pallet of cod liver oil tablets in the warehouse and for years he'd taken a capsule every day. One day he'd opened a tub to find the gelatine had spoiled, leaving the contents to ooze to the bottom of the container. That marked the end of his self-medication and his joints had started aching ever the more.

With each step his joints eased off. It was always hard for Ali to get going in the morning these days. He would shuffle around much like the undead outside until his ligaments and muscles had eased off.

Only in his mid-forties and Ali felt that every morning he awoke he was on the steep slope to old age. The cold metal handrail made his stiff fingers tingle unpleasantly. He let out a shallow cough that echoed off the rough brick walls in the empty stairwell.

If I feel so bad just waking up, he thought, *how must those dead fucks outside feel?*

Ali spoke to the empty walls as he hauled himself onto the last step, "Maybe that's why you moan."

At the top of the stairs he swung the door open, flooding the stairwell with natural light. It took a few seconds to adjust to the brightness and when he did he saw the whole group there.

Sarah, her light brown hair whipping in the wind, stood shoulder to shoulder with Ryan at the edge of the roof. Ryan looked cold. He stood there bare footed, wearing only his flimsy boxer shorts. Slightly behind them was Nathan, arms folded close to his chest and appearing as cold as Ryan despite wearing jeans and a t-shirt. Behind them Ray stood with the elf-like eight year old Jennifer, now the second youngest of the group since Samantha's baby had been born. At the back George and Elspeth stood not far from the door.

Elspeth cradled her granddaughter in her arms. Her dull grey hair and the weathered lines around her eyes and lips seemed to disappear when she held the girl. She held her tight to her chest the way she'd held the infant's dying mother not so long ago. No doubt these past few months had been the hardest she'd faced since settling here, the newborn girl a constant link with the daughter she had lost.

It struck Ali that the sweet infant in her arms must stir a conflicting bundle of emotions for her—the joy of a granddaughter and a reminder of the cost of her birth.

Elspeth's daughter, Samantha, had hooked up with Ryan. Ali had never used any romantic terms to define their relationship. Ryan, Samantha, Sarah and Nathan were all a similar age. It was inevitable than in such close proximity, with youthful hormones brewing, that there would be a pairing. Nathan had hit on Sarah, unsuccessfully as far as Ali could tell, but Ryan and Samantha had come together. He had heard them in the echoing warehouse even when they'd tried to conceal their trysts. The warehouse was big but there were few private spots.

"What's going on, George?" Ali asked the old man next to him.

"Sarah's seen a helicopter." George flashed a smile that showed he'd taken the time to put in his false teeth.

"There's music playing," Elspeth helpfully added.

Ali was taken aback. "A helicopter?"

He cocked his head slightly and listened. He took a few paces further onto the roof and stopped by the water butts. His long black beard bobbed in the gusts of wind. With his thick hands he stroked the hair tame. As he stood there holding the point of his beard he picked up the music drifting on the wind.

The army of corpses below also heard it. From their besieging positions around the warehouse, some of the undead had started wandering towards the noise.

Nathan stood slightly hunched against the cold. He asked, "So what do we do? Light a signal fire or something?"

"They might think it was just an accidental fire," Ryan pointed out.

Nathan turned round, running his gaze over the rest of the roof. "Maybe we could use the solar panels like signal mirrors?"

"They're not looking for us—they're not looking for *anyone*," Sarah said, her voice carrying a note of dismay. "They're not expecting anyone left alive."

"So what are they here for?" Ray asked, speaking up for the first time.

Ray was a logical man. Happier working out problems on paper than engaging in the practicalities. Ali remembered when they'd first arrived here Ray had spent the best part of a week cataloguing the pallets of supplies within.

With his index finger Ray shoved his glasses further up his nose, as much a habit as a necessity. "If they're scavengers they're shit out of luck," he said. "There's nothing left. We've picked this place clean."

"Wasn't much to pick," Nathan complained.

Ryan shrugged his heavyset shoulders. "So how do we signal them?"

Sarah was stolid. "We don't. We go to them."

"*Go to them*, girl?" George's overly loud interjection startled Ali. The power behind that old voice was stronger than Ali had heard in some time. George shook his head, nodding in the direction of the music. "We don't even know who they are."

"He's got a point," Ryan agreed. "They could be worse than those things."

"They might shoot us as soon as help us," Elspeth added.

Sarah turned her attention away from the ruined city to look at her comrades. "It's been years since we've seen any marauders and none of them were in helicopters. Anyway, they're advertising their presence with the music. It's like they want to cause a commotion to shake the place up." Sarah paused and pressed her tongue to her bottom lip in contemplation. Finally she said, "No. This has been our only chance of escape in years and it may be our last."

"Sarah, think about it," George said, taking a half step forward, "We're safe in here." With an arm carpeted in grey hair he gestured back at the warehouse door. "The moment we open the shutters there'll be no turning back. They'll be in here and there won't be no way of stoppin' 'em."

Sarah shook her head slightly. "How much longer will we be safe in here?"

No one answered. No one wanted to confront the truth.

Ali wasn't the smartest of men but he'd picked up on whispered conversations over the past couple of months. He'd watched as the gaunt bespectacled man had scurried around the warehouse with his clipboard in hand.

"Tell them straight, Ray," Sarah demanded, breaking the silence.

Ray muttered into his chest like a chastised school boy, "I don't know."

"Ray!" Sarah barked.

"Maybe four or five weeks worth of food," Ray admitted, "and that's rationing out even thinner than now."

Elspeth's face dropped, shocked by the revelation.

The predicament wasn't a shock to Ali. Like most of the survivors he had been complicit in his ignorance, preferring to ignore the inevitable for as long as possible. Ali had pushed aside the thoughts of how perilous their existence was. He knew the food would run out but he knew there was nothing they could do about it. Each winter he had foraged among the decaying buildings trying to find supplies of food. As the years dragged on they had to forage further afield. The incident with the cod liver oil capsules had brought things into sharp focus. Knowing their plight last winter he'd gone out further than ever before. He and the younger ones had fashioned a sledge and set up a series of waypoints. It was the longest any of them had spent away from the warehouse since they'd arrived. Day after day they picked through the frozen dead and frost shattered rubble in a vain attempt to bolster their dwindling supplies. But the town had already been gutted.

When the first thaws of spring released the dead from their icy prisons it was time to retreat. And as the snow of winter had melted away, a steady trickle of undead had found them, like migrating birds finding the same nesting site year after year. In previous years even the most concerted winter cull had proven futile. Come spring the undead would return. Slowly at first, a handful at a time, but before long there were thousands crushed up against the fences. Summer was still at least a month away but already the warehouse was swamped.

Ali tuned back in to the conversation to hear Nathan complain, "Ryan's guzzled the last of the Jack."

"Nathan!" Elspeth chided from next to him.

Ryan faced the group from the lip of the roof and asked, "What do we do?"

He stood there, his skin numbed from the cold, casting his gaze across everyone. Ryan was hoping that someone could come up with a better plan, but as he looked at his emaciated friends no one did.

"Fuck it," Nathan said, breaking the awkwardness. "Sarah's right. We have to go to them."

Ali stroked his rowdy beard flat and took a deep swallow to lubricate his voice and said against the wind, "Hold on."

It seemed that even the baby in Elspeth's arms went quiet as everyone turned to look at him.

"You're seriously suggesting we go out there?" Ali looked over the heads of his audience into the distance where the chopper had been spotted.

Sarah's voice was acidic, "What else would you suggest?"

Sarah had been quite cold towards him in the early days. Ali was used to it; he'd always been an outsider and maybe that suited him. Now looking out at the people he'd been thrown in with—*incarcerated with*—people he would never have chosen to be with, he realised these were the closest friends he'd ever had. Always quiet, always reserved, Ali had kept himself to himself but in the close confinement of their sanctuary the time had worn down many barriers. After those first fearful months they'd started to grow together. Week on week, month on month, year on year the barriers had melted away. Every one of these people were his friends and Ali knew they would all die if they didn't make the right decision.

He asked the crowd, "You're thinking things are so bad that it justifies going out there?"

Sarah caught Ray's eye before speaking. "They will be in a month."

Ali could see what Sarah was trying to do. She was trying to force the group to the same conclusion she had. But he knew that the older people, George and Elspeth, wouldn't budge if they felt pressured.

"There are thousands of those pus bags between here and there. One bite, one scratch and that's all it takes to turn you." Looking around, Ali checked that the gravity of what he had just said had sunk in. He continued highlighting the unknowns to his companions. "You plan on dodging those things long enough to get to a helicopter full of people who are mystery to you?"

Ray shuffled nervously but other than that the group was silent.

"As Elspeth said, they may not be friendly, they may want to shoot us, they may refuse to take us. What then?" Ali paused for a response.

"We don't have time to argue this," Ryan said. "Who knows how long they'll be there."

"Is it truly worth the risk?" Ali asked. "Do you want to wait here and starve to death or take the chance?"

The congregation on the rooftop started looking at each other. Ali could see people were starting to seriously weigh up the two options, the slow death through starvation or the risk of trying to get help.

"I only say that because everyone has to be sure what choice there is."

Ali leant back against a water tank and waited for the group to decide. He already knew the only option. Starving to death would drive everyone mad. They'd end up fighting each other for crumbs. He remembered his grandmother telling him of a famine when she was a girl. He remembered her arthritis gnarled fingers jabbing out at him as she told of how she'd eaten the rats that were gnawing on her brother's corpse. Ali never knew how true her stories were, but the fear he had as a boy sitting on the floor looking up at the ancient matriarch was with him again.

Even if their bid for safety failed at least they would die trying. And that was one thing his grandmother had instilled in him: keep fighting because in the end all you have is what you fight for.

Slowly the group started to look more solemn as one by one they came round to Sarah's side.

Sensing the change in mood, Sarah said, "Okay, leave everything. Only carry a weapon. It's not far to the square but there's a lot of them and we'll have to run the whole way. Nathan, Ryan, get all the Molotov cocktails we have left. Let's try to thin them out."

Ali smiled as he watched Sarah pull the group together. She had a knack for taking charge, a natural leadership. She was smart and pretty even with the trendy lip piercing.

Ali took a moment to survey his friends. Ryan and Nathan were already rushing to the floor access to get the petrol bombs. They were young men, strong with youth. Ryan was physically bigger than all the rest of the survivors but Ali worried more about him than anyone else.

The past few months he'd hardly spent a day sober as he'd tried to drown out the pain of his loss. Elspeth, he knew, had suffered Samantha's death more deeply than the rest. The other survivors had lost a friend but Elspeth had lost a daughter. But there, clutched in her arms, swaddled in a cream shawl, was her reason to push past the pain.

Looking at their faces it was obvious that Ray, George and Elspeth were lost, frozen by the enormity of the group's decision. Ali knew he would have to ease them into action.

"Jennifer," Ali called out to the small girl, "let's go downstairs and get dressed properly before we go out."

Stretching out an arm, Ali offered the eight year old a hand. He guessed she was about eight, no one could be sure. The orphan knew she was four when they'd found her but she couldn't say when her birthday was so her age was an ongoing estimation.

"Come on," Ali called to the rest of the group. "Best we hurry."

CHAPTER TWO
HEAD COUNT

A jump of static on his radio pulled Cahz away from scanning the terrain.

"Don't know what make worst noise—you or the dead," Angel announced.

Cahz cast a look around, puzzled by the Russian sniper's comment.

"You come down here and say that, Angel!" came Bates' angry response.

Cahz craned his neck to see Bates down on the ground. The young soldier was standing in the middle of the car park where he'd been dropped off, the capture net beneath his feet. Cahz grinned as he heard Angel let loose some Russian obscenity. Bates, agitated, stood with one foot atop his battered ghetto blaster, gesturing at a nearby office block, his weapon slack by his side. It was a good natured exchange of insults, but it was just that kind of lapse of concentration that got people killed.

"Stay on station, Bates," Cahz said, breaking into the exchange.

"Angel, speak English!" Bates replied, ignoring Cahz.

"Burak!" Angel cursed.

"Oh, that's it!" Bates voice hissed over the radio. "I know what that one means! I'm coming up there to kick your ass—"

"Bates!" Cahz snapped. "Stay on station."

"Roger that, boss," came back Bates' cowed response.

"Those two are like my parents," Idris offered.

Cannon laughed, remembering the end of the gag.

"They argue a lot and don't have sex?" Idris offered.

Cahz didn't respond. He was still looking out of the window at Bates on the ground. The wisecracking soldier was still looking agitated on the cargo net. It was all displacement, Cahz knew, a distraction from the reality of their surroundings. You needed a certain level of detachment to visit these ghost cities, but too much and you became oblivious to the dangers shambling around.

Again the blurt of static grabbed Cahz's attention.

"Bait, this is Angel. One Whisky Delta, seven o'clock, one hundred yards out."

"Don't start with me!" The frustration in Bates voice was obvious even through the poor radio communication. "Don't call me bait! You know it makes me jumpy."

"Is your name," came Angel's response, the sarcasm dripping from her Eastern European accent.

"It's *Batesssss*! You leave out the S on purpose."

Cahz whispered "Fuck sake," before toggling his mic.

"Bates, Angel, this is Lieutenant Cahzalid. You will observe proper radio discipline. Is that clear? No more horseshit!"

After a few seconds Bates replied to Angel's contact using the proper protocol.

Confirming she understood Cahz's annoyance, but without admitting her part Angel too reported back, "This is Angel. Multiple contacts all vectors."

"What's the count, Angel?" Cahz asked, but before he could get an answer a shot rung out.

He whipped round trying to ascertain the threat. He couldn't see where the shot had come from nor its intended target.

"Did you see anything?" he asked the other occupants of the chopper.

"Can't see anything kicking off, boss." Cannon admitted.

"Who fired?!" Cahz barked into his mic.

"Me sir," Bates replied.

Cahz looked down at Bates through the glass foot well of the helicopter. "What the hell was that for? I didn't see any W.D.'s in your immediate vicinity."

"No, there weren't," Bates said. "Caught one that looked like John Prage a hundred yards out. I just had to pop one in his head."

"Who the fuck is John Prage?" Cahz immediately realised he'd regret asking that question. "No, forget it. We don't have time. Angel, say again. What are the numbers?"

Bates didn't hear or didn't care that Cahz didn't want to know. "He was this prick I used to work with. If anybody deserved to get bit it was him."

"Shut the fuck up, Bates, or you're on report," Cahz snapped.

Bates had the sense not to cut in.

Cahz repeated his question: "Angel, what's the count?"

"Too many, sir. Suggest we abort and find clearer ground," Angel reported. "There's also smoke. W.D. must have set off something flammable."

Cahz looked over at Idris, the helicopter pilot. "Spin us around to get a look."

"Sure," Idris replied.

The chopper dipped slightly and made a gentle turn.

Looking out over the ruined city, Cahz could see a precession of grey corpses snaking their way around the derelict cars and other debris to the lure below. He craned round to talk to his right-hand man.

Cannon had shifted slightly, his head cocked in the opposite direction from the last time Cahz had looked. The sour expression Cannon wore owed more to the discomfort than his gruff disposition.

Before Cahz could speak, the bear of a man piped up, "There's too many of them, boss."

"Something must be drawing the Whisky Deltas in," Cahz said, thinking out loud.

"But what, boss?" Cannon asked. "World's been dead a long time."

"I haven't seen this many in one place since that op' in Norfolk." Cahz looked through the view port at his feet, at Bates standing on the cargo net below. "It's academic anyway," he said, more to himself than any of his crew. He turned to the pilot. "How are we for fuel?"

"We're good. Why'd you ask?" Idris said.

"It's early and the weather's clear. If we've got the fuel we can try for an alternative site."

Even with the helmet and mic obscuring his face, Cahz could see Idris suck in his cheeks as he considered the option.

"We've come pretty far out for the operational range," Idris said. "As long as we back tracked and found something on the way home..." Idris paused for a moment, making a circling motion with his index finger as he calculated something in his mind. "Yeah, if we head for home and spot a landing site we overlooked on the way back I can give you twenty, maybe thirty minutes."

Cahz looked back at Cannon. "What you reckon? Twenty minutes enough?"

"Pushing it—we'd be closer to thirty," Cannon surmised.

Cahz checked his watch. It was still early and he estimated there would be another twelve or so hours of daylight. He turned his attention to Idris. "If the fuel tanks can take an extra thirty minutes we'll still make it back in time for chow."

Idris nodded. "Yeah, if the weather stays good, half an hour isn't going to tax the bird too much. But I don't need to remind you weather reports aren't as accurate as they used to be."

"If we spot a viable site on the way back all well and good. Failing that we miss out on the employee-of-the-month bonus."

Cannon gave a snorting snigger at Cahz's quip.

Cahz flipped the radio on his shoulder to transmit to the two on the ground. "Angel, Bates, we're bugging out. Angel, is your position secure?"

"Yes, Lieutenant," Angel replied.

Cahz addressed everyone over his microphone: "Let's move before those W.D.'s and that fire give us cause for concern." He looked out of the window at the rolling black clouds of smoke. "Okay then. Bates, you're first up. Confirm your harness is secure and clean."

Bates spoke into his radio, "Affirmative, Lieutenant. We're good to go."

Cahz watched the pockets of smoke. As he watched, they grew, but they didn't look like a normal fire. The smoke seemed to be concentrated into patches rather than carpeting an area as he would expect. They looked like the Indian smoke signals from an old western. He hadn't seen anything on the way in, and now as he watched, a fifth distinct plume of smoke started to rise up above the buildings. He couldn't see the actual fires behind the ruins and he had no time to investigate.

"Cahz!" Angel hollered over the radio, a tremor in her voice. "We've got live ones!"

Cahz, alert from Angel's exclamation, looked around at the multitude of undead below. He mulled her words over in his mind. *Live ones.* Did she mean the dead were particularly active or had she spotted survivors?

"Say again, Angel."

"Multiple humans fighting their way toward Bates. Seven, maybe eight." Angel's voice dropped. "Ah jeez, they just lost one. Coming in on four o'clock."

Cannon lent forward from the back of the chopper. He asked, "What do we do, boss?"

Cahz looked down at the derelict buildings. He shifted his position to get a better view of the streets. There were walking dead down there in the thousands. Is this what happened to the lost retrieval team? Had they landed trying to save survivors only to be overwhelmed? Could there be survivors from the lost team among the living on the ground?

Cahz cupped the radio mic in his hand.

"Angel, give them cover fire."

***

With as much power as he could bring, Ali swung his steel pipe down on to the back of the zombie's skull. The head crumpled, yielding to the force of the pipe. There was a cylindrical indentation imprinted on its cranium as the zombie staggered to the ground.

As it toppled, it's hands grasped tight to George's shirt. Dragged by the extra weight, the old man was pulled off balance.

Straining against the fall, the old man let slip a gurgled moan, a moan all but lost to the guttural cries of the surrounding undead.

Ali lashed out with his pipe smacking a zombie across the temple. He cried, "Ray, help George!"

Ray bent down, arm outstretched. "George, George!"

George recoiled away and grunted.

"George!" Ray barked as he scooped up his friend's frail body. "You've got to help, buddy."

George didn't. His face was pale and locked in a grimace, his right hand clutched to his chest.

"Move it!" Ali called out between swipes.

"Chest," George panted.

Ray had the old man under the arm and was hauling him to his feet. He pleaded, "Not now, George, not now."

George gave a heavy shudder and the stiffness left his body.

"George?" Ray gasped, staring into the old man's watery eyes.

A withered hand appeared over Ray's shoulder and grabbed his coat.

"Hell!" Ray jumped, letting go of George. He burled round, shrugging off the zombie's grasp.

Unable to see what was going on, Ali called out, "Ray?!"

"It's George," came Ray's stunned reply. "I think he's dead."

Ali reached back and grabbed a fist full of Ray's jumper. Pulling him forward, Ali bellowed, "Move it or we'll be dead, too!"

"But… George?" Ray stammered.

"Move!" Ali commanded as he raised his weapon again.

Throwing his arm down he whacked another walking corpse square on the forehead. There was a crunch and the lip of the pipe raked down the zombie's face. The dark skin split apart, revealing a canyon of yellowed bone framed by the wet muddy post-mortem flesh.

"Where are the others?" Ray screeched, his voice pitched high with terror.

"Up ahead." Ali made a small jump into the air to get a slightly better perspective. "I can see Ryan's head."

Ray cast around, trying to peer through the throng of dead cannibals. "Where's the helicopter?"

"Shut up and fight!" Ali battered the next undead assailant out of his path.

For every zombie Ali floored it seemed that there were a hundred more closing in on him. The sweat was streaming down his face, saturating his bushy eyebrows and soaking into his beard. His shoulder ached, his arm throbbed and his palms stung from the force of the hammering. The thought of being devoured alive by these malodorous monsters kept him lashing out.

"We'll never make it," Ray blurted.

Ali turned to cajole his friend and as he looked round he saw a zombie, its teeth bared. It threw itself at Ray. Too far ahead to do anything, all Ali could do was shout a warning.

Just as it was about to chew down on Ray, it cocked its head as if confused.

Then it simply keeled over.

Ali suddenly became aware of shots ringing out.

A second zombie was hit. It fell spraying a wet trail of infected brains behind it.

"Come on! We'll make it!" Ali whooped triumphantly.

Buoyed on by the sniper's intervention, Ali surged on through the crowd.

A prepubescent girl in a grimy pink top with her arms outstretched came staggering over like a sleepwalker. At the last moment Ali dodged her bony fingers and planted his pipe straight across her face.

He didn't stop to see if he'd floored the zombie. He didn't have to immobilize every one of them—he merely had to clear his way to the plaza.

The next zombie stepped into Ali's path. It was an old woman with wild grey hair populated with twigs, old leaves and other tangled up pieces of detritus. She hissed through a gash in her cheek as she lunged at him.

Ali sidestepped her and elbowed the deceased crone in the head as she passed. The flesh under the blow squelched and the old woman fell, her arms flailing out furiously all the way to the ground.

A thrashing arm caught Ray by surprise, tripping him.

"Ali!" Ray bellowed as he tumbled to the ground.

Ali glanced round to see a mob of zombies close in on Ray. A shot rang out and one of the mob members collapsed, but it was futile. Ali knew there were too many to shoot. All he could do was outrun them.

Ray cried out, "Help me!"

Ali froze. A strong gust of wind rushed passed his face. Down the street over the heads of the undead he saw a glorious sight. A blue and white helicopter was descending into the square. The morning light bounced off its windows and sent sparkling beams off in every direction. As the chopper softly lowered he could see people inside. With one last effort he could barge past the hundred or so zombies between him and safety.

"Ali!" a voice from behind begged.

Ali spun round to see Ray on all fours. The clearing Ali had bludgeoned was rapidly diminishing as the surrounding zombies closed in on their stricken meal.

Ali looked over his shoulder at the descending helicopter, then back at Ray. He bounced back on the balls of his feet and doubled back to his friend. As he passed he took relish in stomping on the old crone's face. Barrelling forward he flung his arm round wildly, clattering three or four zombies with his pipe.

The tactic hadn't worked as well as Ali had hoped. None of the zombies had been destroyed and none had been forced back. Ali swung out again this time with more focus. He clobbered the zombie directly in his path over the head flooring him. As the creature started to fall he kicked out at the next closest, pushing it away and then driving through the gap.

In front of him were a crowd of zombies, all with their backs to him, forming a knot. Both hands on the metal pipe, he brought the cudgel down with all his might. The zombie collapsed and Ali thrust his free hand down to grab Ray.

With an inhuman bellow, Ali jerked as hard as he could.

Ray's scrawny body shot up through the gap. Ali maintained his grip and backpedalled, pulling Ray with him. Ray struggled to find his footing as he was dragged along.

"My glasses!" Ray panted. "I can't see!"

"Forget 'em," Ali spat.

The path ahead was now awash with rotting corpses and although he could hear the throb of the engine he could no longer see the helicopter.

Needing all of his strength, Ali let go of his friend and planted both hands firmly around the base of the pipe. He swung the pipe as he pushed forward. Like some ancient berserker he cleaved at the enemy with a feral rage. Again and again his weapon battered down.

"*Get… out… of… ma… fuckin'… way…*"

With each word the metal pipe swung.

But with each blow he was moving forward less and less.

Ray screamed from behind, "Ali!"

***

The skids of the chopper kissed the pavement. Cahz threw open his door and hopped down onto the abandoned parking lot. As he shut the door he caught the concerned look on Idris' face. The pilot had a rule about landing in country and that was DON'T.

Already the smell of rot was assaulting his nostrils—the fusty mix of decomposing flesh and rank bile. Back on board the ship that served as his and his team's home base, surrounded by hundreds of miles of open sea, the collapse of man's supremacy rarely impinged. Here, feet on the fractured tarmac, it was obvious the dead held dominance.

"What's the plan, boss?!" came a shout from Cannon above the noise of the engine.

Rather than trying to yell above the din of the rotors, Cahz made a simple hand gesture and the two men jogged off.

The ground beneath his feet was strewn with debris. Broken glass, litter, indistinguishable hunks of metal, a thousand and one household items discarded during the Rising. A twist of aluminium tubing hidden behind a clump of weeds snagged Cahzs' boot, causing him to stumble. He glanced back fleetingly before regaining his stride. He was aware of the adrenalin coursing through his veins, heightening his every sense, almost slowing down time.

Up ahead he saw the stone corner of a tall office building. Around that corner the survivors were fighting through hordes of the undead. From there he and Cannon could be well covered, in easy reach of the chopper and in a good position to help the fleeing survivors.

"Here," Cahz said. "We'll cover them from here."

He turned the corner and a body slammed hard up against him, pressing so closely he couldn't swing his carbine round. Out of instinct his hand grabbed the figure, ready to push them out of biting range. In that fraction of a second Cahz hadn't registered who had run into him.

A young woman gripped by fear and holding a girl in her arms stood panting beside him. Her body trembled in his grasp.

Cahz used his grip to propel her on round the corner. "Go to the helicopter!"

Turning back to Cannon, he said, "Watch my six." He knew his old buddy would have anticipated his tactic but his sense of caution demanded he say it anyway.

Cannon gave a smile and a nod. "Sure thing, boss!"

Cahz turned and took up position. In a different conflict against a different enemy he'd been taught to stick to cover, to stay low, but that was a long time ago. He didn't concern himself with redundant doctrine. This enemy didn't shoot back.

Cahz stepped out from the cover of the building and, standing up straight, braced the butt of the carbine to his shoulder. He peered through the scope and selected his first target.

Not far from him a zombie came hobbling after the young woman he had directed to the helicopter. It was a gaunt creature; a woman in life, now a sagging mass of sticky, syrupy, brown pustulence; wild sprouts of wispy hair on an otherwise leathery scalp, torn dress caked to her rotten flesh. Its lips were drawn back in a snarl, exposing a line of cragged and equally soiled teeth. Its pathetic limp was mirrored in grasping hands, arms glued to its sides, forearms outstretched from the elbows only. The decrepit beast looked like it had been dunked in oil like some wretched sea bird caught in an oil slick.

Cahz pulled the trigger. A spray of bullets ripped through the zombie's face, destroying its head.

"Shit," Cahz said. He thumbed a catch on the side of his carbine and flicked it from burst fire to single shot. He chastised himself for the waste of ammunition. "Get it together."

He aimed his gun again and in two smooth shots he obliterated another two walking dead. Another two shots and the path ahead was cleared for the next batch of survivors.

The two men came lurching towards him, an old woman supported between their arms. Cahz could hear a stream of encouragement from the young men as they hauled the exhausted woman along.

"Keep going down to the chopper!" Cahz shouted to the trio.

Before taking aim again, he surveyed the street. Along the sidewalks, spilling onto the roads, staggering between the mangled cars, came an army of cadavers. All wore the same uniform of tattered brown stained clothes, all with the same pallid grey faces.

Hundreds—if not thousands—of infected corpses, shambling forward, charging in slow motion.

But there among the palsied attackers was a knot of fury. With lighting strikes a tall balding man with dark hair was battling obstinately against the swarming horde.

Cahz braced his weapon and lent his assistance to the fight. Framed in the dark circle of his sight, he took aim and fired. Tracking from left to right he fired, trying to weed out the zombies on either side. He couldn't risk a shot at the knot within the mêlée, so entangled in the combat were the targets that the risk of hitting the men he was trying to save was too likely.

A spray of blood, red and warm and alive, spurted from the brawl. Cahz caught the spurt in his view as he picked targets. Had a shot missed a zombie to strike the survivor? Or had a zombie's bite found an artery?

He knew he couldn't dwell on the reason. All he could do was continue to obliterate zombies.

The scope went black. Cahz pulled back from his blinkered view and took a shocked step backward.

Arms outstretched, head clocked at a crooked angle, a zombie was trampling its way towards him. It was no more than a couple of lumbering steps away and Cahz had only known of its approach because it had blocked his view.

He adjusted his aim and fired. The reanimated shop worker's head lurched back, its brains annihilated by the bullet passing through its skull.

Cahz counted himself lucky. He quickly scanned the surrounding area and focused his attention back on the knot of survivors.

The street was choked with zombies now. Cahz dipped in and out of using his scope, anxiously trying to spot the man with the pipe. He peered through the throng, hoping to glimpse the arm raise that held the sturdy grey pipe. But there was nothing.

"Boss, this is Bates," Cahz heard over his earpiece. "I'm running dry and there's no let up."

Among the legions of walking dead, Cahz could see no signs of a struggle.

"Angel, have you got eyes on the other survivors?" Cahz asked, hoping the view from the sniper's vantage point would bring good news.

A trio of zombies steadily advanced on the street corner. Getting too close for comfort, Cahz floored them with three well-placed shots.

Angel hadn't replied.

Cahz again toggled his radio. "Angel, come in."

"Lieutenant," came Angel's Russian tone, "I have situation."

Cahz turned and scanned the skyline. Silhouetted on one of the rooftops he saw the team sniper. She was standing in a firing position, shooting at something on the roof. In a matter of seconds she had fired a whole magazine from her pistol. Whatever threat she faced, it wasn't finished with her.

Cahz sighted his rifle on her to get a clearer view through his scope. The feathery white clouds and the low sun scattered the morning light, leaving Cahz to see only the dark shadow of her silhouette. Her ponytail bobbed as she hastily reloaded her pistol. Then, without warning, she turned and threw herself off the rooftop.

Lost from view, Cahz drew back from his sight, frantically scanning for her.

There.

Three or four floors from the bottom of the building, she dangled on her safety line.

The rooftop now became full of shambling corpses. As they reached the edge of the roof they slowed, confused by their lack of prey. Then the first of them fell. Whether it had stumbled, was pushed from behind, or just hadn't stopped walking, the result was the same. The corpse tumbled down the face of the building.

The plummeting body narrowly missed Angel as she clung to the building's façade.

Now a torrent of undead plunged from the roof. Dozens of brainless cadavers hurtled the eight storeys to pile up in a heap of splattered and shredded flesh.

Transfixed by the drama playing out across the plaza, Cahz watched on, his heart pounding. The worst of it was he knew there was nothing he could do to help her. Unconsciously his fingers caressed the toggle on his radio. As much as he wanted to call her he knew better than to distract her. The sniper acted alone, compromising her own safety for the sake of her comrades. Cahz turned his attention back to the street corner and dispatched the fresh batch of zombies encroaching on his position.

Back along the street there were no signs of life. No glimpse of the survivors, not even a knot of undead that might indicate a struggle.

Nothing.

Cahz fired a few well-placed shots to thin out the zombies and took one last look into the mob. Reluctantly he turned to his buddy.

"Time to go, big guy," he said as he patted Cannon on the shoulder.

He toggled his mic. "Okay people, time to bug out. Everyone back to the bird."

With Cannon in tow, Cahz jogged back to the chopper. The air had the tart taste of spent powder mingling with the reek of festering bodies.

Cahz kept an eye on the team sniper as he made his way back. Dangling from her line, like a spider, Angel had pulled her side arm and was popping shots into the small gathering of zombies lucky enough to remain mobile after their dive off the roof. Her aim looked clumsy for the veteran shot she was. Then Cahz realised she was using her right hand, her left arm hanging loose by her side.

"Cahz, we've a problem," the pilot's voice came over the radio.

Just yards from the chopper, Cahz didn't bother to reply over the mic.

"Cannon, go give Angel a hand," Cahz ordered.

"You got it," Cannon replied. He peeled off and jogged over to the stricken sniper. He was a huge man, almost as wide as he was tall, but more nimble than a soldier half his bulk. With startling agility he powered over the parking lot.

Gathered around the chopper were the people who had made it through the zombies. They all looked gaunt and exhausted. The young woman, the first to make it past Cahz, was bent double, dry heaving from the exertion. The other survivors didn't look too much better.

The young men had instinctively assumed a picket and were watching nervously the advance of the zombies towards the chopper.

Cahz turned his head and double-checked behind him. A mob of undead had followed him round from the street but their sluggish gait meant there would be a few minutes before they reached the helicopter.

Bates, at the window of the chopper, was struggling to hold a conversation with Idris over the noise of the blades and the nearby ghetto blaster.

"What's the problem?!" Cahz called out as he reached the chopper.

"Are you counting heads?!" Idris hollered back.

The disparate group were strung out around the chopper. The young woman was bent double, the eight-year-old girl she'd been carrying was comforting her with her hand on her back. The old woman was unsuccessfully trying to calm the baby in her arms. Even over the deafening sound of the chopper and the blaring ghetto blaster the child's screeching still cut through it all.

Beside him, trying to look like he was working hard at solving a mental problem, Bates scratched at the short blond stubble on his chin.

Cahz suddenly understood the dilemma. "Ah, shit!"

Before he could ponder the problem further the young woman stepped in.

"Where are the others?" Sarah asked, red cheeked and still gulping for breath.

"I'm sorry, ma'am," Cahz said as mournfully as he could while shouting above the noise. When he saw the woman's face drop he threw in, "I waited as long as I could."

He looked away from the woman and the burning pain in her eyes. He felt guilty for not saving the others but yet he felt worse still for the news he was about to break.

His gloved hand found a seam of rounded rivets running down a length of the chopper's skin. He brushed his fingertips over the tiny bumps as he pondered.

"Could we get everyone on-board and try to find somewhere safe to set down?" Cahz knew how stupid an idea that was even before he'd finished saying it.

"Where?" Idris shrugged, playing through Cahz's suggestion. "Look, we'd be struggling to get airborne with the extra weight even if you could cram everyone in. And if we could take off, where would we get the extra fuel we'd need to get back to Ishtar?"

"What's the problem?" Sarah interjected, catching snippets of the conversation.

"Ma'am, the chopper only seats five, maybe six at a squeeze," Cahz admitted. He saw the woman's eyes dart across the gathered people, taking a mental note of the numbers. "And there are ten of us."

Cahz frantically tried to pull the problem apart. "Don't suppose the girl and the baby will be a problem. They can sit on someone's knee." Looking across the abandoned car park, the army of undead were doggedly drawing closer.

The big soldier, Cannon, jogged up, Angel trailing behind. Along with his own support weapon, Cannon had Angel's prize possession, her sniper rifle, draped over his shoulder. Cahz knew Angel's injury must be severe if she was allowing someone to carry it for her.

Before Cahz could ask Angel what was wrong, the young woman broke in again.

"That still leaves us four seats short," she said, still focused on the problem.

Cannon said something that Cahz missed over the noise and the demands for his attention.

"The kids'll fit in fine," Cahz heard Idris summarise, "but we're pushing the weight limit. We've got enough fuel for the five of us and a few of the pus bags, but they weigh next to nothing. Even if we do stuff this bird full, we'll be short on fuel."

Cannon and the young woman were listening intently, although both cast more than an occasional glance at the encroaching zombies.

"Okay, there's no drag if we don't use the net," Idris said, "but we'll still splash down who knows how short of the ship. And what if the weather turns and we meet a strong headwind? We'll just ditch a whole lot sooner."

The scrawny male survivor, impatient to get moving, spoke up, "Could some of us get carried in the cargo net?"

"No, we can't take the weight or the drag, son," Idris repeated.

"Anyways, you'd die of exposure before we got back to the ship," Bates added. "It's bad enough just getting winched up, but being under that thing for two hundred miles? No way you'd make it."

"No need for a seat for me dear," came a frail voice from behind.

The old woman with the baby looked tearful.

"What do you mean?" Sarah asked.

The baby was hoisted to one side and the old woman pulled her collar down. Where the curve of her neck melded into the shoulder there was an ugly bite mark. Already a deep purple hue surrounded the raged oval of torn skin.

"I'm sorry I couldn't protect her," the old woman sobbed.

Cahz watched confused as the thick set survivor walked up to the old woman. Slowly but purposefully he reached down and eased away the swaddling from the child's face. The baby was screaming. Her cheeks red, her lips pursed, her small lungs howled out a shrill cry. On the corner of the swaddling were wet splodges of blood and across the small child's face the trail of a scratch mark.

"Shit," Cahz whispered.

"Oh God no, Elspeth," Sarah gasped.

"Must have happened when I fell," the old woman said, turning to the man next to her.

The thickset man stood transfixed by the child. With the back of a finger he stroked the infant's uninfected cheek while tears ran down both their faces.

"I'm so sorry, Ryan," she apologised.

"Boss," Bates broke in, "I'm out of ammo and they're close."

"We don't have time for this, Cahz," Cannon agreed, a note of agitation in his voice.

Cahz turned to his men and addressed them. "Okay, listen up. This isn't an order but we've more of a chance down here than they do. I'm giving up my seat."

"Jesus, Cahz, we haven't survived this long to get fucked by a handful of civvies," Cannon protested loudly.

Cahz looked his old friend in the eyes. "Like I say, I can't order you to stay."

"You don't give much of an option, Boss," Cannon said grudgingly. "We've stuck together since this shit came down. If you're stayin' I'm stayin'."

Cahz smiled and patted the big man on the shoulder.

Bates tossed his head and said, "I'm taking my seat."

"I stay," Angel volunteered.

Ryan stepped in. "No, lady. Your arm's busted. I'll stay back."

"Ryan you can't—" Sarah started.

"These boys might have the firepower but they don't know the ground," Ryan argued. "They've got a better chance with one of us to guide them."

Cahz rubbed the sweat from his upper lip with his gloved finger. The zombies were now close enough to see their gnarled teeth framing their gaping maws. A few more seconds and they would be upon them.

There might have been a better way to solve this problem, but Cahz knew they didn't have the time to find it. He said, "That's that settled."

Cahz grabbed the young woman with both hands and threw her into the chopper. The woman was too shocked to resist and the rotors were too noisy for him to hear her protests.

"Okay miss, in you go," Cahz said in way of preamble as he scooped up the young girl. As he shoved the girl into the cabin, he called on the scrawny survivor, "You! In the bird now!"

Nathan was ushered into the middle seat.

"Soon as you can, get back here and pick us up," Cahz said, looking at Idris. His attention then went immediately to Bates, who was retrieving his equipment. "Bates, leave that behind. How much juice is in those batteries?" Cahz pointed at the beat up ghetto blaster.

"Not much, boss," Bates replied with a shrug. "They're rechargeable and they're pre-Zee. If you turn the sound down a bit you might eke out another fifteen, twenty minutes, but I guess about an hour is it."

Cahz gave a nod. "Okay."

"Boss!" Cannon's deep voice bellowed. "Gettin' a bit close!"

The snarling growl of machine gun fire overwhelmed the dawdle of the chopper blades as Cannon cut a sway through the closest zombies.

"You looking for a decoy?" Bates asked.

"Yep," Cahz replied.

Bates produced a modified land mine. It was a green oblong with a slight banana curve. Unlike standard issue mines, Bates had been busy modifying this one. One corner had what appeared to be a travel alarm clock duct taped in place. A pair of clumsy wires, intermittently hidden behind more silver duct tape, wound their way into the back of the casing. Cahz had warned Bates about tampering with explosives on more than one occasion, but now wasn't the time for a reprimand.

"Set a timer on it for, what, five minutes?" Bates offered.

"Make it twenty," Cahz said. "It'll act as a distraction. Maybe pull a few away from us."

Bates made an adjustment to the timer before setting it down and picking up the rest of his gear.

"You packing any more useful toys?" Cahz asked as the soldier perched on the rear seat of the chopper.

"Yeah, sure." Bates lay down his rifle and unfastened the thigh pouches from his webbing. With a smile he tossed the two packs at Cahz. "Two more claymores, two flares, a smoke grenade and one MRE."

Cahz caught the packs by their strapping. "Ain't planning on staying long enough to have to eat army rations. Maybe we can tempt those motherfuckers to eat these instead."

"Smear it all over you," Bates teased. "Then no fucker will want to bite you."

Cannon shouted over the noise with some urgency, "It's gettin' tight, boss!"

Cahz rapped his knuckles on the windscreen to get the pilot's attention. "Get these people out of here!"

Idris gave a nod.

Angel called out from her seat in the front, "Cahz, it's at least an eight hour turnaround!"

Eight hours was a long time out here and Cahz knew it. But he cocked his head and smiled.

"Quicker you go the quicker you get back!" he said.

"Good luck, Cahz." Angel passed out her sidearm and a bundle of magazines. There was an assortment of magazines for the sidearm and one chunkier magazine for her rifle. The larger of the clips bore the unfamiliar Cyrillic writing Cahz had seen on much of her Russian equipment.

Cahz looked her in the eye. "You sure?"

"I want empties back," Angel warned. "Since Izhmash closed, are bitch to get hold of."

Cahz nodded, taking the friendly jibe.

Cahz firmly handed Angel's pistol to Ryan. "Okay, we need somewhere high and defendable. Which way?"

Ryan took the gun in his hand. "This way."

"Stay close, stay sharp, stay alive!" Cahz hollered.

Chapter Three Barrel

"Stay on me!" Cahz hollered.

Elspeth and the baby were being ushered forward by Ryan. Flanking them was Cannon. The further they ran the denser the crowds of undead became. They were less spaced out and now impossible to simply run past.

A dead man stepped into Cahz's path. Using his momentum he swung the butt of his rifle and floored the creature. Its face split open. The dead skin sloughed off, revealing the vomit-yellow bone beneath.

A waft of tart putridity found Cahz's nostrils. He stifled a gag and barged on.

The zombie fell to the ground, but even with the massive head trauma it still flailed. Cahz didn't bother dispatching the creature; he pushed forward through the throng of walking dead, carving a path.

The crack of a pistol made Cahz whip round.

"Don't shoot unless you have to!" he called back at Ryan.

"Have a word with them, pal!" Ryan shot back.

Cahz turned back to the wall of rotten flesh ahead of him. In cold measured swipes he battered the cadavers from his path.

The sound of helicopter blades travelled up a pitch but Cahz was too busy to look behind. The noise rose and the downdraft washed across his shoulders and head.

He battered another zombie across the face. Chunks of rotten flesh broke loose and flew free.

His heart raced. It wasn't the exertion of close quarter fighting, it wasn't the fear of being surrounded by the undead. He felt his stomach sink and his heart pounded as the sound of the rotors changed. He knew the only way out was leaving him behind. He couldn't turn around—couldn't bear to watch the chopper ascend into the morning sky.

But the noise of the chopper stayed, echoing around the square, a constant reminder of his decision sounding in his ear. The noise of the rotors beating their retreat lingered for far longer than he thought possible.

Cahz cast off the thoughts of escape and lunged at the gnarled face of a resurrected police officer. The butt of his carbine impacted with a sharp crack and the skull gave way. Before Cahz could shift his weight, a second cadaver lurched at him. Its withered and necrosis blackened hands latched onto his body armour, clawing to get a firm grip. Unable to bring his weapon up, Cahz pressed his shoulder into the zombie's chest and pushed. The zombie had no strength and no purchase against the shove, but instead of falling back it snagged on Cahz's webbing.

A new zombie stepped up to the entangled soldier. With his rifle caught up in the first zombie's arms, Cahz had lost the use of his primary weapon. He let go with his right hand and grabbed for his pistol. The decayed, bony fingers of the undead scratched at Cahz's body armour as the two creatures ganged up on their prey, eager to deliver a bite.

Cahz flipped the safety off his pistol and jammed it into the fleshy underside of the nearest zombie's jaw. Screwing his eyes tight and clamping his mouth shut, Cahz pulled the trigger.

The zombie's jaw liquefied with the deafening crack of the round discharging. The noise of the blast hammered into Cahz's eardrums. Crushed by the strike on his ear drums, the sounds around became muffled. The only clear sounds where the rasp of his own breath and the galloping thump of his heart. Blown apart by the shot, the zombies head vaporised. A tirade of congealed blood and shredded flesh slapped across Cahz's face.

His eyes still shut tight, Cahz turned his gun to the second cadaver mauling him. The muzzle halted against something firm and Cahz fired. The blast wasn't as loud. His ears were still reeling from the proximity of the last shot.

His target's weight shifted as it keeled over, but it continued to thrash, caught on Cahz's webbing. Cahz drew his sleeve across his face, scraping the worst of the putrefied debris away. He blinked his eyes open and gasped back the foul pus-laden odour. Drips of fetid gunk clung to his lips. Cahz screwed up his face and spat.

Before he could wipe his face for a second time, something tugged at his webbing. Hanging off his body armour by its bony arm, the zombie was struggling back to its feet. Its left arm rendered inoperative by the bullet through its shoulder, it hauled itself up by the arm tangled in Cahz's armour. The pathetic grey husk stared up at Cahz while it tried to find purchase.

Before it could, Cahz levelled his pistol and fired. The headless zombie hung there, dangling from the straps on his webbing.

The bitter taste of rancid flesh crept up Cahz's tongue. He felt the saliva ooze in his mouth and the bile rise in his throat. He tried to spit, but the thick mucus wouldn't leave his lips. Instead it dribbled down his chin and onto the headless cadaver swinging from his chest.

Around him a dozen raw and weeping outstretched arms grabbed for him. Too close and too numerous for him to club, Cahz raised his pistol. He leaned into his firing stance and shot the remainder of his magazine into the crowd. A score of zombies fell inert around him.

"Don't fire unless you have to, eh?" Ryan said from behind him. "That didn't last long."

Cahz unhooked the corpse from his gear. "Change of plan," he said as he refreshed his pistol. "We've got to get in cover. Head for the that building."

"You'll never land a chopper on that roof," Ryan said.

"Then we'll need to be winched off," Cahz replied.

"He's right," Cannon said. "But we'll never get far in these crowds."

Cahz wiped his cheek, smearing some of the pulverised zombie onto his glove. "What's that building there?"

Ryan hesitated. "Offices of some sort?"

"Okay, that's our destination. Cannon, thin it out."

Cannon hugged the heavy machinegun against his side and fired. The buzzsaw noise ripped through the air, obliterating both the sound of the chopper and the moans of the undead. Bullets punched into the zombies ahead, knocking them down like pins.

"Go, go, go!" Cahz bellowed, slapping Ryan on the shoulder.

As Cahz ran off into the machinegun-hewn swathe, Ryan looked back.

The old woman was stumbling through the freshly mown corpses, the baby clutched tight in her arms. Her eyes were red with tears, her footsteps uneasy and faltering.

"Here, Elspeth," Ryan said softly as he put a steadying arm around her.

Some of the zombies stopped by Cannon's burst were starting to get up. Even with chunks torn out of their decaying bodies, unless the bullets had pulped their brains or shattered their spines, they would keep coming.

Cannon let out another burst, knocking over a handful more. He knew that without a head shot they wouldn't stay down, but there were too many to take time picking shots. For now all he could do was waste ammo trying to knock them down and hope it would buy enough space to get through to safety.

Cahz charged forward, his pistol barking as he dispatched the most immediate threats. His lips felt cracked and sore from where he'd wiped the atomised zombie with the back of his glove. His cheeks still felt wet, plastered as they were with infected brain matter. He spat out the saliva building up in his mouth and tried not to swallow the bitter infected tissue that was forming a scum over his tongue. Trying to ignore the fetid taste, he pushed on.

More and more of the undead fell as the party fought their way through. Bludgeoned with rifle butt or shot at point blank range, dozens of walking dead were destroyed or pushed from their path.

With a point-blank coup de grâce, Cahz dispatched the final zombie between him and the office block. It had been a new building before the Rising, a towering icon to corporate power, but like a million other homogenised offices the world over it now lay abandoned. The standardized architect of glass and steel and sandstone now wore a coat of grime. A shabby veneer smoke stained grey with green trails of moss marking the tributaries from burst pipes and leaky gutters. Here and there in the thin troughs between steel and stone a resilient plant clung, its leaves turned skyward in triumph.

The expansive vista-exposing front window was a broken mosaic of splintered glass. A burnt out car sat rusting in the foyer where it had smashed to a stop.

Cahz stepped through the broken window and peered into the gloom. His boots crunched on the broken glass. Instantly a damp chill permeated his lungs and the smell of musty plasterboard hung on every breath.

The sound of the ghetto blaster still wafted into earshot between the dry cries of dead voices. But the drone of the chopper was now overwhelmed by the moans of the hungry dead.

Cahz scanned the lobby, looking past the security desk and the elevators, trying to make out the entrance to the stairs. Loops of conduit sagged from the ceiling like vines in a plastic and aluminium jungle. A steady trickle of water cascaded from a snapped pipe, splashing onto a mushy ceiling tile.

With his boots squelching through the debris, Cahz cautiously skirted the dilapidated car sitting on its four flat tyres. The driver's door was slightly ajar. The windows were smashed in. Down the seams of the metal work he could see the tarnish of rust—or was it dried blood? In the dim light he couldn't be sure.

As he unpicked the darkness a figure stepped out of the gloom. Its arms outstretched, it let rise a wail. Its tough vocal cords pushed out the stale air in its dead lungs, past its goatee framed lips, to form a flattened vowel that bounced off the empty walls, an off-key note that piqued Cahz's fear. The zombie's once neat uniform was now dishevelled. The crisp white shirt bore a large hole across the shoulder. Around the edges the raw flesh had desiccated, forming ragged sheets of dried skin. The crimson deluge that once poured from the wound was now a brown stain that ran down the zombie's chest to merge into the blood-caked trousers.

Fighting against his natural reaction to flee, Cahz took a determined step towards the zombie. The saggy folds of grey skin that drooped from its face became taught as its mouth opened wide. Its jaws held apart in anticipation of a meal. Polluted saliva glistened behind the cracked and blackened lips. As it lurched out of the shadows, Cahz realised the dead security guard didn't have a beard. The dark stain around its mouth was the dried blood of a long dead victim. This wretched being had been infected and upon his defective resurrection he had in turn infected another, the cycle of infection perpetuated. In this one malignant creature, Cahz could see reflected the billions of dead and undead.

Cahz thumped the cadaver hard in the head. The bone crunched with the impact and the butt skidded off the loose skin. As the metal edge slipped down the zombie's face, it took with it the cold dead flesh, exposing the bone beneath. Like a well cooked chicken, the skin and muscle and cartilage sloughed free from the skull.

The zombie stumbled backwards into the shadows from the force of the blow, but rather than toppling to the floor the creature caught itself and came shambling forward again. When it emerged into the light, it smiled an impossibly wide grin populated by broken teeth and yellow glistening bone.

The zombie stepped closer, devoid of a nose and grinning. Its skull still wore small clumps of flesh and sinew. The raw white eyes inside their sockets twitched and darted, peering through damaged cornea, trying to reacquire its meal. The remnants of its human face dangled from its chin like the wattle on a cockerels neck. The slick grey mask of dead flesh quivered and jiggled as the creature stumbled forward.

A bolt of sick rose in Cahz's mouth. He spluttered at the acrid taste, spitting out the milky granules of vomit.

The zombie closed in, arms outstretched, compelled to embrace its meal.

With a grunt of exertion, Cahz delivered a second blow. The rifle split open the skull with a crack and this time the zombie collapsed to the floor.

"Is it clear?" Cannon asked as he drew up with Cahz.

"No idea." Cahz pointed at a set of doors. "Reckon that's the stairwell?"

"Let's give it a try, boss." Cannon jogged over and pushed at the door. "A little help here."

Cahz turned to see Ryan supporting Elspeth as they hobbled into the lobby. At their tail there was already a sea of undead arms clawing for them.

"Fuck!"

Cahz whipped round at the cry to see the stairwell door wide open, light streaming in from the skylight beyond. Silhouetted against the opening, Cannon was tussling with a zombie.

"Get off me, you dead fuck!"

Cahz levelled his rifle at the mêlée. The muzzle danced, trying to track his target as the pair tussled.

"Shit," Cahz spat, unable to get a clear shot. Letting his carbine drop free in its harness, he dashed over to his comrade.

Cannon twisted and succeeded in creating some space between himself and the zombie. He pulled back his hand and let fly a punch.

He bellowed, "Fuck off!"

The punch landed. Contorted by the impact, the creature's head whipped back, its nose flattened and the skin ruptured. The corpse skidded to a halt not far from the crashed car. Cannon stormed over to the zombie and before it could rise up he pounded his boot into its face. The bone buckled and cracked and Cannon stomped his foot down hard again. With successive hammering its jaw snapped and an eye was popped from its socket.

"I guess it wasn't clear," Cannon said, looking at the pulped skull. "Fucker popped out from behind the security desk."

"Come on, Cannon!" Cahz shouted, holding open the stairwell

doors.

"Annoying little shit." Cannon squashed his boot into the remnants of the zombie's face and gave a final twist of his heel.

Cahz looked into the brightly lit stairwell. Golden streaks of sunlight were streaming through the grimy windows.

Back out in the foyer, the first of the pursuing zombies had made it inside the building. As Cannon ran past he jammed the door shut.

"Are you sure it's safe up there?" Ryan asked.

"You're the local expert—you tell me," Cahz replied, looking for a lock to the doors. "Cannon, watch the stairs."

"Sure thang, boss," Cannon confirmed as he stepped past to take up position.

Cahz tried to pause and listen. He couldn't tell if the stairs were a safer option or not. For all he knew he was about to trap himself in with a horde of voracious undead.

There was too much noise for him to pick anything out from the echoing stairwell. The constant moans of the pursuing zombies, the shuffling of feet, the infant crying and the old woman sobbing all combined to form a heart-wrenching chorus of misery.

"Come on. Come on in quick," Cahz beckoned to the stragglers. As soon as the pair were through the door he threw it shut. "How the hell do you lock this?"

"Can we brace something against it?" Ryan suggested.

Cahz could see the barrel of a lock but no key. He looked around for something to bar the door but there was nothing. The stairwell was a mosaic of peeling paint, dirty glass and small clumps of smashed detritus. The hard synthetic fibre carpet tiles wore a film of dust and plaster, muting what would once have been a rich royal blue down to a pastille shade. His eye was drawn to the vivid red of a wall-mounted fire extinguisher. Its colour was still vibrant unlike its washed out surroundings. The only betrayal of its neglect was the specks of rust clinging to the welds around its neck and brackets.

The door thumped, yanking Cahz's mind back.

Instinctively he pushed hard against the door.

"If only the door opened the other way, those dumb fucks would never work out how to get in," Ryan offered.

"Well, it doesn't," Cahz snapped.

The door thumped again as a second then a third zombie added their force.

Cahz kept his back to the double doors, holding them shut. "Look, those pus bags have got no strength but I can't stand here all day."

"Want me to check upstairs?" Cannon asked.

"Go, and take these two with you. You might need the extra muscle."

"There's got to be filing cabinets or something we can use," Ryan said as he bounded for the stairs.

"If you're not back in five minutes," Cahz said, "I'm coming looking for you."

Cannon and Ryan started up the stairs, leaving the old woman behind. The hallway echoed with the clump of boots and the crying of the woman and child.

Cahz unclipped his canteen, twisted the lid off and put the end to his lips. He tipped the bottle up and poured a gulp into his foul tasting mouth. With the thoroughness of a dental hygiene commercial, Cahz swilled the water around before spitting it out onto the floor. There was still a bitter funk lingering on his taste buds. He rinsed a second time but the taste remained.

"I'd murder for some gum," he muttered.

He tipped his head back and let a stream of water spill out over his face. He gave a shudder like a wet dog tossing the water droplets away. He brought up his arm and dragged his face across the sleeve. His face still felt polluted, unclean with the remains of the dead plastered to his skin. Like an obsessive compulsive, he raked his gloved hand down his damp flesh, trying to peel off the contamination he knew must still be clinging to him.

The snug fitting body armour rose and fell erratically with the jittery heaving of his chest. He took a deep breath in through his nose and tried to calm his hammering lungs and the sense of dread. Slowly his breathing became less rapid and he found himself looking at his shoes.

The tan leather was sprayed with all manner of amorphous gunk. Splashes of dark viscera clung precariously to the tip of his boot. He tried to kick off the worst of it by scraping his boot across the floor but to no avail. He closed his eyes to escape the thought of the innards smeared over him, but the darkness behind his eyelids served to intensify the sounds around him. The sobs and wails from the old lady and the child, the muffled strains of Bates' stereo playing to an indifferent audience, the banging and slapping of dead hands against the doors and through it all the incessant chill of the dead's moans.

Cahz opened his eyes. The old woman was still standing there.

"Lady?"

The old woman stood there, immobile other than the shudders that swept across her with each sob.

"Lady," Cahz said more forcefully, trying to gee her up.

Slowly she turned to face him. The wound on her shoulder was seeping. Rather than clear plasma or fresh blood, the viscous liquid that oozed out was an evil, almost black, hue of dark blue.

"Lady, what's your name?" Cahz asked, his voice raised against the thumps and moans from the other side of the door.

The woman took a couple of deep breaths to calm herself. "Elspeth."

"And the baby?" Cahz asked.

"The baby…"

Elspeth looked down at the child she carried. There was a raised red welt along the child's face with spots of blood along the line. The baby's face was flushed from her crying and her eyes puffy from the tears, her pouty lips still quivering even though the effort of crying had exhausted her tiny body.

"She doesn't have a name," Elspeth said. "Sam always liked Lucy or Rebecca but she died giving birth. Ryan..." Elspeth looked at the stairs Ryan had ran up. "Ryan's her dad and he's been avoiding her."

Cahz had wanted the woman to go upstairs with the others so that he had a clear run if he had to leave the door. But Cannon and the man called Ryan could be anywhere by now. He thought for a moment of ordering her up the stairs, but what if she missed the two men and went wandering off into the

building? It was best to keep a close eye on her, keep her under control. That way there'd be no surprises.

"Okay, lady," Cahz said in as reassuring a tone as he could muster. "You stay down here with me and we'll wait for the others to come back."

"Samantha had picked out Rebecca or Lucy as girl's names but I told her to wait and see," Elspeth said, lost in the child's gaze. "You were going to be called Emily until the moment the midwife asked if I told…"

There was a squeak and a thump and they both looked round.

Pressed against the grubby window, a blurred face peered in. Not much more than a shadow through the dirt smeared glass, the zombie pressed its face and hands to the glass, drawn by the movement and the sounds.

The thuds from the door were now joined by the slap of dead palms battering against the glass. The thunderous booms of the thumps echoed up the stairwell and the baby redoubled her wailing.

Against his back, Cahz could feel the constant pounding and now his ears rang with the reverberant thuds of fists on glass.

A bitter, acidic taste still polluted his mouth. He tried to spit it out but even a further rinse of water couldn't shift it.

"What's keeping them?" he muttered.

"Will that glass hold?" Elspeth asked nervously. She looked at Cahz for reassurance as she stepped back against the wall.

"I don't know," Cahz admitted in a flat tone.

He tried to listen for Cannon and Ryan's movements but it was impossible above the noise of the besieging zombies. He looked at his watch to gauge the time then realised he had no idea when the pair had left. He told himself they'd only been gone a couple of minutes; it was simply the adrenaline and fear that made the time pass more slowly.

The door behind him still groaned with pressure. Not enough yet to worry him. The pounding wasn't coordinated but the weight of numbers pressing in was growing. In increments the pressure would build and there would come a moment where he'd have to start pushing back rather than just bracing it. If that happened it wouldn't take much for him to lose his purchase and for the door to swing open. He decided that would be his point of no return. If the door started to jar open he would abandon this position and try to find a secondary point to hold. But was there such a place in the building?

"You been in here before?" he asked Elspeth.

"I don't know… I don't think so. They all look alike, these new office blocks."

Elspeth was right. Even if she could have given him a detailed plan of the building, he doubted it would be much different from his imagination. Stairwells either side of the elevator shafts, open plan offices on each floor. The only surprises being the ingénues places where the undead would choose to hide.

"I didn't do much of the scavenging. Jennifer, George and me would wait outside when the others went in."

"That's fine, lady. We'll just wait here for the—"

A loud crash from above cut Cahz's sentence short. For an instant his muscles tensed, ready to run before he checked himself. He pressed his full weight against the door and listened.

"What was that?" Elspeth asked.

"Be quiet," Cahz whispered.

Again came the booming crash, closer this time, sharper and less muffled. Elspeth took a step away from the stairs, sliding her back along the wall, trying to distance herself from the sound.

The dead at the windows and behind the door heard the noise, too. They paused their incessant banging and listened.

The respite wasn't long, for within moments a moan rose above the silence and the frantic hammering began anew.

Long seconds passed in the empty corridor as the sounds of shuffling and groaning grew louder.

Elspeth looked at Cahz. He could tell from her eyes and nervous curl of her lips that she wanted to say something, anything to break the terror.

Over the noise of the pounding and the moaning, emanating from the landing, came a snarling.

CHAPTER FOUR
DES-RES

"Ali!" Ray screamed.

Ali was furiously battering the zombies around him—too many for him to pause but Ray kept screaming.

A hand touched Ali's shoulder. It was a strangely gentle action, not at all frenzied like the normal clawing. Ali turned, half expecting to see a familiar face, but instead all he saw was the chewed up remains of something that might once have been human. The decrepit cadaver sported ugly chunks torn out of its body like it had been run over by a speed boat, its feeble grasp the result of the disintegrated tissue wrapped around the splintered bones.

The faceless wretch loomed in to try to bite. Too close for a killer blow, Ali swiped his elbow into its temple. Thrown off balance, the zombie fell, but its fingers clamped shut, trapping a handful of Ali's jumper. And as the zombie toppled over it dragged Ali with it.

Ali hit the ground hard.

It was dark. Only small chinks of light penetrated the thick forest of overhanging dead flesh. Behind him came a satisfied chomp and slurp as a zombie took its fill.

Ray's screams were high pitched and childlike in timbre. There were short breaks in the shrieks as Ray guzzled down the air to fuel his cries. Each gulping scream punched into Ali's chest and crushed his stomach in its tight clench. Ali gasped for breath as the terror laden screams pulsed and climbed an octave. Suddenly the cries became stifled, slipping down to a wet gargle.

Within moments a gasping and choking was all that remained of Ray's protests. Gradually even those dull sounds abated until all Ali could hear were the moist smacks of the undead feasting and the agitated moans of those jostling to get their share of the kill.

A zombie shuffled forward to join the sweet banquet and stamped on Ali's beard. As it ploughed forward a clump of hair was wrenched from his chin. Ali clamped his lips shut and rode out the pain, desperate to avoid detection.

The creature, drawn by the smell of blood or the noise of eating or whatever macabre sense drove them, stumbled forward. It kicked at Ali's thigh before sideling away for its meal.

Ali slid onto all fours and looked out at the multitude of dead legs ahead of him. There were innumerable zombies in front of him, too many to fight.

I don't stand a chance.

Then it struck him.

Still on all fours, Ali gingerly eased himself forward.

I may not be able to stand, but I can sure as hell crawl.

Ali pushed forward, his head down, shuffling forward on his forearms like some religious supplicant.

A zombie brushed past him on its way to sup on the feast of Ali's fallen friends. The corpse's leg brushed close enough for Ali to smell it. It was the fusty smell of gangrene, a pungent tang that sucked the hope from the air.

Still edging forward across the broken tarmac of the street, Ali heard something change: the constant beating of chopper blades that had echoed around the dead city. The noise had suddenly shifted pitch.

Ali wanted nothing more than to stand up and to see what was happening, but he knew he couldn't. Instead he continued his penance-like crawl.

He was only a few more inches forward when he collided square on with one of the walking dead.

Ali froze.

The zombie brought its left leg even with its right, shins flat against Ali's head. It nudged forward sheepishly, testing the resistance with its palsied muscles.

Ali held firm, not moving but not actively resisting either. All he could see were the scuffed rubber toes of a pair of ruined trainers.

Once these shoes would have been bright white; now the plastic was torn and stained yellow, the soft leather buried under a layer of filth. An accent of thin red could still be made out under the grime, and above it a logo that once meant something to the dead man wearing them.

Inside the zombie's mind a simple calculation was taking place. All the billions spent on brand recognition, market penetration and mass media brain washing didn't mean much now, to the living or the dead. Like the brethren of cadavers around him, only the deepest primordial sense remained. Through the stodgy infected brain matter it finally came to the conclusion it had met an impasse. And so after an age, the cadaver pivoted and hobbled away.

Ali breathed a sigh of relief as he watched the trainers trudge off.

Shuffling forward himself, he came to a storm drain clogged with rotting vegetation and the flotsam of urban decay. The drain meant he wasn't far from a building and the possible safety within its walls.

Past the drain, only a few short metres of pavement and a dozen or so zombies separated Ali from a derelict apartment building. He and his fellow survivors had long ago looted all the surrounding buildings, but Ali hoped he could find sanctuary inside. The doors had all been forced open during their scavenging, and as long as the wood hadn't swollen shut in the subsequent years he could secure it and take time to think. He just had to crawl to the side of a building and follow it until he found an entrance.

Ali placed his hand on the kerbstone and eased himself on. Slowly crawling between the zombies, Ali desperately tried to stay calm, fearful his laboured breath would attract attention.

His concentration was snapped back to the square as the sound of gunfire barked from behind him.

The helicopter sounded more distant now and he guessed it was airborne.

But the shots sounded closer than the chopper. That could only mean there were people on the ground—well-armed people. Now an impossible thought clawed its way into his mind. Was there still the chance of a rescue?

Ali let a smile take control of his lips. There was a way out of this. He just needed to be smart and—

A bony hand clasped his own. Hauling itself forward with its tattered arms, the legless zombie was at eye level with Ali. The narcotised jaw slumped open to utter a moan. A thick black tongue flicked behind punctured cheeks, but instead of the dry howl nothing came out. No rallying call to alert its fellow undead.

Ali cast his eyes over the crippled ghoul. It had been dragging itself along for so long that its chest was a ragged pulp of grated flesh. And where the ribcage ended so did the zombie. The docked stub of its spinal column whipped excitedly like a Dobermans stumpy tail. And like an attack dog its teeth were bared.

The zombie pulled closer. But still there was no wail from its dusty throat, its lungs presumably left behind somewhere along its crawl.

Ali planted his hands on both sides of the zombie's head. He grabbed hold of the matted and greasy hair and slammed the creature's head down with all the force he could muster. The jaw cracked on the curb and a thick slab of knotted hair and scalp ripped free in his grasp. Teeth and bone spilled onto the road followed by thick black ooze. But the bone shattering force had done nothing to deter the monster. It used all its pathetic strength to try to draw closer. Ali dropped the chunk of flesh in his hands and grabbed hold again. Lifting the cadaver up, he thumped the skull down for a second time. With a sharp crack the zombie's jaw fractured and dislocated, hanging split in two like the mandible of some giant insect. The two halves dangled, anchored to its skull by the infection-wrought mastic muscles. Lashing out between the broken bones, the zombie's tongue flicked and lapped, seemingly unaware it had lost the ability to bite. As it tried to push forward, Ali clasped its head tight between his thick hands. The creature fixed Ali with an unblinking stare. Its eyes were ice white but they burned with insatiable malice. Again Ali battered the head against the ground and again there was the sickening crack of bone, but still the zombie was animate.

Before Ali could attack again there was a focused moan from above. The zombies in the crowd had never stopped moaning, but this one was different. Ali and the rest of the survivors had grown used to the constant low groaning, the low moan of frustration as the dead called relentlessly for food. But there was a second type of call, a quicker louder wail when they caught a glimpse of prey. Ali's ears heard that excited moan. He looked up, knowing he'd been spotted, and as he turned a zombie fell upon him.

Ali pushed off with his legs and lunged ungracefully away from the attacking zombie. But his clandestine escape had been detected. Above, a circle of zombies had turned their attention to him. As each corpse spotted him they too let out the excited moan. In turn the moan rippled out, drawing more and more in.

"This is bad," Ali said as he stumbled to his feet.

He craned his neck up as if offering his throat to the zombies, and then jumped into the air. With the extra few inches height the pogo afforded him, he could see the doorway into the apartment block just metres away.

With their customary moans, the zombies pressed in.

Ali lowered his head and charged. Barging his way past the gathering zombies like a running back, he knocked them flying. With a few pounding steps Ali successfully ploughed his way through the crowd.

Like most of the buildings near the warehouse, this one had been looted by the survivors. He knew that the door would have been prised open and easy to get into.

Throwing the last cadaver out of his path, Ali used his momentum to shoulder the dark blue door open. The lock had indeed been jimmied and it flew open with unexpected ease. The door clattered against the entrance wall and swung back. Ali skidded across the slime coated floor and, thrown off kilter, he flailed his arms desperately trying to retain his balance. With no purchase underfoot and too much forward momentum, Ali's feet slid from under him and he toppled over.

His knees buckled and he came crashing to the floor, smacking his head against the first step. As the pain from the strike found him so did the returning door. The metal runner on the leading edge slashed down his leg, scoring deep into his shin. The pain burnt out his vision, leaving him blinded in agony.

A scream burst from his lips as the pain boiled out of him. Like a rallying call, the zombies gurgled back their own tainted response. The light from outside was devoured as the first wave of ragged assailants stumbled for the door. Forced by the mob behind, the lead zombie lost its footing to the pressure and fell. Unlike a living human being, the creature never tore its gaze away from Ali as it fell. It hit the ground chin first, splitting the rotting flesh from the bone. The creature fell just short of Ali. Unconcerned by its injuries it immediately thrust out with its gnarled arms to seize it prey.

With a primordial scream Ali lashed out with his good leg, battering the zombie away. He backpedalled, kicking as he went scrambling on his backside up the stairs.

The light from the street outside was rapidly disappearing as the zombies crowded in on the doorway. The zombie that Ali had just battered away was proving an effective, if temporary, barrier. The undead fighting their way in were tripping over themselves, their necrotic brains unable to compensate for the hazards underfoot and the shoves from behind. Once down, their withered limbs proved too weak to pull themselves free of the growing stack.

Still facing the pileup of dead flesh, Ali eased himself up using the handrail on the stairs. The gash in his leg was bleeding. Thick rivulets of blood trickled down his ankle and pooled amongst the slime on the floor.

In the close confinement of the hallway the moans of the dead reverberated off the hard walls. The discordant cacophony clawed at Ali's ears. It was the same chorus of desperation that had surrounded the warehouse but here the walls weren't muffling the sound. Here the walls were containing them, amplifying them, making the noise infinitely more disturbing.

Holding onto the handrail, Ali hobbled up the steps. As he turned on the first landing he looked back at the heap of bodies in the hallway. A pair of zombies had untangled themselves from the pile and was making a painful crawl towards the stairs. They would take a while to get themselves upright and shamble after him. He had a few seconds to think, time to find somewhere defendable and work out a strategy.

He looked around the stairwell desperately trying to recall when last he was here. Did he remember the layout? Was there another exit? The noise from the dead driving into the building flustered him. He couldn't think. But he had to act.

Hands supporting his weight on the banisters, he eased his injured leg onto the floor. Careful to test the pain, he straightened his foot out and planted it on the first sodden carpet tile. A whip of pain shot up from the wound. Ali winced against it but kept his balance. With slow, wary footsteps to avoid slipping in the slimy carpet, he made his way to the first door. The hallway smelt damp and rotten; the crumbling plasterboard walls, the decaying household fabrics all mixed with the unmistakable stench of decomposing flesh.

Ali tried to listen for the sounds of a trapped zombie up ahead, but the moans from the horde downstairs drowned everything out.

The door ahead of him was slightly ajar with a strong shaft of golden yellow sunlight visible on the wall inside. Tentatively Ali pushed at the door. It didn't budge. The wooden frame had warped from the water damage and sat snugly in its jamb. Ali pushed harder and when that didn't work he took a step back and charged.

With a screech the distorted door reluctantly swung open a few degrees. Ali wedged his good leg into the opening and levered his body against the door, and with a series of short shoves he managed to push the door far enough to squeeze in.

The apartments hallway led off ahead for a few metres. The

wooden flooring was strewn with the former owner's possessions, a woman's blouse, a black kitten heeled shoe, a hairdryer, its red plastic case cracked open exposing the hard mechanical innards, and a dozen other innocuous remnants. The dank smell was stronger here.

Ali resisted the natural urge to call out, "anyone home?" as he inched forward.

The corridor lead into what looked like a dining/living room from Ali's narrow view. Between here and there were three closed doors. He decided to ignore the closed doors and check out the living room. He stalked through the debris, trying in vain to stay quiet when every footfall made the warped wooden floor groan.

He craned his head round the corner, quickly checking both directions. To his right was the living room, a large bay window with a small balcony affording a view across the street. The sofa and chairs turned to face a long extinguished flatscreen TV. To the left was a small kitchen and dining area with a breakfast bar island forming a barrier between the two areas.

And there it was, under the work surface a large black mass.

Ali froze. He didn't move and neither did the corpse. Plucking up his courage he drew closer. From the bundle of rags under the breakfast bar he could see a fat, mottled leg. It was dark and discoloured, still with a shoe tightly wedged on, the same type as in the hallway. As he peered round he could see the leg was attached to a lump of black rags.

Ali stood over the dead body. His approach had been less than silent; shards of pottery from some smashed crockery crunched underfoot. At the top of the mass was a mess of brown hair poking out from a black lace hat.

"Poor gal," Ali whispered, looking down at the woman in her morning dress.

He nudged the dead woman's foot with the tip of his shoe. The spongy flesh wobbled but nothing more. Ali didn't know how long this corpse had been lying or what had killed her. Judging by the integrity of the dead flesh he assumed she'd been infected and subsequently dispatched. There was nothing to be gained in investigation of her termination. It didn't really matter. All that mattered was she wasn't going to try to bite him.

Right. What can I use for barricade? Ali pondered, stroking his long black beard.

He looked at the sofa. It would be ideal. He reckoned he could even wedge it across the stairwell. With the stairs blocked he would have free range of all of the apartments and any useful material they still harboured.

He bent down and tried to lift the sofa, but it was a quality piece of furniture. It was far heavier than he'd anticipated and far too weighty for him to quickly manhandle alone. Instead he switched tack and opted for one of the chairs. It wasn't as big, but having tested the weight he knew he could easily manhandle it to the stairwell.

Ali threw off the damp cushion and started pushing the chair into the hall. Within seconds the casters were entangled in the abandoned detritus scattered across the floor. A fusty smell wafted up from the rotting wood and textiles. The fabric of the chair was as sodden as the cushion he'd tossed aside. He bent at the knees and, grasping the chair by its arms, he raised it up. As he found his grip on the heavy lift a trickle of water squelched out and dribbled down his wrist. Ali gave an involuntary shudder as the cold water crept its unpleasant way up to his elbow. Ali flicked his arm trying to divert the drip away but the tributary was intent on snaking its way down his elbow. The waterlogged material was adding even more weight to the substantially constructed chair.

Ali took his first faltering step and as his foot hit the ground the gash in his leg flared up. The exertion had increased his blood pressure and he could feel warm blood dribble down his ankle. Puffing out a short breath, Ali ignored the pain and struggled to the hallway.

The door frame looked narrower and narrower with every step and as he drew closer the back of the chair obscured more and more of his view. Finally the inevitable happened: the chair struck the wall. Ali stood there for a moment, trying to gauge the situation. He made a small step to his right, and feeling the bevel of the door frame slip past the back of the chair, he tried again. This time the chair slid through but as he drew level his thick fingers bashed against the edge of the door frame.

"Shit!"

He realised that although the chair would narrowly squeeze through the gap, his hands on either side wouldn't.

He set the chair down for a moment to assess his position. His leg throbbed and his lungs were pumping from the exertion of lifting the chair. The wooden surround was only half an inch thick, enough to bar him from lifting the chair through, but he could still push the chair along the warped wooden floor far enough into the hallway to pick it back up and carry it the rest of the way.

Ali looked up at the main door and recalled the trouble he'd had pushing it open. Struggling against the buckled floorboards, it struck him he'd have no chance of prising the door wide enough to get the chair through. There was no way he'd ever get the chair to the stairwell.

Then from through the gap in the door he saw a zombie.

Ali froze. The creature swayed as it stumbled forward. It gazed into space like an addict in a chemically induced trance. It looked straight ahead as it shuffled round the landing.

In profile now, the zombie staggered into full view. Its face was grey with deep lines. Its hair sat in short curls that under the filth could well have been blond. Then, without turning its head, it shuffled past the half open door and continued up the stairs.

Ali stood there, his heart pounding, his jaw open. The impaired creature had failed to spot him. Just a few metres away and it hadn't even bothered to look through the doorway.

A voice inside his mind suddenly bellowed, "Shut the door!"

Ali vaulted the chair. As he landed a jolt of pain from his leg thundered up into his skull. The shock stole the strength from his muscles. His injured leg slid away from him and he toppled to the floor. The broken hairdryer shattered under the weight of his impact, but the hard metal parts punched him hard in the chest. Ali spluttered out a wheeze as the air was thumped from his lungs. He rolled over, tears of pain clouding his vision. The water stained ceiling above undulated and throbbed in rhythm with the throbbing of his head. A low groan issued from Ali's mouth as he tried to snatch his breath back.

A second groan joined his.

When it sounded a second time he could hear feet dragging against the mulched carpet tiles. His face contorted by the pain, he rolled over onto all fours. With a steadying hand to the wall, he pushed himself up. A tight grimace was clasping his lips shut. He panted for breath as he slid along the wall.

As he reached the open door, he came face to face with the zombie. No longer in profile, Ali could see the right side of its face was peppered with holes. The tone in its face hardened and the necrotic muscles pulled back its jaws. As its mouth widened it looked for an instance as if the zombie was breaking into a smile.

Ali threw his whole body at the door. The collision shuddered through his aching bones and flesh. With a reluctant squeal the door started to move. A dark shape loomed from the landing outside and dry moans echoed up the corridor.

"Shit," Ali gasped as he heaved against the door.

The warped wood of the floor screeched as it gave way and outside the cries of the dead raised to match it.

Just inches from shutting, a dead arm thrust its way in. Ali kept pushing, pinning the dead flesh between the wall and the door. The blue tinged arm flailed and pawed at the air, desperate to capture the living being it knew was inside. Ali leaned against the door with all his bulk, but no amount of effort would close it now.

Just inches away from Ali's face, the arm continued to thrash. The appendage had been trapped above the elbow, leaving the zombie no real range of movement. It flailed up and down, causing the corner of the door to rip into its perished flesh. The translucent skin buckled and puckered as it split and peeled back. As the paper-thin skin curled away it revealed the raw wet infected meat underneath.

A waft of choking decay found Ali's nostril. The curdled human fluids and the slow mouldy rot of its flesh assaulted his senses like a mix of rancid blue cheese and fresh vomit, astringent and gut wrenching.

Ali stifled a gag and mustered his fortitude. If he opened the door a crack he might be able to push the zombie's hand back through the door and close it before it could reach out again. But judging by the excited moans there were already more undead outside. One of them might just as easily grab Ali's arm and start gnawing down on it. If he retreated to the living room there was no door to block them off. Ali guessed he could up end the couch and use that to block the opening, but he wasn't confident he could do it quickly enough to block them off. He could hide behind one of the closed doors in the hallway but he had no idea what was behind them. A bedroom? A closet? And would he want to be trapped in a closet with no way out?

Ali kept his weight against the banging door behind him. There was little enough pressure from the zombies on the other side. He had time to think.

Something snapped with the twang of an elastic band breaking. Ali looked round to see the zombie with its arm wedged in the door had succeeded in sawing through a tendon. Part of the forearm now looked flat and limp, the tension lost. Along with shavings of skin and thick black ooze, the door now had a morsel of finely grated muscle clinging to it.

"If I wait long enough you'll saw your own arm off. Save me the trouble, eh?"

The zombies on the other side retorted with their customary clumsy moans.

CHAPTER FIVE
LOCK

The door behind Cahz shook violently. The mob of hungry dead pushed desperately to get in. Individually their putrid muscles held little strength, but behind that fire door were probably hundreds of rotting infected corpses, all adding their impetus to the pressure.

But Cahz wasn't paying them any attention. With his right heel jamming the door shut, he'd lent forward, his carbine raised and pointing up the stairway.

The snarl came again, this time accompanied by a growling.

"What is it?" Elspeth asked, taking a worried step back.

Cahz didn't answer. He couldn't answer; he had no idea what was making that sound. There was a loud bang from somewhere up on the first or second floor; not a gunshot, more like a door being kicked open. Then came a screeching noise as something heavy heaved its way towards them.

The snarling gave way to grunting and the sound of something metal clattering echoed down the stairwell. Cahz kept his weapon trained on the stairs. He listened intently for a clue to how close the threat was, but Elspeth and the child's sobs combined with the ragged moans to overwhelm Cahz's senses. A bead of sweat escaped the corner of his eyebrow and trickled down his cheek.

With a tremendous crash something thunderous came barrelling down the stairs.

Cahz opened up, firing a three round burst into the skin of the foe. The bullets popped straight through, punching a neat hole in the grey aluminium.

The filing cabinet lay wedged at an odd angle, almost as if it had been killed. With a reluctant squeak a drawer slid open and a cascade of paperwork tumbled to the floor.

"Fuck!" came a voice from up the stairs.

"Boss?!" came a second.

"For fuck's sake didn't you dicks think to warn me?!" Cahz shouted back angrily. He was as mad at himself for being so jumpy and for wasting the ammo as he was at Cannon and Ryan. "I could have killed you!"

Cannon clambered over the blockage. "Shit, boss, no need to be so jumpy."

Cahz thumbed at the door. "Cannon, there are half a million ravenous corpses behind this door. Of course there's a need to be jumpy!"

"Okay, okay. Point taken," Cannon apologised as he started manhandling the long tall cabinet down the last of the steps.

"What took you so long?" Cahz asked. "Trouble?"

The cabinet thumped with each step as Cannon and Ryan hauled it to the bottom. Cannon looked over his shoulder, still heaving at the oblong of aluminium. He said, "Trouble came and went from this place, boss."

"What's that supposed to mean?" Before Cannon could answer, Cahz pointed at the cabinet. "Anyway, what are we going to do with this then?"

The grey paint had been scraped clear where it had been dragged along. It sported bashes and bullet holes and it was slightly twisted off true.

"I was hoping it'd be long enough to wedge between the door and the first step." Cannon scratched behind his ear. "But it's not…"

Cahz took a calming breath, and although his heart was still pounding he'd calmed himself down. "It's not a bad idea even if that thing's a little short."

"There's plenty more office furniture up there," Ryan offered. "We're bound to find a desk or something the right size to fill the gap."

"Okay, get to it," Cahz said. "But this time holler down before you start chucking stuff at us."

"Will do, boss." Cannon gave a sloppy salute before nodding to

Ryan to follow him.

Cahz closed his eyes and slumped against the door. With his eyes shut the vibrations from the door against his back were magnified. A dull ache made its presence felt in the back of his head.

He unscrewed the lid from his canteen and took a swig. The slug of water didn't shift the bitter taste on his tongue.

"Could I have some?" The woman's voice was shaky and uncertain.

Cahz held out the canteen. "Sure."

Elspeth was gazing down at the baby. The child had reduced her crying to a more tolerable whimper.

"She okay?" Cahz asked, peering over as far as he could. It was the most tactful way to ask if the baby had succumbed to the infection.

Elspeth rocked the baby gently. "I think she's calming down."

Cahz held in his relief. Both the woman and child were infected and it was only a matter of time before they joined the ranks of the living dead. In just a few short hours the contagion would infest every cell in the woman's body. And maybe less time than that for the child.

Elspeth took a long drink and passed the bottle back. "You'll have to screw the cap back on. My other hand's full," she said, rocking the baby.

On cue there was a slight gurgle as the child made a sucking reflex.

"She's such an angel," Elspeth said.

Even with the nasty looking scrape down her face, Cahz couldn't disagree.

"The others keep telling me how she looks like Samantha, but she doesn't… Well, not that much. She's Ryan's—you can see that in her face." Elspeth was crying now. "She's got Samantha's eyes but that smile's Ryan's."

Cahz nodded and smiled as he lifted the canteen to take another drink.

He panicked and tossed the plastic bottle across the hall. The clatter startled the baby and she resumed her piercing wail.

Elspeth jerked backed. "What is it?"

The canteen rocked to a sloshing halt, the water glugging from its open neck.

"You took a drink, lady," Cahz yelped, "and I was just about to drink from it too."

Elspeth was puzzled. "So?"

"You've been bit…" Cahz's voice trailed off as he realised how insensitive he had just been. The last drips of water trickled over the lip of the discarded canteen, sending ripples across the newly formed puddle.

"Look, I'm sorry," he offered, but it wasn't enough. Elspeth was in floods of tears.

Cahz leant hard up against the door, his head tipped back and his eyes closed. All he could hear were the sounds of crying in front and the moans behind.

Please God, just get them to shut up, please.

There was a loud crack from somewhere outside like the whip of a circus performer.

"What was that?" Elspeth asked.

Cahz looked at his watch. "That'll be Bates' homemade time bomb." The door behind him groaned further at the pressure of the undead pressing against it. "I thought the explosion would waste a few and draw more towards the noise. Guess there's just too many of them to make a difference." Cahz pulled his gloved hand across his face, wiping his chin. He looked down to examine his hand to see if he had removed any of the imagined contagion he felt creeping across his flesh.

"Gardyloo," came a call from above, followed by several loud thumps.

Something heavy came crashing down the stairs. With a sharp crack of plastic shattering, a photocopier tumbled into view. Shards of the beige plastic casing pinged off and flew down the stairs.

Ryan and Cannon quickly followed and kicked the office stalwart the last few feet. It cartwheeled over the last steps to land with an almighty crunch half on top of the filing cabinet.

Cahz lent back against the door, looking up at the ceiling.

"Get that wedged in place," he ordered without looking back at his subordinates.

"Sure thang, boss," Cannon complied.

With a few moments hauling and kicking, the two pieces of office equipment were solidly wedged against the door.

"Okay, let's get away from this noise," Cahz said, rubbing a thumb and finger across his eyebrows, trying to dispel a burgeoning headache.

"Just a minute," Cannon said.

The big soldier stood with his support weapon slung over his midriff and his hands casually folded on top like he was about lead a battlefield prayer.

"Cannon?" Cahz asked.

"There's…" Cannon paused. "Well, you'll see. It's just bit fucked up."

"What is?" Cahz asked.

"Masada," Ryan said.

"Masada?" Cahz echoed, puzzled.

CHAPTER SIX
BALCONY

"Three," Ali said. "Two," a little louder.

"One!"

Ali pushed off from the door and ran down the hallway. He half vaulted, half clambered over the chair blocking the way to the living room. As he landed a rip of pain spread out from his leg, but he ignored it.

The groaning of the zombies now mixed with the groaning of the front door as the weight of numbers forced their way through.

Ali cast a glance back to see the first of the undead pushed through the widening gap by the horde behind.

He picked up a small coffee table and hurled it at the full-length windows. The cheaply constructed table bounced off the glass and split in two as it crashed to the floor. The window remained intact except for the kaleidoscope crack that radiated from the impact point.

Ali stomped his foot into the weak point and the crack widened. He suddenly had an image of his foot knocking a neat hole through the glass—a hole that would lacerate his calf and leave him snared, unable to escape.

He picked up the larger half of the broken table and started hammering at the crack. Shards of wood splintered away with every swipe. As he hammered at the glass, the cracks zigzagged out longer and thinner, but with each blow the joint in the ruptured table gave a little more. Finally Ali battered the window and the table disintegrated in his hands.

He screamed as slivers of wood slashed into his skin. He looked down at his wounds to see toothpick-sized splinters of jagged wood in his palms and fingers. Blood wept from some of the larger punctures as he plucked out the slivers.

There was a thud in the hallway. As he watched he saw a pair of hands come into view. The pallid skin and the accompanying moan told him that the zombies had reached the chair obstructing the hall. It wouldn't be long before they managed to clamber over it.

He looked back at the window. The crack almost reached both the top and bottom frame. Then he noticed something and his stomach dropped. The crack was only on the first layer of glass. The window onto the small balcony was double glazed and the outside pane was undamaged.

Ali held his head in his bleeding hands and let out a shriek of frustration.

For a moment the zombies stopped moaning, their retarded brains trying to process the scream. Was it one of their own? Why did it sound so different to the ubiquitous moan? None of these were questions contagion addled neurons could cogitate. Exhausting their stodgy logic, they simply abandoned the thought and returned to their sluggish pursuit.

"Couch," Ali reminded himself.

He hopped over to the massive piece of furniture and knelt down, putting his hand underneath. He straightened up, taking the strain, and as he did missed splinters dug deeper into the flesh in his palms.

Grunting, Ali pushed the pain to one side and continued to hoist up the settee. It was heavy and he had only managed to raise it a few degrees when the far end slipped. Rather than raising the piece of furniture up on end, it was skidding away along the hardwood floor.

With a thud the first zombie toppled over the chair barricade into the living room. The creature lay there for a moment face and body flat on the floor, its feet and lower legs still caught up in the chair. It wasn't so much stunned by the fall as simply unable to comprehend what it should do next.

A second zombie was clambering through as the first found its composure and started its faltering attempt to get upright.

Ali dropped the couch with a loud clatter.

"Fuck!" he spat out from clenched teeth. He berated himself for not blocking the hall with the furniture while he had the chance.

He took a step towards the closest zombie with the intent of staving its head in when he caught a glimpse down the hallway. Packed against the walls was a throng of zombies, dozens of cadavers swaying as they slowly surged forward.

Ali turned back to the window, his hands shaking furiously, then back to the hallway. He couldn't take on so many zombies and he couldn't break open the window.

"Get a grip!" he barked to himself. "Breathe. Take a breath. Calm down. Think, damn you, think!"

He paced up and down in front of the window, his bloodied hand ruffling his hair.

"Find the key?" he said, looking at the handle for the window. "Where will the key be? No—first, what type of key is it?"

He bent down and examined the lock.

The first zombie was now on its feet and shuffling towards him.

Ali peered at the round brass barrel of the lock imbedded in the handle. A moan from behind made him swing round and as he did he brought his hand down. The handle turned and the window clicked open.

A draft penetrated the gap and caressed Ali's cheek. He looked back at the now open window in disbelief.

Ali cursed his stupidity. "Ah, piss."

He jumped to his feet and flung the window open. He stepped onto the balcony and slammed it closed just as the zombie connected with the glass. The infection filled body stood there pawing at the cracked window, its lips and teeth trying to chew at him, too dumb to notice the impediment.

"Fuck you!" Ali hissed as he flipped his index finger at the cadaver.

The creature watched the gesture only out of its instinct to follow movement.

As Ali lowered his gesture the zombie's hand shadowed his movement. As Ali's hand fell to his side the zombie's hand slapped the handle and the window swung open again.

"Fuck!"

Ali grabbed the handle from his side and pulled the window shut again.

With a thump a second grey skinned face peered out from behind the cracked glass. Ali stood there pulling the handle, watching the window fill up with the dead.

Once the snarling zombies had built up enough pressure, Ali let go of the handle, secure in the knowledge that the pressing weight of the dead on the other side would hold the pane shut.

"Okay, what now?"

He looked out across the street. The ground below was a mass of undead—more zombies than he'd ever seen before. The sea breeze shifted and the stench from below caught his nostrils. He instinctively recoiled, but his gaze brought him back to the window behind. There was now a plethora of dead faces gawping back. The wind whipped round again, bringing with it the smell of smoke from one of the many Molotov cocktails that had been thrown to thin out the undead. Other than the smell of burning, there was no sign of the helicopter, the sound of its whirring blades now lost to the distance.

All the exertion had suddenly made Ali feel lightheaded, like he had stood up too quickly. It felt like hours since they had all stood on the roof of the warehouse debating whether or not to break from their safety.

He looked at his watch. There was a thin smattering of blood obscuring the face. He rubbed his left arm under the armpit of his jumper and re-examined the smudged but readable timepiece. It was eight o'four in the morning. Just over forty minutes had passed.

Ali pushed a long breath out and shook his head. He was exhausted. He slumped down against the window. He wasn't safe on the balcony. He knew he couldn't stay here for long.

Maybe just a minute… while I catch my breath.

He twisted his ankle round to get a better view of his slashed leg. There was a brown crust starting to form in the deepest parts of the gash. The skin looked raw and pink. He didn't think it went all the way to his muscle but he didn't want to check. A steady trickle of blood was still flowing from the wound. If it was serious Ali really didn't want to add that to his mental list of All The Things That Are Fucked Up Right Now.

Ali looked up at the balcony above. He would have to climb up there, find somewhere sheltered and safe, somewhere he could tend to his injuries, somewhere he could think.

The noise of the zombies slapping the windowpane seemed distant.

Ali lent his head back against the glass and closed his eyes.

***

Ali woke with a start. Juddering awake, he frightened the seagull perched on the balcony railing. The scraggy grey and white bird flung its wings out and cawed abusively from its yellow beak.

"Shoo!" Ali hissed, waving his hand at the bird.

Voicing its displeasure with a vulgar squawk, the brash sea bird snapped its beak and took flight.

The scavenger was no doubt scrutinising Ali for signs of life, intent on an easy meal. With the demise of man, these opportunists had been forced to revert to an honest living rather than just scrounging the scraps left by civilisation.

Ali rubbed his sore head. His brain felt like it was a hammer drill trying to bore its way out of his skull.

There was a bang from the window behind him and Ali turned round to see a solid sheet of dead faces staring back. Pressed behind the glass, the patient zombies had seen his movement and taken a fresh interest in him.

Slowly Ali backed up from the window until he felt the railings behind him.

The grating where he'd lain was awash with fresh blood. He looked down at his injured leg. His jeans were soaked, a dark patch encircling his calf.

Gingerly he peeled the material away from his leg to look at the wound. The flesh was still raw and inflamed but the gash itself looked dark with clotted blood.

Ali nodded to himself, satisfied that although he'd probably lost a lot of blood, it couldn't be that serious if it had stopped by itself. And he'd woken up.

How long have I been out?

He tilted his stiff neck down to check his watch. An hour had passed since he escaped from the flat and passed out.

In the street there still stood thousands of moaning zombies, their cries mixing together, forming a continuous low grumble. Occasionally one would utter an excited moan, higher and louder, and the call would ripple through the mass of undead.

But there was no sign of human life. Earlier when he had struggled through the crowds of the infected there had been gunshots. Although the chopper had gone there must have been people left behind. And armed people at that.

Ali scanned the city, hoping to see something that would indicate a rescue party. He tried to stand up to get a better view, but his legs were numb. It may just have been the awkward position he'd been in or it could be something more serious. If it was something more severe than a dead leg, he knew it wouldn't be long before the seagull mustered up the courage to come back pecking at him.

Ali grabbed hold of the railings and eased himself up. The mesh floor of the balcony was coated with blood and through the gaps he could see a knot of eager zombies ogling him, their faces covered in the spilt blood.

He gripped hold of the railing and looked over at the throng. There was an element of jostling in the crowd as the zombies pushed and clawed to get under the drip. They stood there, their crimson-daubed faces upturned to the balcony, their mouths wide open, lips drawn back, teeth bared.

Suddenly a revelation hit him. Ali recoiled from the railing, bathed in cold terror. Their dead lips weren't drawn back ready to attack. The blood-splattered zombies were smiling. They were happy. A surge of vomit churned in his stomach. Unlike the surrounding cadavers they weren't moaning—they were revelling in the taste of human blood. His blood. The dead creatures were experiencing pleasure from the taste of his blood.

"Fuck," Ali heard himself whisper.

But in spite of his revulsion it made perfect sense. He knew the zombies were driven to feast on human flesh. He had often seen them moaning and crying out at their prey but he had never stuck around to watch them feed. He'd always been too busy trying to destroy them or run away to watch their reaction to eating.

"Calm down," Ali instructed himself and he drew in a deep breath. "Focus on staying alive."

He scanned the nearby buildings. There was nothing; no indication of life. Ali consoled himself that he didn't have a commanding view from this floor. Rescuers could be just behind a building out of sight only metres away.

Then Ali had another dark thought: What if the gunshots weren't rescuers? What if the people in the chopper had abandoned his friends? Maybe the occupants of the helicopter had refused to take them but had instead given them guns and told them to fend for themselves?

Ali shook his head, having pondered the idea. Why would the people in the chopper abandon them and give them weapons? That wouldn't make sense. Why waste the guns and why risk the chopper being shot at by the angry people they had just left? It made no sense.

Ali knew he had to push to one side the useless fretting about his companions and get on with the task of his own survival.

Looking up, he could see the four other balconies above him. There was a similar line of wrought iron platforms running parallel to him in the identical row of apartments next to this, but the gap between his current position and the closest one was five or six metres away. Even without an injured leg it would be an impossible leap.

"Upwards and onwards," Ali geed himself on as he clambered up.

He examined the railing and the possible footholds. Using the frame of the window to steady himself, he first sat on the railing. He reached up but was a good distance short of the overhanging balcony. A light gust of wind fluttered past him and Ali held his breath. It wasn't a long way down. If he were to fall he knew he'd survive. But he knew he wouldn't survive for long. He'd land like a crowd surfer in the welcoming arms of the dead below.

Ali swallowed down his nervousness and eased his good leg onto the handrail. With one hand gripping the rail and the other flat against the rough brick, Ali pushed up. Gritting his teeth against the pain, he squatted on his haunches on the perilously thin guard rail.

With great trepidation Ali let go of his hold and placed both hands on the wall to steady himself. Slowly fighting against the pain and the fear, he straightened his legs and stood up. It was only a difference in height of around six feet, but his heart thumped like he was on the peak of a mountain. He gulped down a breath, trying to push back the vertigo. A light breeze wrapped its way around him. His unruly beard fluttered in the draught and fear spurred him into action.

He stretched up and found the balcony overhead, giving a sigh of relief at finding the extra purchase. He pulled his gaze away from the ochre brickwork to look up. With his height the next storey up was only inches away from his face and he was easily able to get his elbows between the rails and onto the decking. He gripped the bars like a dejected prisoner and tested his weight and grip.

"You've just got to go for it."

He swung his good leg level to the decking and jammed his foot in between two railings. He threw his left hand up, using the momentum from the swing and found the top of the railing. Grunting from the exertion, he pulled himself over the railing and landed with a thump safely onto the deck.

He lay there like a landed fish gasping for air staring at the underside of the balcony above. Even though his leg throbbed he let slip a childish giggle of delight.

"Made it," he wheezed.

After a few moments gaining his composure, Ali got back to his feet. He walked over to the window and gazed in. The sunlight and the dark interior combined to turn the glass into a dull mirror. He placed his hand to his forehead and lent into the window, hoping to shade the worst of the glare.

The room looked abandoned. Items of a normal life left behind by their dead or fleeing occupant. Ali rapped on the windowpane with his knuckles. He wasn't adhering to some long lost etiquette, he wanted the noise to draw out any zombies that might still be inside.

After waiting long enough for any shambling half skeleton to investigate, he tried the window. It was locked shut.

Still grasping the handle he looked up to the next balcony.

"Onwards and upwards," he sighed.

He repeated the climb and made his way to the next balcony. But again the window was firmly closed.

He waited for a moment to regain his strength. Above him was the final floor.

He didn't know what he'd do if that window was shut. He looked over at the adjacent terrace of balconies. The gap was too wide to jump but he'd seen a movie once where the hero had jumped diagonally, landing on the balcony one level down and across.

But Ali's leg throbbed, his joints ached, and he didn't feel much like an action hero.

"One last climb," he said.

He saddled the guard rail and started his third ascent.

In a few seconds he'd repeated his climb and was standing at the top floor balcony. He was delighted to see the window was open a crack. But the initial thrill evaporated as he tried the handle. This window too was locked shut.

Undeterred, Ali wedged his fingers in and pulled. The window didn't budge.

Ali berated himself for losing his steel pipe in the throng below; with a little leverage he might be able to pop the window open.

As he stared at the adjacent apartments, contemplating his chances of successfully leaping the gap, the metal baluster in his grasp twisted slightly. Ali's mind sparked. Bending down he methodically checked each of the thin metal struts that joined the decking to the handrail. The four on each corner were sturdy structural columns with the ones between forming a safety screen to prevent someone from accidentally falling. Some of these were loose. They turned in their seating.

Ali examined the construction of the balcony. If he could buckle the handrail up he should be able to pop out some of the metal bars.

He lay down on the deck, his head wedged against the wall, his fingers stretched down to find purchase through the gaps in the deck, and then he kicked out hard. He smacked the underside of the handrail with his heels. The metal rattled but nothing gave. Ali stuck his left foot through the bars and twisted to lock himself tight against the recoil of the kick.

This time Ali lashed out with one foot. With his more secure position, more of the energy went into its target. Ali kicked again and this time he felt something yield. Furiously he kicked and kicked again and with each strike he felt the metal buckle.

With a dozen more angry boots the handrail started to budge. Ali squatted in front of the misshapen baluster. The light metal welds had snapped and some of the bars were detached. Ali grasped hold of the most likely candidate and twisted. With a few good yanks the three-foot metal rod was dislodged.

He wasted no time in slotting the bar between the window and the frame. He took a square stance and purposefully pulled back with both hands. The plastic frame started to creak and deform. Ali kept the pressure up, leaning back and pulling with all his might. Something started to give—he could feel movement through the metal shaft.

Invigorated by the prospect of success, he found more strength and pulled harder. There was a sudden crunch and the makeshift crowbar was catapulted out of the Ali's grasp. The bent metal bar flung off into space, slicing through the air like the blades of a helicopter to land in the zombie-carpeted street below.

The tension suddenly released, Ali stumbled backward where he collided with the damaged handrail. He threw his hands out, grasping for anything before his momentum carried him over the railing.

Unable to stop, he flipped over the balcony. As the sky flashed overhead his grip found purchase. Then came a jolting wrenching through his shoulders as the momentum yanked at the joints. He hung there for a spilt second before his fingertips slipped free.

Ali started plummeting again. He was watching the balcony above fly away. As he fell a couple of the loosened bars burst free and were sent tumbling to the ground with him.

Ali flailed his arms out, trying to grab hold of anything to arrest his fall. His arm connected with something impossibly solid. The force of the impact was numbingly violent. His whole body twisted from the impact and he collided hard with the metal deck of the balcony below. The two metal bars that had fallen with him clattered off the decking and continued their journey to the crowd of zombies below.

Ali started laughing. Like an action hero, he'd survived by a piece of miraculous luck. Granted, it hadn't seen him favoured enough to get him to the adjacent apartments, but he was still thankful. He laughed until he realised just how much pain he was in. The laughter turned to coughing, and when that subsided, Ali groaned.

After an age and a couple of aborted attempts, Ali hauled himself up to sit against the wall. His injured leg throbbed and now his shoulder did too. There was a lump on the back of his head and a massive headache to testify to the force of the impact. He looked down at his hands. They were bloody and scratched and now he noticed the nail on his index finger had been ripped off about halfway. He felt sick looking at the raw pulp of his nail bed. He dropped his hand out of sight, grateful that the pain from elsewhere was masking his missing fingernail.

He looked out over the thoroughfare packed with undead. They filled the road from here to the offices across the street. The front windows were smashed in and the zombies were packed inside just as thick as outside. To his right he could see the plaza they'd been trying to get to. The helicopter and its promise of rescue were long gone. And still there was no sign of the people who'd been shooting earlier.

Up to the left, back towards the warehouse, Ali could just see the odd patch of tarmac. The zombies were thinner on the ground up there but there were still thousands of them. The odd waft of grey black smoke drifted across the street, some of the petrol bombs were still burning and hopefully still incinerating zombies.

"What now?"

He could climb back up and try the window again, but even if he forced his way inside there would be nothing of use to him. All the food and weapons had been scavenged from here years ago. Could he survive until the helicopter came back? And what if the helicopter never came back?

Ali looked across at the dilapidated office block, its sandstone walls grimy with soot and moss and all the other discolouring that five years of the apocalypse and a lack of maintenance had accumulated. The maintenance crews, the cleaners, the office workers and a hundred other careers had all amalgamated into one profession: denizen of hell. Most of the undead that had congregated wore the same uniform now: tattered brown rags, pale blue skin and a gormless open maw.

Here and there Ali could still pick out the odd noticeable individual. A soldier in a bio-chemical suit with his gas mask torn off, a hiker with his backpack still secured by its shoulder straps his thick jacket with white puffs of stuffing poking out from the rips, and Ray—

Ali shook his weary head and let out a lonely sigh.

Among the zombies gawping up at him was Ray. There were raw chunks of flesh gouged from his body where the zombies had ravished him. His familiar glasses were missing and his face was caked in his own dried blood, but it was unmistakably Ray. Ali's friend these last four years was now reduced to a mindless corpse.

Even with a hundred hungry ghouls feasting on his bones he had revived before the ravenous mouths had time to consume him. And no matter how fresh the kill, once they had reanimated no zombie would eat them.

"I am truly sorry, my friend," Ali said.

He closed his eyes.

CHAPTER SEVEN
CHAMBER

"What the fuck happened here?" Cahz said, stepping over a dead body. Once through the broken gap in the makeshift defences, he had been confronted by an extraordinary scene. It looked like the stairwells had been barricaded and sealed off. The office furniture piled up to block the entrances and the space created by their absence resembled a campsite. There were tents, camp beds and piles of provisions all laid out in an orderly pattern. The only thing that wasn't orderly were the blood splatters, bullet holes and dead bodies.

"Defence in depth," Cannon said absently, looking at the make do redoubt.

"What are the tents for?" Elspeth said absently.

"Privacy I guess," Ryan offered.

"The Whisky Deltas break in?" Cahz asked, looking round the breached stronghold.

"Nope, not a single W.D. in here." Cannon nudged a corpse with his foot. "These poor bastards have rotted to mush. The roaches and flies have seen to them."

"W.D.?" Ryan asked.

Cannon answered without acknowledging Ryan, "Walking Dead."

Cahz continued to prowl round the site, occasionally pulling open the flaps on tents with the muzzle of his rifle. He prodded at a flap of leathery skin on a cadaver's skeletal rib.

"That's an exit wound," he observed, looking at the shattered bone. "This guy died from a shot to the chest. What the hell happened here?"

"When we found this place," Ryan looked across at Elspeth, "What, four years ago?" Elspeth shrugged. "Well, the corpses were in better condition. You could see some had their throats cut, others shot." Ryan gestured to a stack of crates. "There was food and water and guns and ammo and everything you'd need to hold up for months. Ray called it Masada."

"Masada?" Cannon asked.

Cahz stepped back to the group. "First Jewish uprising against the Romans in something like fifty A.D."

"Ray reckoned the same thing happened here," Ryan added.

"Do one of you want to fill me in? I ain't that clued up with Jewish history," Cannon grumbled.

"There was a Roman siege at a place called Masada. The Romans built a massive ramp to breach the defences. It took months to build but when they finally got over the wall everyone was dead. Even though they had plenty of supplies, rather than being captured and crucified or sold into slavery they decided to commit mass suicide."

Cannon kicked a corpse with a gunshot wound to the head. "Yeah, well, nobody shoots themselves in the cheek to blow their brains out."

"At Masada they drew lots," Cahz said. "Each man would kill his family and then they in turn would kill each other until only one man remained. Then he would be the only one who had to commit suicide."

"So you're saying the same thing happened here?" Cannon asked. "It was Jonestown massacre all over?"

"That's how Ray and Sarah saw it," Ryan answered. "Surrounded with no way out, they committed mass suicide."

"It's a bit unlikely, isn't it?" Cannon wonder aloud. "Could it not just as easily been looters?"

Ryan shook his head and pointed at the crates. "There were still a ton of supplies when we found the place. Kept us fed for a month. No way looters would have broken in, killed a group of heavily armed people, and then left without ransacking the place."

"They all drank the Kool-Aid," Cannon said reluctantly. "Still it's a bit sick."

"Technically it was Flav-R-Aid," Ryan mumbled.

"Hell, Cannon, we've seen a dozen things just this fucked up over the years," Cahz pointed out.

Cannon chewed his lip. "Suppose."

"Well, let's make this place secure," Cahz said. "We need to be sure we can get to the roof and check it's suitable to land a chopper. Ryan, you know this place better than us."

Ryan nodded his agreement.

"You and Cannon check that out. Go scout things out up there. I'm going to start making an inventory of what we can use in here."

"No point," Ryan said. "We gutted the place of anything useful."

"I want to know that for sure. You guys might have missed something. Now get a move on."

Cannon gave a nod and turned for the stairs.

"Cannon," Cahz said. Cannon stopped and whipped round. "Go up one staircase and down the other. Don't go onto the other floors, but keep your ears open for other residents. We'll sweep the place clear only if we need to."

"Got it boss." Cannon made a salute and jogged away.

Ryan hesitated. He looked at Elspeth and the child she cradled.

His daughter was still whining, her cheeks flushed, the scratch down her face puffy and prominent. Elspeth looked cold and grey. Her skin had a waxy sheen to it and her eyes looked sunken. Ryan had seen that pallor so many times before. The condemned look of the infected.

"You comin'?" Cannon called back.

Elspeth was Samantha's mother and they shared the same hair and the same eyes. And now Elspeth shared the same haunted expression Ryan had seen on Sam when she'd realised she was going to die.

"Yeah, sure," Ryan said softly and turned to follow.

Cahz slung his carbine behind him and marched up to the crates.

The various wooden and plastic boxes weren't as ordered as he'd first thought. Cahz guessed that at one time they had been neatly stacked, but that Ryan and his friends had seen no need to tidy up after their foraging.

He squatted down on his haunches and gave a huff before opening the first one.

Inside was an array of bandages and other basic first aid.

"Here," Cahz said, offering a Mepore dressing.

"Oh, what's the point?" Elspeth sighed.

Cahz nodded and tossed the dressing back.

"It doesn't hurt now anyway," Elspeth said.

"Gone numb, huh?" Cahz didn't look back to make eye contact. Instead he opened the next box.

"After all this time…" Elspeth sucked in a sharp breath. "I

mean... Well, I don't know what I mean. We'd survived all of this, Samantha and me." She looked down at the sleeping child in her arms. "It was a shock when she died. I thought I could console myself with my granddaughter. There was always a reminder of Samantha. But she reminds me too much sometimes. It's all so unfair. I mean, who dies in childbirth these days..." Elspeth paused for a moment. "I mean, no one should die in childbirth in this day and age, what with the medicines and machines and doctors. If we'd have had them Samantha wouldn't have died. She'd be here to look after her baby girl just like I looked after her." Elspeth looked up, her eyes wet with welling tears. "That's how things are supposed to be. Not this nightmare." She took in a deep breath that transformed into a sob. She started crying.

Cahz looked round from his rummaging. Elspeth was sitting with tears streaming down her cheeks. Her short salt and pepper hair combined with the deep wrinkles from her weeping made her look like a pensioner. Cahz guessed she was actually younger than that from the way she talked and the way she had run the gauntlet of zombies.

He gazed at her blankly, trying to decide what to do. He could go across there, sit down next to her, and put a comforting arm round her. But what would be the point of that? Cahz didn't know her, had only just met her and there was no point investing time in getting to know her as she'd be dead in a few hours.

He might as well go over there and put a bullet in her brain—wouldn't that be the kindest thing to do?

As prudent as it was, Cahz knew he shouldn't dispatch her. Elspeth was a longstanding companion of Ryan's and he'd no doubt want to say his goodbyes.

He sucked in a brisk draft of air through his teeth. He turned back to the first crate and retrieved the dressing.

"Let me have a look at that," he said as he walked over.

"I'm sorry," Elspeth sobbed.

Cahz pulled back the blood soaked collar. The bite mark beneath was black. The contagion's spread was marked against her pale skin by the tendrils of dark veins. He unpeeled the dressing from its packaging and gently placed it over the wound. The stark white plaster showed the contrast of the greying dead skin and infected deep blue blood vessels.

"Nothing to apologise about, lady," Cahz said, staring down at his boots. "Whole world's shit and there's no rhyme or reason to it."

"I was supposed to look after her." Elspeth looked down at the baby. The child's face was still raw looking with a thick red welt.

"You did your best. Sometimes that just isn't enough." Cahz

paused a long moment. "I was about to try and empathize with you, lady—tell you about the people I let down. But it's not the same."

Elspeth glanced down at her blood stained blouse. "No, it's not. You've not been infected."

Cahz straightened at the comment. He felt the tainted mucus in his mouth rise. He shook his head. "There's nothing anybody can do for the infected."

"There is one thing," Elspeth butted in, looking down at his side arm.

Cahz saw where Elspeth was going with this train of thought.

"How do you want to play it?" he asked.

"I don't know. I just know I don't want to be a nuisance. I don't want to come back and… well, you know."

Cahz did know.

"When?" he asked solemnly.

Elspeth took a deep swallow. "Not right now, if that's what you mean."

She gently stroked the baby's uninjured cheek. The small child pursed its lips and made a sucking motion in its sleep. "She's gorgeous, isn't she?"

"She sure is."

Cahz meant it. Even with the nasty scratch covering one side of her infant face, her wide eyes and pug nose were still cute. He felt a cold shudder run down his spine at the thought of having to shoot such an angelic face.

He picked himself up and made his way back over to the supplies.

"Best sort through this stuff," he said, trying to distance himself from the child and the appalling notion.

"Find anything useful, boss?" Cannon asked, looking at the heap of crates.

"Nothing much. The most important things are these." Cahz stood up and ushered Cannon over. "There are six of these five gallon water bottles," Cahz said as he gently kicked the first container with his toe. The water inside sloshed against the clear walls.

"Will they be safe to drink?" Cannon asked.

"Should be fine," Ryan said. "Water doesn't go off so as long as the lids are on tight. There might be a bit of a taint off the plastic but it won't kill you."

"You know that for sure?" Cannon asked.

Ryan thumped his chest. "Never done me any harm."

"If you're worried we can drop a couple of purification tablets in," Cahz said.

"We got some?"

"Over here. There's a ton of camping equipment." Cahz looked over at Ryan. "You and your pals obviously didn't need it."

Ryan peered into the open crate. "We had as much of this shit as we needed. It was mainly food and weapons we took, when we could find them."

"Any medical supplies boss?" Cannon asked.

"Yeah, boxes of the stuff," Cahz replied. "Why, you needing something?"

"Got some gloves and some disinfectant?"

"You carrying an injury?" Ryan asked, suspicious of the big soldier.

"Nope. I just want to get the crud off my kit." Cannon looked down at the gore soaked body armour and the smudges of gunk on his uniform. "I don't want to wipe my nose and get the infection off this shit."

"Here." Cahz tossed two tissue box sized containers over in rapid succession.

Cannon caught the first box with ease but fumbled slightly to keep hold of the second. When he finally had both under control he read the packaging.

"One hundred vinyl gloves." Cannon turned the second box round. "And alcohol wipes."

"Closest thing to a disinfectant I've found," Cahz said.

Cannon sat down on the edge of a crate and started opening the boxes.

"I suggest we all take the time to clean ourselves up," Cahz said looking round at everyone. He saw Elspeth lying on a camp bed oblivious to the conversation, cradling the infected child. In reality he knew he was only addressing Ryan. It was too late for them.

"So there's no chow?" Cannon said as he scraped at his body armour with what looked like a moist towelette left over from an in-flight meal. The wad of tissue was becoming more and more discoloured with every pass. Streaks of black, brown, red and even green began accumulating on the white cloth as Cannon went about cleaning.

"Don't know how you can think of food right now," Cahz confessed.

"Just taking stock. Need to know our assets and liabilities."

Cannon kept working at the sodden fabric as he spoke.

"We do have dinner, courtesy of Bates." Cahz held up the webbing Bates had passed him. "But it's early for lunch just yet." He placed the pouches down with the rest of the useful material scavenged.

"Fantastic," Ryan said, eyeing up the pack.

"And I think we should be saving that," Cahz added.

"Saving it?" Ryan asked. "What for? I mean, your man's coming back in a few hours and I'm fucking starving."

Cahz sat down on a crate. "He is, but it'll be a while."

"Well, how long?"

Looking down at his watch, Cahz went through some mental arithmetic. "If all goes well I'd expect to see him sometime after seventeen hundred hours."

"And if it don't go well?" Cannon said slowly.

"Worst case scenario, old Captain Warden won't let him fly without six hours shuteye," Cahz answered.

"That's a full day then," Ryan said.

"We've got a secure location and enough water. We've got one MRE and they're quite generous so even split between four that ought to keep your belly quiet." Cahz levelled his last comment at Ryan.

"Come on, I've not eaten a proper meal in…" Ryan paused. "Well, for fucking years."

"You'll be right at home with the MRE then. It ain't a proper meal," Cannon quipped.

"You're lucid and mobile. I don't doubt you're hungry, but the longer we save the food the better," Cahz said.

"Why if we're getting picked up in a while can I not have some now?"

"No, we'll wait and eat it tonight. That will give us the energy we need when we need it. For now just sit tight and wait."

"You forgettin' something, boss?" Cannon looked over at Elspeth.

Cahz gave a sigh and nodded.

"Lady," he called over.

Elspeth was looking drawn and groggy.

"My name is Elspeth," she said indignantly. "You haven't used my name once."

Cahz realised that he'd been avoiding using her name. Maybe in his unconscious mind he'd reasoned it would be easier to deal with a nameless zombie.

"Sorry Elspeth, but this concerns you." Cahz lowered his tone.

"Have you decided how you want to go out?" Even when forced to address the issue directly he still couldn't help but use euphemisms.

Elspeth straightened up. "I don't want to be shot, if that's what you're asking. At least not until I've come back."

"That's fine, Elspeth," Ryan said. "I'll keep an eye on you."

"I don't want you to kill my granddaughter either," Elspeth added. "Not while I'm alive."

Ryan hung his head and bit his lip. He knelt down beside her and reached out his hand. Gently, so as not to disturb her, he moved some of the swaddling away from her face.

"How's she doing?" Ryan whispered gazing at the cherub like features.

"She's been able to fall asleep, bless her," Elspeth said. "Look, Ryan, it's not right her not having a name. I know you've had it hard with Samantha's death, we all have."

Ryan knelt there, quietly looking at the child.

"I don't expect a christening or anything like that," Elspeth added. "I mean, God stopped listening a long time ago. Ryan," Elspeth said more firmly, "Ryan, it's not right not naming her." She looked Ryan in the eye. Her old translucent skin showed the snaking lines of contaminated veins beneath.

Ryan's bottom lipped trembled involuntary as he thought about Sam.

"You can't let her die without giving her a name." Elspeth passed the bundle over to her father. "Samantha would have wanted you to."

Ryan took the sleeping child with shaking hands. He bit at his lip trying to keep the tears in.

"Oh Elspeth!" Ryan blurted out and started crying.

Elspeth put her arms around the young man and hugged him close.

Cahz nudged his colleague and whispered, "Show me the roof."

Cannon nodded and the pair made their exit.

CHAPTER EIGHT
PURCHASE

"Can't sit here all morning," Ali said as he stood up.

For lack of a better idea he had decided to try the partially open window again, this time a little more cautiously. He scrambled up onto the broken balcony and dislodged another makeshift crowbar. He wedged the metal bar into the open window and again applied pressure, this time more evenly and warily.

As soon as he started he could hear the PVC frame of the window groan but nothing more.

He pushed a little harder. Still the window didn't budge.

Ali started leaning into the push then pulsing the force to try and fatigue the joints and bolts keeping the window locked. The third time he applied tension there was a faint ripping sound, like a strip of fabric being torn. Ali pulled on the bar again and this time the noise was slightly louder.

He put the metal rod down and examined the gap. The plastic surround was buckled and chewed and the metal joint the window pivoted on was scraped but still intact. It hadn't budged.

Ali stood resting for a moment with his hand on the frame. He stroked his long beard with his free hand debating if he should keep at it or formulate some other plan.

Something was sticky against his fingertips. He pulled his hand back from resting on the window frame and looked at it. Pressing his thumb to his grubby fingertips they felt tacky from the sealant. Ali now looked closely at the window frame where he'd been leaning.

The weathered white surround wasn't flush with the wall.

Changing tack, Ali grasped hold of the edge and pulled. The plastic flexed under the pressure and then started to creak. He tugged at the surround and little by little it started to give.

He stood back and wiped the sweat from his forehead. The gap around the edging was tiny but wide enough now to force his crowbar in.

He jammed the metal rod in and started prying at the window frame. The plastic and glass and metal groaned and splintered and popped.

Ali worked back and forward like an oarsman on some ancient galley. Back and forward, back and forward, teasing out pulses of pressure with each stroke. The plastic buckled and cracked until suddenly there was a crunching noise like a fissure cleaving through ice.

Ali stood back again to see a spindly line of cracks on the glass radiating out from the corner he was working on. He rubbed his greasy palms against his thighs and resumed his task.

Within a couple of minutes the first of the four sides of framing snapped away. Beneath the façade was the raw brickwork and behind the cavity the inside wall. With the inside of the glazing unit exposed, removing the last three sheets of plastic edging was relatively easy.

Soon Ali stood triumphant in front of the exposed brickwork. Only a few wedges of packing secured the window in place and there were gaps between the glazing unit and the wall large enough to squeeze even his thick fingers through.

With a mighty kick he battered the window. The glass cracked and the clunk of the impact echoed around the sill but the window didn't topple into the room.

He scratched his head. He remembered his mother telling him not to do that or he'd go bald. He'd never expected this innocuous habit would lead to the barren patch on top of his head but no doubt his mother would have taken it as evidence that she was right.

"You're going to have to come out somehow," Ali said to his inanimate adversary.

Guessing the weight of the unit was a two-man lift, Ali stepped to the side out of the window's way. He slipped his thick fingers into the top edge of the frame at his side and braced his body against the wall. He took a deep breath and pulled.

At first nothing happened, then a wedge of packing material snapped and popped out. With that the whole thing screeched and started to slide. Ali flung the plastic frame away from the wall with all his strength. The last few strips of wooden packing disentangled and the huge window unit toppled out, like a tall oak being felled. Instinctively Ali took a step back as the double-glazing unit impacted with the twisted and damaged railing.

The glass shattered and crunched. The whole balcony shuddered with the impact. The metal squealed at the mistreatment.

Ali stumbled as the decking twisted and wrenched against its fixtures. Then the unit tumbled back towards him and collided with the deck. Ali jumped back flat against the wall as the force of the impact reverberated through the whole building. With a loud ping a retaining bolt snapped and the balcony lunged downward.

"Fuck!" Ali screamed as he grabbed for the empty window.

He pushed off with his feet but the energy of his spring was lost as the decking sheared its last brackets and went into free fall. A tortured screech of metal shot out as the metal body pivoted away from him.

The smashed window unit slipped from the decking and clattered its way down the side of the building. With a dull squelch it collided with a clutch of unsuspecting zombies in the street below.

Still attached to the wall by one wrought iron tie, the balcony hung, uneasily swinging to and fro.

Ali gasped for breath and hung on to the side of the wall. He had both hands tightly gripping on the exposed brickwork left bare when the window had sheared free. His arms were sore, from the wracked shoulders, to the battered elbows to his aching wrists and hands and all the burning muscles in between.

The pain, Ali surmised, would only get worse.

The last support ruptured with a screech and the decking smashed its way down the side of the building. It bounced and tumbled as it fell, skelping off the balcony below. Ali looked down just in time to see the metal decking splat to a halt in the mob of undead.

Determined not to meet the same fate, Ali tried contracting his arms to pull himself up but he lacked the strength. Sweat cascaded down his forehead with the effort of holding on and he desperately wanted to wipe the stinging perspiration from his eyes. He felt out with his feet, trying to find a toehold.

He strained his neck looking down for some kind of purchase but his body obscured the view. He could easily drop down to the balcony below but he might not be able to climb up again. What's more, the balcony below could have been weakened to the point of failure from the debris that smashed off it. The extra weight dropping onto it could be enough to cause it to collapse.

Ali knew his best option was to get through this window.

Taking a frantic second look to his right, he saw the railing from the flat below protruding from the wall. Ali swung out his leg in an attempt to gain the purchase he needed. The brick overhead crumbled, sending a shower of grit tumbling into his face. Ali spluttered out the dry dirt from his mouth and tried to bat away the dust in his eyes. The masonry crumbled again, taking the security from his grip. He slipped. His foot hit the railing and slipped free. As his fingers slid loose of the brickwork, Ali threw his foot out again. It connected with the railing. Quickly he pushed against the solid footing and heaved. He kicked out with his injured leg. Fear robbed his senses of the pain as he pushed against the brick. Using the push he scrambled up the wall.

Throwing his elbows over the lip of the windowsill, he tumbled through the gaping hole in a cloud of plasterboard and masonry.

He squirmed his way to the floor, wheezing from the lungful of powder. A dry hacking cough rasped its way out of his chest as he belched out the dust caught in his throat. He lay on the dirty floorboards gasping and clutching his chest, spluttering dark droplets of spit from his lips with each breath. As he lay on the bare floor he had a sudden disturbing thought.

He craned his neck up and called out in a trembling voice, "Is anyone home?"

Ali didn't expect a response, at least not a human one.

Motes of stour wafted in the empty room, lit by the strong morning sun. The wind whistled past the exposed brickwork accompanied by the groggy moans outside, but the apartment was quiet.

He blinked back the particles of dirt from his eyes as he rolled over onto all fours. As his breathing steadied, twinges of pain burst along his nerves. Now that the adrenaline was subsiding the various disparate injuries were vying for his attention.

Slowly Ali stood up. He dusted himself off. With a few watery blinks his eyes started to focus on his surroundings. This room was a barren copy of the first floor room he'd escaped. No breakfast bar, no cupboards, no furniture or flatscreen TV. The room was dusty and empty. There were paint-splattered sheets against one wall and a couple tins of paint accompanying them. The power sockets and lights were hanging limp from the wall, suspended by a few inches of electrical wire.

To replace the inoperative lights there was an adjustable stand with a caged light bulb. The power cable for the portable lighting trailed off down the hall. Quietly Ali followed the wire round. The hall was as empty as the main room but Ali was relieved that although the lock had been smashed open, the main door was firmly shut.

"Looks like your decorator won't be finished on time," he quipped as he opened the closest door to him.

The door swung open to a gutted bedroom. A number of the floorboards were up and piled up to one side. A drum of white sheathed electrical cable sat in the middle of the room, reminiscent of a coffee table. Sitting on top of the makeshift table was a toolbox.

Ali opened the lid and looked inside. There was an array of screwdrivers, a couple of tools that looked like pliers and what Ali guessed were numerous ends for phone lines or the like. Riffling pass some kind of meter Ali found a few rolls of electrical tape and a slim black and yellow retractable knife.

He smiled as he held the cheap plastic tool in his hand. It was a disposable blade, the type where you could snap off the leading dull edge and push the fresh blade from the hilt. But this simple tool would increase his chances of surviving a hundred fold. It would be a useless weapon against a zombie, but a blade had a thousand uses in any survival situation.

Buoyed on by this small quantity of luck, Ali scanned the rest of the room.

The morning sun was shining strongly through the bedroom windows and on the windowsill was a plastic bag. Ali stepped over to the window and opened it up. Inside were the unwanted and unwelcome remains of some contractor's packed lunch. Along with the discarded wrapper of a chocolate bar and sandwich, long since devoured, were the less palatable items of the workman's lunch. The largest item was the half drunk bottle of what would once have been a carbonated fizzy orange. Ali twisted the cap off but there was no hiss of gas. The drink had gone flat, possibly years before.

Like a wine connoisseur Ali held the bottle to the light and swilled the contents around. The liquid was translucent but clear of any foreign bodies and not cloudy. He placed his nostrils over the lip of the bottle and sniffed. There was still a sweet fruity odour from the contents.

Ali placed the bottle to his lips and took a swig. The drink was flat but a few full gulps and Ali let out a satisfied gasp. Even a stale, warm and flat drink was still ambrosia to him.

Next Ali examined the foil wrapper of the unopened low salt, low fat granola bar. There was a huge list of ingredients that Ali wasn't at all sure could be all that healthy but eventually he found the sell-by date. The bar was three years out of date—not that that would stop him from eating it.

The only other item was a crumpled packet of cigarettes. Ali picked the pack up and gave it a shake. Something hard rattled inside. He flipped the carton open and inside were two cigarettes and a lighter.

"Way hay!" Ali found himself shouting.

He didn't smoke and even if he did he reckoned the tobacco would be ruined. What had excited him was the lighter.

The transparent pink body of the disposable lighter showed an ample reservoir of fluid. Ali gave it a shake before flicking the igniter down. With a click of the flint a tall yellow flame burst forth.

Not since a long forgotten childhood birthday did he think he'd been so pleased to receive such a cheap gift. He had never received any formal survival training, only the lessons he'd learned from staying alive, (which, considering the dead wandering around outside, was no mean feat.) With a knife, a lighter and some ingenuity, Ali knew he could survive the day. One thing his otherwise stoic grandma had taught him was to treat each day as a gift.

Stuffing his newly found trinkets into his pockets, Ali moved on to check the other two doors in the hallway.

The first door was a dark and empty closet. There was no natural light and of course the power had been dead a long time. Ali guessed this side of the apartment must back onto the mirror version apartment next door.

He moved to the last door and tentatively opened it. The door swung to with a loud creak. As the diffused light of the hallway crept in, something caught his eye. The bathroom was as vacant as the rest of the apartment: A bath, a sink, a toilet and no other fixtures, not even a toilet roll holder—but there was one extraneous item sitting on the toilet cistern.

Ali stretched himself into the gloom, keeping a foot wedged against the door less he lose the source of light.

He snatched up the dusty paper and brought it back into the bedroom. Sitting down on the roll of cable, Ali carefully unfolded the newspaper. It was remarkably well preserved for being abandoned some four or more years ago. The pages were still crisp and rustled as Ali flattened them out.

CRISIS! The headline cried in thick bold letters.

Ali smiled as he read the half truths and fantasies that were passed off as news. Even as the world had collapsed the media was turning a buck. He remembered the trouble the copywriters had had keeping up the panic. Every day dozens of broadsheets and tabloids had to think up a new and more frightening headline to trump the last. After **THE DEAD WALK!** there was very little impact any others could make. And for once the scaremongering of the media was deficient.

Ali opened up the paper to see a picture of the Eiffel tower listing and broken, smoke billowing from the Parisian skyline. The unenlightening article was entitled 'Paris falls'. The one telling line wasn't in the piece, it was under the picture. In small letters it read 'Representation'.

Ali smiled again, looking at the mocked-up photograph.

"Why's the Eiffel tower bent?" he asked the newspaper as if he expected it to answer. "What are the dead doing gnawing at the steel girders?"

Ali laughed at this notion. He gnashed his teeth at the newspaper and laughed. He laughed at the world that had to re-enact scenes from war of the worlds to enthral ignorant readers.

Ali laughed until he became aware of how lonely a sound it made echoing off the bare magnolia walls.

CHAPTER NINE
STOCK

Cahz looked down at the city from his vantage point. It was a different sight to the one he had experienced flying over at daybreak. The height of the chopper was comparable to the elevation of the office block he now stood on, but it was very different. Maybe it was the changing light—the pinks and golds giving way to broad daylight? Maybe it was the fact Cahz knew he was stranded.

Cannon interrupted his commander's thoughts. "So, boss, what do you think?"

Cahz slowly circled round the flat roof. "I'm no expert, but it sure looks big enough."

"Good. So, what now?"

"What now, indeed," Cahz replied, looking at the bristling mast of satellite dishes and aerials. "We'll need to fell these antenna."

"Blow it with one of Bates' claymores?"

Cahz stepped over to the steel structure and tried to rattle the solid struts. He rubbed his chin. "Hmmm… I don't think the claymore will have enough power to take it down. There was some D.I.Y. store stuff in one of the crates. If we can find a torch, or even just a saw in there, we'll be fine."

"If not?" Cannon asked.

"Adapt, improvise, and overcome," Cahz replied.

Cannon gave a snigger.

"It might not be enough though," Cahz said, looking down at the canyon between the office block and the next. Half a dozen storeys below, the streets were packed with the undead.

"How do you mean?"

"I don't know anything about wind shear and that sort of stuff," Cahz admitted and he spat over the edge of the office block. The white spit tumbled down the gap between the two buildings for a moment before being whipped violently to one side by a gust of wind.

There was still a bitter taste on his lips like he'd spent all morning licking envelopes. He scraped his tongue against his teeth, trying to abrade the taste away. The frothy white spit was caught by the wind and dashed against a window long before it hit its intended targets on the street.

Up here their moans were softened somewhat by the wind. However, the stench wasn't tempered by the breeze. The wind direction had changed from their dawn insertion and was now blowing out to sea. With it came the reek of the rotting dead mixed with the tang of smoke.

Cahz looked out onto the horizon. Just beyond the ragged skyline and the random pillars of smoke was the ocean. Out on that ocean was their base ship, a refuge in the middle of nowhere. Safety.

"Wish I'd paid more attention sitting up front all these missions."

"Wind shear?" Cannon parroted. "It doesn't feel that windy to me."

"Not to me either. Just some LZ's I thought looked fine, Idris would veto 'cause of wind shear or cross winds or something like that. I didn't pay any attention. I don't know how to fly, so I didn't bother to ask." Cahz gave Cannon a friendly tap on the shoulder. "Still, buddy, it looks good to me and at the worst I'm sure we could get winched out one at a time." He cocked a finger at the communications tower. "I'm sure we'll be sound just as long as we get rid of that thing." He took a few steps away from the edge of the roof and looked out over the city. "We can hold out here until the pickup. We've got water and some food. The entrances are secure. We just need to sit tight and wait."

"Makes me wish I'd brought some cards with me," Cannon said. He burbled up some phlegm and shot it out at the throng below just as if he were ridding himself of a cherry pip. Turning back from watching the spit's descent Cannon caught Cahz's eye. He said, "We do have one problem, boss."

Cahz turned back from his companion and looked towards the

service entrance that led back into the building. "Yeah, I know. Elspeth."

"She's gonna turn."

"I know."

"You know what needs done," Cannon said, his voice betraying none of the emotion behind the issue.

Cahz only nodded. It was normally Cannon who was the quiet one, but Cahz sensed he wouldn't leave the question.

"Lieutenant?" Cannon pushed.

Cahz knew Cannon was nervous. The big man was almost always in control always, confident his sheer strength could get him through. But Cahz knew the man was uneasy the minute he stopped referring to him as boss.

"I know, buddy. I know," Cahz said. "I'm not going to ask you to do it."

"It's not that," Cannon replied. "I'll do her if you ask me. But when?"

"She wants to wait until she's gone. I can respect that, but you're right, there are issues with that. Do we lock her in a room? Set watch over her?" He turned to look his friend in the eye. "Do we cable-tie her to a radiator? There's no good way to do this."

"There never is," Cannon said. "But it needs done."

Cahz could see Cannon was waiting for an answer, a nice clean plan of events. All he could tell him was, "I don't know, buddy. I guess we talk to her and Ryan." He slapped Cannon on the shoulder again. "We'll work it out."

Cannon stood stoic and unmoving. Cahz sensed that the friendly pat wasn't the conclusion to the matter he'd wanted.

In the deep pause that followed, Cahz couldn't even see Cannon breathe.

"What is it?"

"The child?" Cannon said.

Cahz's shoulders slumped as he thought of the angelic looking child. The soft pink skin framed by the grubby swaddling and the infected welt running the length of the left-hand side of her face. He let his hand slip from his friend's shoulder.

"I'll do them both," Cahz said, looking down at his carbine. As he gazed at the slick black metal he couldn't help but see the faces of the people he'd killed. Since the Exodus from the mainland, he hadn't needed to administer the coup de grace. It had been years since he'd last been called upon to administer a mercy killing or watch over a friend to prevent their return. But all that time didn't diminish the clarity—the look in their faces as he pulled the trigger. He'd forgotten the names of many of those he'd dispatched, but never the faces. Some of them cried. Some wore false smiles to try to help make it easier. And the ones who he'd guarded until their resurrection, in a way they were the easiest. He wasn't shooting a human being. With their pallid skin, gaping maws and their vacant eyes, Cahz was destroying a monster, not the person they had once been.

"You ever read *Of Mice and Men*, David?" Cahz asked, surprising himself calling Cannon by his first name.

"Nope," came Cannon's short answer. "Why?"

Cahz thought back to Candy's dog being shot.

After a moment he said, "It's not important."

***

Ryan was pacing up and down, rocking the baby, when Cahz and Cannon returned.

"She won't stop crying," he said.

Elspeth lay on a camp bed, apparently asleep even with the racket. Cannon unconsciously walked round to cover her, just in case her sleep turned into something more permanent.

"The infection?" Cahz asked.

"No, I just think she's hungry," Ryan said. "It's way past her feeding."

"You didn't bring any baby food?"

"Well, no, I didn't think to. I threw on some clothes and grabbed an armful of Molotov cocktails. That was it." Anger started to rise in Ryan's voice. "I didn't think any of this would happen."

"Okay, fair enough. None of us thought today would turn out the way it has," Cahz said, trying to diffuse the antagonism.

"Is there some powdered milk in that ration pack?"

Cahz looked down at the army issue meal. He hadn't expected to open it so soon, and besides, was there any point feeding an infected child?

Cahz berated himself for having such a callous thought. "No, there's not," he said.

Worried that Ryan might doubt his honesty and expose his emotional bankruptcy, Cahz slung his weapon and sat down on a crate. He unfastened the pouch Bates had given him and slipped out the insipid khaki brick of plastic. Printed along the top were the words 'peelable seal'. Cahz ignored the advice and pulled his knife from its scabbard. Although the packs were supposedly designed to be opened by hand, the only man Cahz had ever seen do so was Cannon and even that was as part of a bet to see if anyone could. Cahz placed the tip of the knife to the wrapping, but before he pierced it he read the batch number.

"Shit, Cannon, this thing's only a year out of date!" he called out enthusiastically.

"Where the hell did Bates get that from?" Cannon asked. "I've never seen a single Post-Rising MRE."

Cahz slashed open the packet. "Crafty little bugger. Do think he's been hoarding them or does he have contacts off ship?"

Cannon shrugged.

Cahz spilled the contents onto the crate lid beside him. An assortment of different packets slid to a halt. "What can we give the kid?" he asked as he spread out the contents like a pack of cards.

Cannon reached down and picked out an item. He stretched over and passed it to Ryan.

"A dry cracker?" Ryan said, puzzled as he read the label. "She can't eat a cracker."

"Mash it up in a cup with a little water or chew it like a mama bird. Either way it'll do for now."

Ryan looked at the packet and then back at Cannon. "Okay," he said sheepishly, realising how sharp this otherwise dumb-looking marine had been. "Will you hold her while I…"

"Sure," Cannon said with a surprisingly kind smile.

"Anyone mind if I snaffle the gum?" Cahz asked, holding up the tiny red film bag with two solitary chiclets.

Neither of the other two men objected as Cahz tore open the packet and popped the contents in his mouth.

"Whoa there!" Cannon called out suddenly.

Both Ryan and Cahz froze. Cannon was staring at Ryan crushing a handful of crackers.

"Don't waste them all," Cannon said.

"But she's hungry," Ryan countered.

"Well mash up a bit at a time. There's no point wasting them if she won't eat it."

"He likes the crackers," Cahz explained.

"How else are you supposed to eat the peanut butter?" Cannon's look was strangely serious. Evidently he actually was looking for a genuine suggestion from Cahz.

"Could you not just suck it out of the tube…?" Cahz's lacklustre suggestion trailed off as he noticed Cannon's stern look.

"Ali made a great Thai Satay with a jar of peanut butter and some canned coconut milk." Ryan paused for a moment, looking at the ceiling. "At least that's what he called it. Real spicy but nice. He made it a few times until we ran out of something. Couldn't say what it was but it wasn't right after a while. Maybe the coconut had spoiled."

"Well, thank you for the recipe tip," Cannon said.

Cahz started to drop the individual packets back in to the open plastic pocket.

"What's the main meal, anyway?" Cannon inquired.

Cahz picked up the big rectangular box and orientated it to read the label. "It's spicy penne pasta," he answered between loud chews of the gum. He held up the empty wrapper for Cannon to see the bold writing below the menu designation. "It's vegetarian."

"Penne with vegetable sausage crumbles in spicy tomato sauce," Cannon quoted from memory.

Ryan looked up from stirring the pulped-up cracker. "Doesn't sound that appetising."

"It's not bad," Cannon countered. "Quite meaty-tasting for a vegi meal."

"One thing we've got Iraq and Afghanistan to thank for," Cahz quipped.

"Why's that?" Ryan asked. He presented his child with the first spoonful of mush.

"Wanted us boys to feel like we were being looked after. Keep up the morale," Cannon said. "I guess they thought it made up for not issuing proper body armour."

Cahz nodded in agreement. "One less thing for us grunts to moan about."

"Let's have a look," Ryan said, holding a hand out.

Cannon picked up the rectangular brown packet. "Not much to see," he said and passed it over.

"You two serve together then?" Ryan asked.

"No, we only met after all this shit started," Cahz said. "We've both done tours overseas, but Cannon here was a civvie when we met up."

Cannon's silence gave Ryan the impression that the big man didn't want to talk about their first encounter and when Cannon broke the silence only to inform him, "She's dribbling," Ryan thought it best to leave the subject.

"She seems to be enjoying that," Cahz noted.

"Yeah, it's doing the trick," Ryan admitted.

Ryan idly flipped over the bland package and looked at the utilitarian information printed on it. "Hey, have you guys read this?"

"Yeah, sure," Cahz said.

"No, I mean really read it," Ryan said with a snigger.

"Why?"

Ryan put on his best anchorman voice and read, "Restriction of food and nutrients leads to rapid weight loss which leads to: Loss of strength, decreased endurance, loss of motivation, decreased mental alertness."

"So?"

"Well, come on," Ryan said, back to his normal voice. "It's like it's describing a pus bag."

"Hmmm," Cannon puffed. "I suppose." He turned to his commander for his reaction, but Cahz was looking the other way. "Boss?"

Cahz turned back from looking at Elspeth. "Not very tactful."

"Ah shit," Ryan said, the humour in his voice crashing down.

Elspeth lay on an aluminium tubing and dull blue fabric camp bed, shivering. Her pale skin was laced with dark polluted tracks of infected veins and pricks of cold sweat dotted her face.

"We need to keep a watch over her," Cahz said.

"How long since she was bitten?" Cannon asked.

Cahz looked at his watch. "Must be close to two hours now."

"What you reckon?" Cannon asked. "A bite that close to her neck…"

Cahz turned to Ryan. "How old is she?"

"Um… mid-fifties," Ryan said, uncertain. "I think?" He shrugged. "To be honest I don't rightly know what year this is."

"You got the wheel of death on you?" Cannon asked.

"Nope. Thing's never that accurate anyway," Cahz said.

"What? *Wheel of death*?" Ryan asked.

"Yeah, there's a mortality calculator. It's like those math wheels made out of card. You line up the dials and it's supposed to give you a time of death from the infection," Cahz explained. "High command thought they were a good idea to issue to troops. Truth is, they done a damn good job of reminding you not to get bit."

"The wheel's only got one outcome," Cannon added.

Cahz turned to his companion. "You've seen as many as I have; what do you guess? Two, maybe three hours?"

Cannon's eyes flickered as he worked on some calculation in his head. "'Bout that."

Ryan looked across at his de-facto mother-in-law. She looked to be in a deathly malaise. Her eyes tightly closed, a lock of sweaty, sodden grey hair falling across her face. He could see the family resemblance to his lost love. She had Sam's eyes—Ryan corrected himself—Sam had Elspeth's eyes. He looked down at the baby girl he was feeding. She gazed up at him with that familiar resemblance.

"She'll turn any time now, won't she?" he said in a flat voice.

"We could put her in that office," Cannon said, looking at the glass fronted meeting room.

"Good call," Cahz noted. "We can keep an eye on her and when she comes back she won't be able to surprise any of us."

"That makes sense," a faint voice said.

Everyone looked round at Elspeth. Her eyes were still shut, but it was plain she was awake.

"Okay, La—" Cahz stopped himself from addressing her as 'lady' again. "Okay, Elspeth, I'll help you up."

"Thanks for looking after me," Elspeth whispered.

"I haven't done anything," Cahz said.

"But you will," Elspeth replied.

CHAPTER TEN
APARTMENT

Having detected no movement through the spy hole, Ali cautiously opened the door. He eased it off of the snib as best he could to minimize the noise.

As the door cracked open he peeked round to get the best of the widening view. He heard the moans and the hammering below as the zombies still held vigil over the flat he'd escaped into. He was poised to slam the door shut at the slightest provocation, but nothing happened.

The landing was damp and musty. One of the frosted glass windows on the stairs was broken, the safety glass pixelated into small clumps. Ali heard a sound, a soft cooing then saw the faint movement of a shadow passing. Even with his heightened anxiety he stood his ground and scanned for the movement. The cooing came again and through the broken glass he caught a glimpse of something outside.

Ali stepped forward, beyond the psychological safety of the flat. As he did the shadow fluttered and took flight; it was then he realised a pair of pigeons were nesting on the window ledge. Unlike him they had apparently grown indifferent to the zombies' eerie cries.

Ali edged further onto the landing, stepping over a rivulet that trickled its way from some burst pipe down its own set of miniature Niagara Falls to the bottom floors. When he reached the banister he slowly peeked over the end. Down below on the bottom two floors there was a mass of undead. They appeared to be jammed in their attempt to pursue him into the flat. The ones at the front had failed to negotiate the shut window, but their calls were still drawing in more of their brethren. They seemed uninterested in exploring the rest of the building, simply jamming themselves tighter and tighter into the first floor apartment.

Then Ali noticed that not all of them were slavishly following the moans. On the third floor a lone figure stumbled its aimless way. It bumped off walls and tripped up and down stairs, oblivious to the commotion the queue outside the downstairs flat was making. The creature made a random stumble that jerked its head backwards.

Ali ducked back in and froze. He waited, breath held, waited to hear the creature make a warning cry or to hear it shuffling closer. He waited until he could no longer hold his breath. When he released it he did so with an even and quiet exhale.

Not wishing to chance his luck, Ali moved on to the next flat. As quietly as he could, he pushed the door open. The moment he did a foul odour flooded his nostrils. It was the unmistakable stench of decay. At this point Ali regretted not being able to grab a metal rod before the balcony collapsed. The knife had a stubby and flimsy blade, no use for dispatching a zombie.

With measured steps Ali crept into the apartment. Instantly he saw that this had been a home; there was a carpet in the hall and pictures on the wall. He pushed past a row of coats hanging by the door and into the apartment.

The well-appointed living room diner wasn't the source of the stench, so Ali backed up and checked the bedroom first. With a well-practiced motion he steadied himself before he eased the door open. The assault on his nostrils came with a vengeance. Sprawled across a blood-splattered bed was a headless corpse. Ali stifled a gag as the stink clawed at his throat. Then he saw the decapitated head. It was resting on its side just in front of the bedside table. Only it wasn't resting. The jaw still worked up and down its milky eyes transfixed on Ali.

Ali backed away and closed the door.

"Get it together," he chided himself. "You've seen this all before and there might be something of use in there."

Okay, maybe there is, but there are another two flats on this floor.

Ali made a deal with himself. "If there's nothing useful in those I'll come back and search this one."

He nodded to himself and left the apartment.

***

Ali stripped off naked. He felt safe in this apartment with the door well barricaded. He tossed his soiled clothing aside and sat down on the edge of the bed. In the strong light of the east-facing bedroom he examined the gash on his leg. The cut was about three inches long, but not as deep as he'd first feared. It was throbbing relentlessly now that the adrenaline from his escape had worn off.

He tossed back a handful of headache tablets found in the medicine cabinet in the bathroom. He flipped the lid off the bottle of water and took a long drink which ended in a satisfied gasp.

Ali looked round at the crowded bedroom. It was the same size as the other ones he'd seen this morning, but the weight bench took up a lot of the space. On the wall were a number of certificates and photos which Ali assumed was the previous occupant. "This is to certify that Frank Topalow…" read a litany of awards. A large man with a beaming smile stared back at Ali. Sometimes he was shaking someone's hand, sometimes Frank was pictured with a trophy or medal, but in all the pictures he was wearing his martial arts gi.

Ali wondered if all that proficiency had actually helped the man survive. Frank was obviously physically fit and able to handle himself, but had that been enough? There was a picture of him in the living room fishing with a friend on a stretch of river. It was a good bet that he knew somewhere secluded to lie low.

Being a fighter the ex-tenant had a comprehensive store of bandages and medicine, a large array of which was now scattered on the bed. Ali had even found some fishing line and half considered using it to stitch the wound. The lack of a needle had been a relief.

Ali ripped open a waxed paper sachet containing an antiseptic wipe. Even before he'd torn the top free he smelled the waft of alcohol. The smell made him pause. It foreshadowed the pain he was about to experience, the pain he was about to induce. The skin around the gash was red and inflamed. His dark leg hairs were caked in dried blood, with some poking into the wound. Looking at it made him feel queasy.

"Best get on with it," he said, as if addressing the injury.

He took another swig of water and poured the remnants over the wound. He winced as the cold water washed down his leg.

Breathing fast now, he drew the wipe over the exposed flesh. He took a hissed breath of air through his teeth.

"Fuck, fuck, fuck, fuck, fuck!" he stammered as the alcohol

burned the lesion. "Balls to that!"

He threw the blood stained wipe across the room.

He picked up the wadding and bandage he'd set aside and gingerly wrapped the wound. Once that was done he lay back on the bed and listened to his own breathing for a few minutes.

Other than his breathing and the occasional whistle of wind, it was peaceful. Even the drones of the dead sounded distant and unimportant.

Ali gave an expansive yawn and rolled over onto his side. With his eyes still open he could see the pair of camouflaged combats draped over the weight bench. In no way did Ali suspect the last tenant of being in the military; the camouflage was that intentionally washed-out fashion type. If the pictures were a fair indication, Frank had been a good twenty years younger than Ali, but fortunately a similar size. As it was, Ali was grateful for the previous tenant's lifestyle. There had been ample medical supplies and a block of a dozen bottles of mineral water in the kitchen. He'd been able to get some clean clothes and soaped up his hands and face using some of the bottled water to escape the worst of the stench he'd picked up battling the undead outside.

Ali lay on top of the bed covers in this long since abandoned apartment, grateful for this respite. He pulled the duvet over his naked body and closed his eyes.

Behind his eyelids Ali's mind whirred. The scavenged granola bar and the tubs of body building protein powders he'd found in Frank's larder wouldn't sustain him. There was enough water to last a couple of days and he could always siphon the toilet cisterns if he got desperate. Below there were almost a dozen apartments he hadn't explored, but were they worth the risk? After all, they'd been gutted years ago. With the zombies stowing out the ground and first floors it would be risky to sneak around—and for what? Ali knew the food and weapons had been scavenged from here years before.

He'd have to move on if he was going to survive in the long term, but the dead outside made an insurmountable barrier. But there was one reason for staying put: The chopper. It might come back. Had his friends reached it? Were they safe now? Would they come back and look for him? Or, as Ali feared, did they think he'd died? If they thought he had died like Ray or George, what would be the point in coming back?

It was these worries that prevented Ali sleeping. His head pounded with the thoughts circling like vultures.

He gave up and raised himself up from the bed. He rubbed his face, trying to erase the thoughts.

"I need to get these out," he mumbled as he stood up from the bed.

He slipped on Frank's clean clothes and padded through to the main living area. Finding a marker pen on the fridge door, he started writing on the pristine white wall.

At waist height he wrote in thick capital letters 'SITUATION'. Beneath that he listed everything he had: the lighter, the knife, even down to the outdated newspaper. When he'd finished writing down everything he thought would be useful, he started another column, titled 'OPTIONS'.

CHAPTER ELEVEN
CATCH

Cahz shifted the gum to one side of his mouth.

"How is she?" he asked.

"She's asleep," Ryan said. He was sitting with his back to a crate, his baby in his arms.

Cahz had meant Elspeth, but he could see she too was asleep. She lay on a camp bed in the glassed-off room which had no doubt been the office manager's. Her skin was now pale enough that she might be mistaken for dead if it wasn't for the occasional shiver and the fact she wasn't chewing on the window trying to eat them.

Cannon too had picked out a comfortable spot and was dozing on the floor, the camp beds proving too small for his huge body.

"Funny—I left all this to Elspeth back at the warehouse. I was too drunk to care the last few months." Ryan looked up, his eyes red with tears. "I just wish I'd spent the time with her rather than getting pissed into oblivion."

Cahz wasn't a counsellor. He didn't want to get wrapped up in this stranger's regrets, but he didn't want to be heartless and just cut him off. He knelt down in front of him, about to give him a speech about everyone having it tough, when his nostrils twitched.

He screwed his face up. "What's that smell?"

"Jesus." Cannon opened one eye and snorted, "That's vile."

Ryan took in a sniff. "It's her. She needs a change."

"Don't suppose you brought a nappy bag?" Cannon chipped in.

"God, that's rank," Cahz said as he stepped away.

Ryan looked blankly at Cahz, "What do I do?"

"Looks like you're due some quality time with your daughter," Cannon smirked.

"I'm serious. I've got no idea."

"No kiddin'," Cannon said. "I'll help."

Ryan started to offer the child over.

"No, no, no. I said I'd *help*. I didn't say I'd *do it*." Cannons tone was firm. "I'll make you a nappy. You clean that shit up." He bent down and opened up the crate full of first aid supplies. Eventually he tossed out some sterile wipes. "Use these for the shine. Go find some paper towels for the rest."

"I'll find some paper," Cahz volunteered, mostly so he could escape the smell.

Ryan started tugging at the poppers on the babygrow.

"And make sure when you undress her you keep her clothes clean," Cannon warned.

"Okay," Ryan said. He slowed down, taking more care.

Like a bomb disposal expert Ryan started on the undergarments. He gently ripped the sides of the disposable nappy and lifted the now squirming giggling child's feet into the air. "God, would you look at the colour of that," he said rhetorically, sliding the soiled nappy out from under the girl.

Cannon knelt beside him. "That's nothin'. The first banana is what scares the bejesus out of you." He unfurled a large sling style bandage and started folding it.

"How do you know so much about kids?" Ryan asked.

"Some paper towels." Cahz offered the bundle to Ryan and shook his head.

Ryan looked at Cahz for a moment, puzzled by his stern look. Cannon was silently working his origami-like magic with the square of cloth.

Ryan went back to cleaning the baby. He made the first wipe and then sat looking around, perplexed as to what to do with the dirty paper.

"Stick it in to the nappy," Cannon snapped.

"Yeah, okay," Ryan said hesitantly. Gingerly he continued cleaning the mess.

Cannon nodded at the triangle of cloth on the floor in front of him. He said, "You ready for this?"

When Ryan nodded, Cannon slipped the improvised diaper under the child's bottom. Cannon then placed a sheet of gauze between the girl's legs. With a few deft folds and a safety pin, Cannon managed a neat fit.

"That's impressive, old boy," Cahz said.

"Thanks, boss," Cannon replied. Then he turned to Ryan and motioned at the used diaper. "Now would you get rid of that?"

"Yeah, sure," Ryan agreed.

Clasping the diaper between thumb and forefinger and carrying it at arms' length, Ryan marched over to a window. When he flung the window open the constant moaning grew louder. Ryan popped his head out and looked down at the assemble cadavers.

"Hey pus face!" he shouted.

The zombies below raised their arms and burbled unintelligible sounds from dead mouths at the human beyond their reach.

"Little present," Ryan said, dangling the nappy at arms' length. "Bombs away!"

And with that, Ryan let go.

The excrement-filled ordnance plummeted down the side of the office block. With a satisfying splat it landed square on a zombie's head and ruptured open. The shit-smeared towels blew off, sticking to the zombie's shoulders and a few adjacent zombies as well. The nappy sat on the zombie's head, steadily releasing a stream of khaki brown gloop down its face.

Ryan beckoned Cahz and Cannon over. "Look at this poor fuck."

The zombie looked bemused, not comprehending what had happened or how it should react. It looked to and fro as if expecting a helpful suggestion from one of the surrounding creatures.

The three men hung out of the window and laughed while the zombies continued their futile clawing at the air. A gust of wind whipped a shit covered towel and slapped it clean across a zombie's face. Blinded, the creature moaned more franticly and stumbled around. Not intelligent enough to pull it free, the blind zombie jostled the others in the crowd, striking out randomly, bumping like a wild pinball. The three men fell around in fits of laughter, pointing and snorting as they tried to catch their breath.

"Ah, classic," Ryan gasped as he returned to his daughter.

The baby was merrily kicking out on her back like a stranded turtle. She wore a smile that exposed a few peggy teeth as she empathically joined in with the mirth. Ryan picked the tiny girl up and held her under the armpits, looking at her angelic smile. The girl met his eyes with a mesmerising stare. Her blue eyes locked onto his in an intense unblinking gaze.

Ryan's smile widened as he studied his rosy-cheeked girl. Then his joy collapsed as he remembered the significance of the scratch down the right side of her face. He pulled the baby close to him, resting her head on his shoulder. The baby flung an arm out and grasped tight to the arm of Ryan's t-shirt before nuzzling into his neck.

"There, there," Ryan said instinctively as he gently bounced the child. "There, there."

The baby smacked her lips and closed her eyes, calmed by her father's warmth.

"What now, boss?" Cannon asked.

"Nothing, I guess," Cahz replied. He nodded to Elspeth's quarantine. "We wait for her."

"You want to take turns watching?"

"No need while she's locked in there. But I guess we'll all feel safer if one of us keeps an eye on her."

"Who's up first?" Cannon asked.

Cahz looked at his watch. "I'll do it for the next hour."

Cannon sauntered back to his spot on the floor. "Give me a nudge then. I'm going back to sleep," he said.

Cahz turned to Ryan. "A nap is a good idea. It could be anywhere between nineteen hundred and o'six hundred before we get picked up. Best we're rested and alert for tonight."

Ryan nodded and went back to sitting against the wall, cradling his child.

***

"Cannon!" Cahz shouted through the smoke. "Where are you, buddy?!"

Cahz edged forward, heading for the stairwell, praying it hadn't caught fire too. He called out again, "Cannon!"

But the only thing he could hear was the crackling of the flames.

Cahz reached the fire doors and swung them open. The way ahead was clear. He held the door open and called into the thick smoke, "Cannon!"

A figure emerged from the billowing black clouds.

Elspeth's eyes were blank but her lips were drawn back, exposing sharp needle teeth.

"What the—"

Before Cahz had time to think, Elspeth had leapt on top of him.

Cahz tried to throw off her cold grip, but he couldn't shift her rigor mortis fingers. Flailing wildly, he toiled to heave her off, but in his struggle he stepped back and missed his footing on the stair. He fell backwards, tumbling the whole way, the zombie biting and scratching as he fell.

With a heavy thump Cahz hit the ground.

"Fuck!" he bellowed, snapped out of his slumber.

He sprang to his feet and anxiously looked round.

"Easy, tiger," Ryan said calmingly as he popped another cranberry into his mouth. "Bad dream?" The cellophane rustled as he grasped with one hand at the dried fruit while cradling the baby in the other.

"You okay, boss?" came a more concerned voice.

"Sure, Cannon," Cahz said, standing dazed in the converted office.

He looked around to see things exactly as he'd left them: the crates, the camp bed, and Elspeth still in her glass cage.

"Just a bad dream…" Cahz stopped dead.

He rushed over to the window and looked out at the street below. There were still thousands of zombies besieging the building. He turned and ran to the other side of the room and did the same. The back of the office block looked down at a relatively quiet employee car park, but behind the wire fencing, packed in the alleyway, was a thick mob of zombies.

"The roof!" Cahz barked as he ran for the stairwell.

"Boss, you've got me spooked. What's going on?" Cannon asked as he pounded up the stairs after Cahz.

"Smoke. There was smoke in my dream," Cahz said, worry in his voice.

"So you had a bad dream. Ain't no other kind nowadays," Cannon replied, jumping two steps at a time to keep pace.

"Met a special forces guy in the field once." Cahz didn't look back as he vaulted up the stairs. "He told me about a course on intuition his unit were sent on."

"Don't get you, boss," Cannon said flatly.

"They pulled a whole unit out to go on a course run by a civvie psychologist. The crux of it is they were taught if you get the feeling something's wrong then something is wrong." Cahz thundered up to the roof access door and flung it open. "And I've got that feeling."

Cannon barrelled up behind Cahz onto the sunlit roof. As he took in his first breath of the outside air, he could taste it.

Cahz walked calmly to look over the building's edge.

"Shit," he said. "Just what we freakin' need."

Cannon drew level with him.

Down below, the adjacent office block was on fire. The flames were unimpressive, their orange glow tempered by the bright sunlight and only visible on the ground floor, but a lick of smoke was twisting its way up.

"Maybe it'll burn itself out," Cannon said hopefully.

Cahz said, "Even if it doesn't spread, do you think you can land a chopper at night with smoke all around? Idris won't even know we're here. We set off a flare and he's never going to spot it."

He pointed to the narrow alleyway between the buildings. Other than the throng of zombies there were a number of skips.

"See there," Cahz asked, pointing.

"Yup," Cannon confirmed.

"Full of trash that was never collected. It'll catch. And that's a gap for the flames to bridge and get to us. Hell, those W.D.s down there will dry out with the heat and combust. One of them could burst into a flaming torch and the fire could spread that way."

"We're fucked then," Cannon said softly.

"We're not fucked," Cahz said confidently. "There's plan B."

"What's plan B?"

"Don't know yet," Cahz said. "But we'd better come up with one."

CHAPTER TWELVE
FISHING

With his aching leg resting up on a stool, Ali reclined in an easy chair and took a swig of black coffee. He'd learnt to enjoy black coffee back in the warehouse. Some of the others had become accustomed to the powdered whitener but he'd never made the adjustment.

The strong smell of his drink mixed with the smoke from the small fire he'd set on the cooker to boil the water. He could have made the campfire anywhere in the apartment, but an atavistic bent instinctively called him to the cooker. In all the destruction, the rubble and collapse, Ali still clung to an ingrained sense of cleanliness.

He took a deep inhale and savoured the wafting odours from the mug. It was a good smell, a comforting smell.

The jar he had found in Frank Topalow's kitchen was almost empty, which no doubt was why it had survived the winter salvaging. Ali wasn't sure if the coffee was any good or not; it was certainly on a par with the past-its-sell-by-date stuff he'd been used to. It had been a long time since he'd tasted fresh milk or anything other than freeze dried coffee. In fact, it had been so long since he'd had a good coffee it was no longer possible for him to retrieve the memory. But the drink was a calming influence, an island of normality, a source of fortitude.

Ali smiled as he recalled his dad always took his coffee black. Sitting here, the smell of black coffee transported him to childhood memories.

It reminds me of the old country, Ali recalled his father saying once. At the time he thought it odd. Ali didn't remember anything of the "old country". All Ali could recall was a hazy memory of a fraught plane flight. He was bored and his parents snapped at him for "misbehaving". Ali couldn't remember his misdemeanour, but he could still see his father's eyes burning with anger as he snatched his arm and dragged him to his seat. His father wasn't a violent man and the shock of such force had stunned Ali into silence. Looking back it was obvious why his mother and father had been so distraught. But to the five year old boy it had been unfathomable.

He took a bite from the granola bar washed it down with a swig of his drink and focused on the now. The meandering scrawl on the wall looked like a convoluted family tree with branches and sub-branches frantically splitting off and multiplying. Over the previous hour Ali had listed all his options and resources, all the pros and cons, everything he felt he should take into account before making a decision. He'd watched Ray do this numerous times back at the warehouse. Ray loved to use charts and diagrams to demonstrate his point or to support his decisions. Ray had had some kind of middle management job for a corporation before all this. Many of his fellow survivors had sneered at Ray's pseudo-intellectual approach, but Ali had found it helpful. Today he was glad he'd taken the time to ask Ray about his techniques.

One branch in particular was ringed numerous times where Ali had come to his conclusion. WAIT FOR CHOPPER. Splitting off from that heading was IS IT SAFE? and FOR HOW LONG?

Ali had no way of knowing if it was safe. All he could say was he was safe for now. The how long would depend on what supplies he could find.

"Find vantage point to wait for chopper," Ali read off the actions points he'd written for himself.

The bedroom in this flat had a wide enough view that he could see most of the plaza, but this was far from ideal. Although he would be able to see a helicopter land, he'd have no way of signalling it from here. And what if it didn't land? What if it just circled overhead looking for survivors?

Ali looked around at the flat. It was comfortable and pleasant. It was an inviting thought just to stay here for a few days, but Ali knew that he couldn't. He knew he would have to find a rooftop vantage point from where to keep look out and where he could signal.

"Supplies," Ali said out loud. "I need supplies. I need food and warm clothing and something to signal the helicopter with."

He put the coffee cup down and took the last bite from the bar.

He gave a grunt of displeasure as he eased his leg off the stool and stood up. Picking up the marker pen, he confronted the wall.

He drew a thick line off from WAIT FOR CHOPPER.

"Get clothing from flat," Ali said as he wrote the words down.

"Signalling." Ali tapped the end of the pen against his bottom lip. He saw himself, pen to his mouth, reflected in the smoky screen of the TV set.

"Ah-ha!" he exclaimed.

He walked over to the defunct media centre and picked up the first DVD from a pile of obsolete disks. The front cover was pink and white like the icing of a fancy cake and in stark contrast to everything else in Frank's bachelor pad. Ali thought he recognised the attractive woman on the cover from some medical drama but even after reading her name he couldn't place her.

"Never underestimate the power of a chick flick," Ali laughed as he looked over at the fishing photo. "You been entertaining, Frank?"

Ali popped open the case with a crisp snap and a glossy leaflet proclaiming "other great titles" slipped free and fluttered to the floor. In spite of the aches, he bent down and picked up the insert and carefully slid it back into the case.

Ali laughed at himself. Some modicum of civilised life still controlled him. He had just spent the best part of the morning looting Frank Topalow's home, defacing the walls and stealing his coffee, yet he felt compelled to retrieve the advertising material from inside a DVD case. He shook his head in disbelief at his own actions and clicked the central lug, freeing the DVD. He held up the shiny disc and peeked through the hole in the centre.

"Perfect."

He put the case back down where he'd found it and walked back over to the mind map on the wall.

SIGNAL MIRROR = DVD he wrote in the next branch.

Then he went on, mouthing the words as he wrote them, "Set signal fire—find kindling (easy) & rubber (or something easy that makes black smoke)."

Ali marched back over to the media centre. He plucked the lighter he'd found earlier from his pocket and picked back up the now empty DVD case. He flicked the flame on and held the corner of the case to it. The plastic bubbled and melted like wax, giving off dark wisps of smoke. He took his thumb off the lighter and blew out the burgeoning flame. The room was filled with the acrid smell of burnt plastic.

Ali looked at the now warped and singed cover.

"Sorry, Katherine," he apologised, reading off the cover. "I doubt you'd have gotten a sequel anyway."

He turned back to the wall and circled the heading "Food".

Other than the granola bar he had just consumed, the only other food (if you could call it that) was the body building powder.

Using his pen like a baton, Ali double-checked the case of water. There were ten bottles left, one he'd drank, the other he'd used to make the coffee. The remaining ten would be more than sufficient to last out a couple of days, but the demolished granola bar would never be enough.

"I need to find a safe place, like a roof, for the chopper to pick me up." Ali chewed at the end of the pen. "But I can't sit up on a roof for two days without food."

He paced over to the window and looked out at the zombie-infested street.

"The apartments below will have been picked clean and it's not like I can go to the corner store."

Ali spotted the picture of Frank and his buddy wearing green waders with wide grins on their vacation-rejuvenated faces.

"A fishing trip wouldn't go amiss." Ali paused. He picked up the picture and smiled.

"Fishing."

***

Ali looked out of the gaping hole where earlier this morning a window had been. He scanned the throng of undead below, looking for the zombie he'd spotted earlier today. There was still the smell of smoke on the wind, a remnant of the Molotov cocktails.

From the fourth floor it was difficult to pick out one cadaver from the homogenous group of undead, all dressed in their decay induced uniforms of brown and grey. Then he spotted the familiar soldier, the one in the tattered chemical suit. Ali scanned around the area hoping, the two hadn't been separated too much by the ebb and flow of the swarm.

Ali smiled. "There you are."

With one hand on the electrical cable and the other on the makeshift hook, he started swinging his arm. Ali tested the weight of the metal bar he'd bent to form a massive fishing hook. When he felt confident about his throw he let the hook slip.

The hook sailed out the window and down to the throng, snaking a trail of electrical cable behind it as it fell.

Suddenly the cable stopped uncoiling as the hook hit the ground. A wave of moans lifted up from the zombies who had spotted the objects descent, and when Ail peered from the window a further surge of moans rippled out.

Ali gently tugged on the cable and started pulling. Hand over hand he drew the cable back, testing it for the snag that would indicate he'd caught his prize.

The cable came up unimpeded.

Ali pulled up the hook and cast it out for his second try.

CHAPTER THIRTEEN
FIRE

"Ryan," Cahz called as he and Cannon returned to the office.

"What is it?"

"We need to make plans to leave," Cahz said.

"Building next door's on fire," Cannon added before Ryan had time to ask why.

"Christ." Ryan ran a hand through his hair. "Now we're surrounded?"

"I know, but we're going to have to come up with something." Cahz marched over to the stack of crates. "First thing, we need to get organised."

"What you looking for, boss?" Cannon asked, watching Cahz ransack the supplies.

Cahz paused and looked back. He shrugged. "Honestly, I have no fucking idea. We need to gather what we can while we can."

"There's not much of use among this stuff—I mean if we're moving out," Ryan offered. "There's medical supplies and camping equipment, but if we're getting picked up in a few hours we're not going to need any of it."

"*If* we get picked up," Cannon said in a flat voice.

Cahz stopped his rummaging, but kept his attention on the contents of the crate. After a long pause he spoke. "Our time in country is dependent on two things: Luck and ammunition. Since we can't depend on the first, then we'll need to rely on the second." He looked up at Cannon. "How much ammo have you got?"

"About eight hundred," Cannon answered. "And that includes rounds for the pistol."

"We'll concentrate on living long enough to get picked up," Cahz said. "If it doesn't happen, we worry about it then."

Ryan and Cannon looked dumbstruck.

"We okay with that?" Cahz asked.

"I guess that's all we can do," Cannon said.

Ryan was less convinced. "What if we need some of this stuff? Shouldn't we take it with us just in case?"

"It's going to be tooth and nail out there," Cahz answered. We can't afford to carry any dead weight."

"But we'll need some of this stuff if we miss the pickup," Ryan complained.

Cahz sat down on one of the closed boxes and looked up at Ryan. "Cannon, what's the survival time of a downed team in country?" he asked.

"Ten hours," Cannon quoted.

"Ten hours," Cahz repeated. "Held up in a nice cosy hotel like this, we'd make the pickup easy. Out there, most fully armed and prepared teams don't even last ten hours. Look around, Ryan. We ain't a fully prepared team. We're three guys with a few guns. Now I appreciate you've survived out here for years, but you've been locked away in your makeshift fortress, not out on the street."

"Then why leave?" Ryan demanded. "The fire might not spread. I've seen it tons of times. Some fires catch, others just fizzle out. We might be okay."

"He's got a point, boss," Cannon said.

"It might not spread—I'm no expert. But even if it doesn't, we'll never get spotted by the chopper. With smoke and the updraft from the flames, it'll make a pickup impossible," Cahz explained. "And that's the best case scenario. If that fire jumps and sets this building alight, how do we get out then? The undead will be enough to contend with without doing it in choking smoke or roaring flames. And before you even ask if we can stay just as long as we can, think about what would happen if the building starts burning after dark. We'd be evacuating into an infested city in pitch black." Cahz stood up. "No, we move out now while it's still light and while we still have some control over the situation."

Ryan nodded and gave a shallow smile. "So what's the plan?"

"First we gather what useful kits we can," Cahz said. "Then we work out an escape plan." He rifled in one of his thigh pockets and produced a map. "We need to take into consideration where's best to get a pickup." He pulled out a pencil from a pocket on his body armour and made a light mark on the paper. "You know the area better than we do and it's not detailed enough to show anything but major roads and towns." Cahz handed the map to Ryan. Ryan took it and examined the chart as Cahz continued, "Now, I've drawn a line from our current location all the way to the coast. That's the direction I expect the chopper will come in from. Idris, our pilot, is a stickler for that sort of thing—likes to follow the same routes to make search and rescue easier. We need to stick to that line as close as possible to have any chance of intercepting our pickup. So what is the terrain like? Are the bridges blown? Are the roads blocked? Is there somewhere elevated where we can signal? Is there space for the chopper to land? Have a good long look and think things through, 'cause if we can make it out of this building, we'll need you scouting the way."

Cahz turned back to Cannon. "Have a look through this stuff. See if you can find anything useful."

"What about them?" Cannon pointed out.

Cahz looked at the baby and then at Elspeth. He ran his hands through his hair. "Ah, shit," he grumbled.

He took the flavourless gum out of his mouth and flicked it away. The minty-ness had gone ages ago, but it hadn't totally removed the foul taste in his mouth.

Cahz lay down his carbine and hauled off his body armour. He unholstered his pistol.

"What you doing?" Ryan asked.

"Why'd you take your armour off?" Cannon asked.

"I don't know, Cannon… I don't know." Cahz was agitated. "She ain't dead yet and I don't feel right marching in there and killing her dressed like an executioner. Okay?"

Cannon made a submissive gesture with his hand and said nothing.

"You're *what*?" Ryan croaked.

He got to his feet, still holding the baby. As he took a step forward, Cannon swung his arm out to form a barrier.

"Cool it, Ryan," Cannon ordered. "You know it needs done."

Ryan started to object but couldn't find the grounds he needed. Elspeth was infected. Even looking at her he knew she wouldn't have long. He could also see it as a mercy.

He bowed his head and stepped back.

***

Cahz closed the office door gently behind him. The smell of death hung in the air. It was a sharp tart aroma, like a mouldy grapefruit mixed with stale urine. It was a smell that clawed at the back of his tongue and made him want to gag.

"Elspeth," he said softly, swallowing back the nausea.

When she didn't stir he called her name a little louder.

"Elspeth."

Still nothing.

Cahz knelt down beside her. Her skin was pale and translucent, the veins underneath an insidious black entanglement of infection that he knew pervaded her every fibre. Beads of sweat dripped from the tip of her nose and landed in a damp patch on the canvas camp bed.

Cahz listened carefully for the sound of breathing. Elspeth's lips were dark and cracked. A steady stream of frothy drool trickled from the corner of her bruised mouth.

He swallowed down nervously. He leaned closed to her mouth and, holding his breath, he cocked his ear, listening for any sound. A faint rasp struggled from her lips and her eyes flickered gently behind her closed eyelids.

The puff of breath was foul. It smelt sulphurous and dank.

"I'm sorry to do this before you've gone, but you don't have much time left anyway." Cahz paused, hearing his pathetic excuse. "Maybe it is better this way. I mean, you won't have to come back as one of those things."

Cahz clicked the safety catch off his pistol, "I'm sorry, but we… I don't have the time to wait for you. I hope you understand if I'm to get Ryan and Cannon and me out of this. I…" He stopped himself. "The truth is, it's easier this way. You're one less thing to worry about. I'm sorry, Elspeth."

Elspeth's eyes began to open, very slowly. The whites were bloodshot, but her irises were still a bright blue.

"It's okay," she whispered. Her eyes slowly began closing again.

Cahz blinked away a tear. He pointed the gun and pulled the trigger.

He stood up and drew his sleeve across his face, wiping away the tears. His ears buzzed with the deafening thump of the shot. The roar of interminable pressure reverberated around his head.

An ugly black pit the size of a coin was oozing blood from Elspeth's temple. The blood wasn't the usual crimson red, but darker—more corrupted. Her eyes had flickered open and rolled back, leaving just a crescent of blue iris visible. Beyond, the cream coloured office wall was sprayed with a fountain of that visceral fluid. Sliding down the wall were chunks of grey meat and shredded skin. A clump of scalp with tendrils of fine white hair slithered its way to the floor. Robbed of sound, the dripping blood was all the more discordant. Cahz watched for a moment, the angry buzzing in his ears blotting out all other noise. It separated him from the moment and yet dragged him in. Trickles of contaminated blood, stark against the pale infected skin, dribbled down her lifeless face. As he watched a dry wad of sickness caught in the back of his throat.

Cahz turned and looked out of the office window.

Ryan was rocking the baby. Even with the bark of the shot impairing Cahz's hearing, it was obvious by the way the baby's face was contorted that she was crying.

Cahz looked down at the gun in his hand. It was a black lump of hard cold metal in his grasp.

He opened the office door, his gaze firmly locked on the crying child.

Gulping back the anguish, Cahz marched up to the others.

Cannon was saying something as he walked up, but Cahz couldn't hear what above the ringing in his ears.

"Put her on the ground." Cahz wasn't sure if the words had come out but from Ryan's shocked reaction he knew he'd made his intent clear.

Ryan shook his head and backed up.

Cahz levelled the gun at the screaming child. Her pink skin was flushed red with howling. He couldn't hear him say it, but Cahz knew Ryan was pleading.

"Put her on the ground and step back!" Cahz shouted. Tears were streaming down both his and Ryan's face.

With the child shielded by his own body, Ryan pushed out at Cahz.

The distraught father was mouthing the words, "Fuck you!" through Cahz's deafness.

Cahz grabbed Ryan's wrist with his free hand and twisted the arm into a lock. Ryan screamed as he fought against the pain, but he couldn't stop from buckling. On his knees on the ground the crying baby was an easy target.

Cahz placed his finger over the trigger.

"Ahhggghh!" Cahz bellowed in pain as his arm was snapped into a lock.

Cannon pushed his commander to the ground, ripping the gun from his grip.

"Look at her!" Cannon shouted. "Look at her!"

The room was full of shouts and cries becoming more audible, less distorted all the time as Cahz's hearing cleared.

"Look at her!" Cannon offered a hand to help Cahz to his feet.

Cahz was hauled to his feet and took a step closer to the baby.

"Look at her skin," Cannon demanded.

He looked back at the office where Elspeth's corpse lay, then back at the child. The baby girl was still gulping in lungs full of air and belching them out as great shrieks. Her soft skin was flushed red from the distress.

"She's not infected?" Cahz said in amazement.

"She should have died hours ago, a kid that young." Cannon put a hand on Cahz's shoulder. "I realised it when I saw you with Elspeth."

Cahz reached out his hands in a silent request to see the child.

"Is she immune?" Ryan asked as he passed her over.

"No one's immune," Cannon countered, a hint of uncertainty in his voice.

Cahz took the child in his arms and rocked her gently to soothe her. As the girl started to calm down he walked over to the window to get the best light.

The scratch down the child's face wasn't as puffy or red as he remembered it. He peered closer at the wound. It had obviously started at her temple and been dragged down to the cheek just above the jaw line. All the way down were flakes of dead skin and small wells of congealed blood. The deepest part of the wound was where it stopped. There was a deep gouge that ended in an ugly lump of scabbed black blood.

Cahz continued looking at the injury—looking long and hard.

"Cannon," he finally said, "pass me the tweezers from one of the first aid kits."

"Here," Cannon said, passing them over.

Cahz took the tweezers and gripped the terminal scab. With a quick pluck he pulled the lump of scab away. The baby started howling again.

Looking out of the window, Cahz examined the tip of the tweezers. He gently turned his wrist to get the best angle of light.

"Well, fuck me!" Cahz exclaimed. "Look at this."

"That's what caused the mark?" Cannon asked, peering at the bloodied lump on the end of the tweezers.

"Let me see," Ryan said, barging past. "What is it? For fuck's sake lemme see."

"It's a shard of glass," Cahz declared, a tone of triumph in his voice.

"She's not infected," Cannon whispered.

Ryan gasped. "When Elspeth fell… It wasn't a claw mark—it was some broken glass on the ground." A huge smile erupted on Ryan's face. "She's not infected!"

He stretched his arms out and Cahz passed the child over.

Ryan hugged the baby close. "Oh my gorgeous baby girl." He planted a wet kiss on the obviously bemused child's forehead. The girl started whimpering at the unexpected attention. Ryan rocked her in his arms, tears of joy streaming down his cheeks.

"Stick your pinkie in her mouth," Cannon suggested.

"What?" Ryan asked.

"Stick your pinkie in her mouth. It'll help to calm her down."

Ryan gave a huff. "Why didn't you suggest that earlier when she was bawling?"

"*Because*," Cannon said, "I didn't want you to get bit and infected."

Ryan turned to the manager's office. "It would have meant a lot to her if she'd known. She wouldn't have died thinking she failed Sam and the baby." He placed a hand over his mouth and shuddered. He stood staring at the execution. "Poor Elspeth." His voice quivered. "She doesn't even look peaceful."

Cahz looked back at the dead woman. Her mouth was agape and the trickle of blood from the bullet wound in her forehead had run down into an eye before pooling and dripping off onto the floor.

Ryan wiped away a string of mucus from his nose and snorted back the grief.

"Cannon," Cahz said, "pull a sheet over her or something."

Cannon gave a nod. He picked up a discarded sleeping bag and proceeded into the office.

Cahz stepped in to snap Ryan out of his distress. "Okay, let's gather what stuff we need, then we'll plan how to get out of here."

He looked around for something to busy Ryan with. His eyes settled on the large plastic water containers.

Standing in front of him, Cahz placed his hands on Ryan's shoulders. "We're going to need water. I lost my canteen, so if we can find some more—"

Ryan broke in, "I spotted camel packs."

"Good. Fill a couple for each of us."

From behind, Cannon closed the office door and rejoined his commander. Elspeth's corpse was now hidden under a puffy green sleeping bag.

"We'll need mêlée weapons in case we run short on ammo," Cahz said as he watched Ryan rummage one-handed through a crate.

Cannon nodded. "I'm on it."

"Oh, and guys," Cahz added loud enough to get Ryan's attention, "see what else you can find and we'll pool it all together. Ten minutes."

***

The three men stood around a fan of assorted objects on the floor in front of them. There was nothing extraordinary among the kit; some water packs, rucksack, crowbar, wind up torch and a few other bits and pieces of civilian camping equipment.

"No point getting a rucksack. There's not enough stuff here to merit sticking in a bag," Cahz said, disappointed at the haul.

"The rucksack ain't for the kit," Cannon said. "It's for the little one."

"You're not stuffing my daughter in a bag!" Ryan said defensively.

"Think about it," Cannon said.

"What? No!" Ryan protested, looking at Cahz for support.

"She'll be comfortable and warm and safe," Cannon countered. "What's more, you can keep both hands free."

"It's a good call," Cahz said.

Cannon grinned. "Think of it like one of those expensive designer papooses."

"Yeah that fuckin' helps," Ryan said stubbornly.

"I made up a few diapers from the first aid bandages and stuffed them in the side pouches," Cannon said, smiling, obviously pleased at his foresight.

"Okay, now the hard part." Cahz stepped up to the window overlooking the rear parking lot. "How do we get out of here?"

"You thinking the car park?" Cannon asked.

"Could we hotwire one of the cars down there?" Cahz thought out loud.

"I doubt it," Ryan said. "We sucked the tanks dry to run our genny years ago. Anyway, they'll have rusted solid sitting out there."

"Yeah, guess you're right," Cahz agreed. "I think the car park is our best option though. The alleyway is packed with W.D.s, but they're only five or six deep."

"No point going out onto the main road," Cannon added. "There must be thousands of them there by now."

"Hey, we can still use the cars!" Cahz said excitedly.

"How do you mean?" Ryan asked.

"Listen: the chain fence between the lot and the building on the other side of the alley. We roll two cars through the fence either side of that doorway." Cahz pointed at the back entrance of the building on the opposite side.

"Yeah, the cars will block the path of the of pus bags," Ryan said, grasping the plan.

"We'll still have to take out the ones trapped between the cars before we force the door open," Cahz elaborated.

"I don't think it's going to work as well as you think," Cannon put in.

"Why not?"

"Well, as soon as the cars break the fence they can walk round them into the parking lot, then come at us from there."

"I know, but we don't need much time. Just enough to clear a path and get through that door."

"Ryan, what's in there?" Cannon asked.

Ryan rubbed his forehead. "Um… I think the bottom floor's a shop and the ones above are offices and apartments."

"Will the door be open?" Cahz asked.

"I doubt it. We usually went in the front. Better light."

"What about the fire?" Cannon asked, looking out at the stream of smoke.

"It's the building next door that's on fire, but it's likely to spread." Cahz lent on the windowsill. "It doesn't look like there's any smoke coming from the building opposite the car park and it might even work to our advantage."

"How do you figure?"

"The W.Ds coming down the alleyway from the street have to get past the fire. Now it might not be hot enough to incinerate them, but the smoke and noise is going to disorientate them." Cahz stood up straight and looked at his two comrades. "The ones further back on the left might not even spot us."

"Fair point," Ryan said. "But once we're in the shop, where then?"

"Show me the map," Cahz said.

Ryan pulled the map from his back pocket and unfolded it.

"There's a railway marked on here running through town." Cahz scanned the features trying to spot the black-hashed line.

Cannon placed a thick fingertip on the page. "There."

"How far is that from here?" Cahz asked Ryan.

"Not far." He moved his finger back from the line to the plaza.

"What, five streets over? But why the railway? It's not like we can catch the five fifteen out of here."

"Think about rail lines running though urban areas." Cahz didn't see any recollection on Ryan's face, so he went on, "They've always got high fences to stop kids from wandering onto the lines."

"How's that help us?" Ryan asked.

"The dumb pus fucks can't get in either," Cannon answered.

"They'll still get in at the stations and the like, but we'll only have to worry about the path ahead. And because it's flat it'll be much quicker to move along."

"Okay." Ryan didn't sound convinced, but he didn't offer anything better.

"The rail line leaves the city and follows the coast north. We can come off it somewhere about here." Cahz pointed at a square on the map. "And find a good pickup point in that area."

"One thing, boss," Cannon pointed out, "that's about fifty klicks over unfamiliar terrain in infested country. We're going to have to move some."

Cahz nodded.

"And I hate to piss on the parade," Cannon added, "but if we're still on the move after dark we're screwed. Even with night vision it's a tall order to go wandering around infected territory at night, and we don't have night vision."

Cahz sighed. "I hear what you're saying, buddy. We'll just have to find somewhere suitable to hold up."

"Look, if we're just marching off to find somewhere in the suburbs to hold out, why walk all that way?" Ryan asked. "We could just find another building like this to barricade and wait out."

"I've thought of that. But what if the fire spreads? What if the smoke's too thick for a pickup? No, we're best to get as far from the city centre as possible. Even if the fire wasn't an issue I'd still want to put some distance between us. There's thousands of W.D.s out there. The more space we can put between them, the safer I'll feel." Cahz looked at Cannon. "I also figure that by getting closer to the coast, we'll double our chances of a pickup."

"How do you figure?"

Cahz explained, "If we stay in the city and the rescue turns up, Idris'll look for a while then bug out. We miss that, we miss our ride home. If we can get out of the city we can signal him on the way in. If we miss him we can catch him on the way out."

"I don't know if I follow your logic on that," Ryan said, "but I can see the point to getting out of Dodge. The streets here are swarming with the dead. It'll be quieter in the country."

"We ready to go then?" Cahz asked.

"We got five minutes?" Ryan said.

"What for?" Cahz asked.

"I want to take a dump in one of those chemical toilets before we go running through a city full of dead fucks trying to eat me."

Cannon laughed. "He's got a point, boss. I'd rather take a crap where I didn't have to worry about getting bit on the ass."

"Fine," Cahz said with a smirk on his face. "Anyone got a newspaper?"

***

"Shit! You've got to look at this!" Ryan waddled into the office hoisting his jeans up.

"No one wants to look at your shit, Ryan," Cahz chastised as he adjusted his body armour.

"No, outside." Ryan fastened his belt and ran back out of the office.

Cahz and Cannon found Ryan in the side office that had being used as the latrine. Ryan had already opened the window and was waving frantically.

"What is it?" Cahz asked, unable to see past Ryan's broad shoulders.

"Ali!" Ryan bellowed at the top of his lungs. "Ali!"

Cahz pushed past to see a bizarre sight. Across the street a zombie was dangling from a line halfway up a building. At the top of the line a man with a thick black beard was hoisting the creature up to an open window.

"What the fuck's he doing?" Cannon asked.

"Ali!" Ryan waved furiously.

The man across the street continued pulling the zombie up. The creature had its arms outstretched, trying to grab at the man is it spun round on the line.

"What is he doing?" Cahz echoed Cannon's query.

"Looks like he's tying it off," Ryan said. "He's bashing that pus bags head in!"

With a few short thwacks the zombie slumped.

"Ali! Ali!" Ryan cried.

The man across the street stood at the window and waved back in wide over-exaggerated sweeps.

"Ali!" Ryan called joyously. "It's Ali," Ryan beamed as he told the two soldiers.

"We gathered that much," Cannon quipped.

Below, the crowd of undead were feverishly moaning, exhilarated by the prospect of living flesh. The man across the street yelled something unintelligible back.

"I can't hear him," Ryan complained. "Shut the fuck up you pus bags!"

In frustration Ryan pointed to his ears and shrugged.

CHAPTER FOURTEEN
AVENUE

The sweat dripped off Ali's thick eyebrows as he pulled on the electrical cable. The soul ripping frustration had evaporated to the elation of finally hooking his quarry. Now all Ali could feel was the burn in his muscles and the pain in his fingers as he hoisted the zombie up. The undead were usually lighter than when they'd been alive. Ali assumed some level of desiccation or wastage set in.

When everything kicked off all those years ago, Ali had delivered a vanload of stray dogs to a research centre. He didn't like to think of the poor animals' fate. Intellectually he knew they were dead already; with no family to adopt them they were only days away from being put down. But he could guess their end wasn't going to be peaceful in the gloved hands of the lab technicians.

He'd stood there in the bustling lab shocked and stunned by the frantic going-ons. Soldiers and doctors in blood-smeared HAZMAT suits. State of emergency broadcasts being repeated through the public address system.

It was here he had encountered his first zombie, a naked and emaciated looking waif of a woman, her skin brown and wrinkled, her eyes a frosted white. She was wheeled past him strapped to a gurney. Her chest was sawn open and there was just an empty cavity where her organs should have been. The scrawny creature still snapped and thrashed against her bindings.

Ali had been frozen by her gaze; that bleached-out stare that somehow expressed a malignant jealousy. Ali listed and watched in a stupor. Occasionally he was pushed out of the way by an anxious orderly or commanded to stand clear by a soldier, but no one questioned why he was there or told him to leave. Mingling among the chaos and raised voices were the moans of the captive zombies. Back then Ali had found the cry more pitiful than terrifying, an imprisoned soul pleading for help, begging for release. Like the sirens' call it drew in Ali's compassion.

He had found himself at the doorway to a lab. A caged zombie pressed against the Perspex of its prison. It moaned constantly, its expression one of confusion held behind the unfathomable invisible barrier. Ali stood and watched, aching to help, unaware of the creature's deadly compulsion. It was the high pitch yelp of a dog that broke the trance and compelled him to leave.

The zombie dangling from his fishhook held the same look of confusion as it spun round on the line. Unable to arrest its rotation, it lashed out every time its orbit brought it back to face Ali. It too gave out the same pitiful whine, but in the convening years Ali had learned to loathe that noise.

Now as Ali heaved he heard an unexpected sound.

"Ali!" a faint voice carried over the moans of the dead.

Ali ignored the audio hallucination, more concerned by the burning of his muscles. Gritting his teeth he continued to pull on the cord.

"Ali! Ali!" the distant call came again.

"Oh my God!" Ali gasped, convinced now the call was real.

The cord in his hands slipped slightly before he regained his poise. Focusing on his catch, Ali brought it up to the level he wanted and tied off the cable. Rotating slowly, the tethered zombie lashed out, trying to snag him. Ali timed his aim and as its arms spun out of reach he leaned in and bludgeoned the back of its skull. He knew when to stop hammering when its stiff arms fell limp. Happy the zombie was dispatched, he stood up and scanned the street.

"Ali!" came the call again and this time he spotted where it had come from.

Across the road on the first floor up, Ryan was waving frantically from an office window.

Ali gave a long over enthusiastic wave back and called his friend's name. His joyous shouts rebounded over the heads of the zombies that filled the space between them. The thousand-strong crowd of zombies joined with Ali's cries in making their own exclaim as best as their decayed bodies could allow. Ali could see two other men behind Ryan. He squinted and peered at them, trying to recognise who they were. Neither man looked like any of Ali's compatriots from the warehouse. They were too well built, with short cropped hair and sandy coloured military style uniforms.

Soldiers?

"Soldiers," Ali said with a firm voice. "They're soldiers. That means a rescue," he exuberantly told the body that was spinning on the wire. "Well, it's too late to rescue you, my friend."

Ryan shouted something over the zombie-filled chasm.

"What?!" Ali bellowed back. For emphasis he held a cupped hand to his ear.

An incomprehensible string of shouts came in reply.

Ali shook his head and shrugged. "I can't hear you."

Ryan started pointing out of the window. Ali followed the direction to the plumes of smoke belching from the neighbouring building. Ryan made a serious of baffling hand gestures, trying to communicate some message, but Ali couldn't make sense of them.

Again Ali shrugged his shoulders.

With his index finger in the air Ryan made a circular motion like he was keeping an invisible hoola hoop aloft.

Helicopter?

"Helicopter?!" he shouted, mimicking Ryan's action.

Then Ryan made a thumb like a hitchhiker over his shoulder.

Instinctively Ali pointed in the direction Ryan had indicated.

"The helicopter is over there?!" Ali squinted his eyes as he tried to make out anything to confirm his interpretation.

One of the soldiers tapped Ryan on the shoulder and there was a short exchange between them. Ryan thrust his arm in the air and then made a thumbs up sign.

Still perplexed by the meaning of their conversation, Ali copied the signal.

He was still standing there dazed by the brief encounter long after Ryan and his two companions disappeared.

He looked down at the dead backpacker dangling in front of him.

"What you make of all that?" Ali asked. When the creature rotated away from him, Ali huffed, "Didn't think you had anything to add."

He bent down and took a long look at his catch. His make do hook had snagged under one of the pack's shoulder straps. Ali pulled out his knife and was about to cut the strap free when he suddenly stopped.

"Idiot."

Ali backed up and retrieved some cabling. He tied the wiring to one of the straps on the backpack and secured the other end to his wrist.

"I don't want this hard-fought catch getting away from me now, do I?" he said to the cadaver as he sliced through the shoulder strap.

With a soft rip the last few strands of fibre snapped under the weight of the dead hiker. The centre of gravity on the hook bucked and the dead body slipped out of the undamaged strap. Like the dummy from a cheap action movie, the lifeless corpse tumbled to the mass of zombies below.

***

Ali sat in what had become his chair in Frank's apartment. The backpacker had proven to be a gold mine: camping provisions, gas stove, sleeping bag and even a domed tent. He was spooning in the last of the beans from a can he'd liberated and trying to figure out what had just happened.

Now he knew the chopper was coming back and there were other people in the same predicament as he. And he knew he could camp out on a rooftop in comfort. But had Ryan's signalling indicated the chopper would return to some other location, or that the three of them were leaving in that direction?

There was no point worrying as there was nothing Ali could do about it. At least if Ryan got rescued he could tell the pilot to come pick him up.

The only worry for now was the fire.

Could it spread to my side of the street?

He decided no, it couldn't. He didn't think it would jump such a wide firebreak as the main road. It might light a few zombies, but he doubted the stone, steel and glass of the apartments would be combustible against such a weak ignition source.

Ali had a newfound sense of safety. He now had food, in the form of the camping supplies, and the likelihood was that the chopper would return.

"I must find something to read," Ali told himself in preparation for his rooftop vigil.

He cast an eye around the living room. It was neat and tidy with even the TV guide appointed its own space next to the remote control. There was a storage tower stacked high with martial arts and action movies. There was the odd loose case next to the DVD player where he'd found the romantic comedy but with no electricity they had all been reduced to a stack of ornate signal mirrors.

Ali's mouth opened wide as an expansive yawn escaped. He used the balls of his palms to wipe away the moisture from his eyes. Like the aftershock to an earthquake a second smaller yawn followed. The sunlight was streaming in from outside, but in spite of that Ali's eyelids were heavy. He set the empty can of beans down on the kitchen counter and returned to his easy chair.

"It could be a long night," Ali justified to himself as he snuggled down.

CHAPTER FIFTEEN
BOLT

Cannon let the blade of the knife slip down to the bottom of the link. The interwoven wire formed a harlequin pattern of squares that made up the car park fence. Each strand of wire was enveloped in a weather bleached casing of green plastic. The plastic had mostly rubbed off at the joints where the cable interlaced, and where it hadn't it was so perished that it dropped off in lumps rather than yield a neat cut under the blade.

Cannon focused on the minutia of his task, the bite of wire against the blade of his knife, the grating of the metal edge as he sawed through the wire. This was not the way he should be treating his knife and he knew it. A sharp knife was an invaluable survival tool and with each swipe he was dulling the blade further.

Still, this was survival, Cannon told himself.

He concentrated on these niggling details rather than let the reality intrude. But every so often he couldn't avoid it. Time and time again clusters of necrotic fingers would poke through the chain. A dead face with skin saggy and blue-tinged would be pressed against the fence, gnawing at the wire. At these moments Cannon's gut reaction was to stop weakening the fence that was holding back the mass of animated dead just a finger's length away.

A dead hand pushed against the wire where Cannon was cutting.

The zombie, utterly focused on the human, didn't notice that it had impaled its palm on Cannon's knife. It poked its nose between the wire and gnashed its crooked yellow teeth. Its vacant, sunken, unblinking eyes transfixed on its potential meal as it pushed against the fence, struggling to get at him. Even though Cannon had wrapped his shemagh around his face, the smell of the creature's rotting innards skulked through the fabric. The monster was so close that Cannon could see the whiskers poking through its dead flesh. The zombie pushed against the fence so hard its skin had started to split at the points of contact.

Cannon pulled his knife back. It slurped as it withdrew from the zombie's soft, bloated flesh. This cadaver was soggy like a sponge. There was a trace of green in the crevices of the creature's skin. Cannon wondered if maybe it had spent some time at the bottom of a lake.

Cannon knew nothing ate the dead—no dog or crow or cockroach or maggot. Nothing found these toxic corpses a savoury meal to devour. One whiff of their necrotic stench was enough to deter even the hungriest scavenger. The only thing that chewed at them was the weather or machinegun fire. But occasionally you would see a zombie, like this one, that had its own flora or fauna. There would always be the odd walking dead that had dragged half a bush with it but this one had a green algae matted to its cracked fingernails like the scum that clung to the walls of a neglected fish tank.

There was one time when Cannon had seen a bobbleheaded mushroom growing from a zombie's suit collar. He'd even helped dredge up a zombie from the ocean, drenched in seaweed, and with a barnacle stuck firmly to its temple.

The wire popped as his knife severed the cable. With the extra space the dead man pushed his whole hand through and grabbed at Cannon's body armour.

Cannon stepped back, but the dead fingers held tight. The zombie snarled behind the fence, ripping chunks out of its own lips as it tried to bite its way through.

Cannon swapped the knife over to his left hand, ripped open the Velcro securing his holster, and pulled out his pistol. He pushed the muzzle against the dead man's forehead and pulled the trigger. As the shot rang out, the zombie slumped to the ground. Cannon shook off the grip, prizing the last couple of stubborn fingers free with the tip of his knife. The zombie's body dangled slightly, suspended by the arm snagged in the wire. What was left of its head tipped back and the mush from its cranium sloshed onto the ground.

As soon as it had fallen away a new zombie filled the gap. Unperturbed by the fate of its predecessor, the replacement zombie slipped its ragged fingers through the mesh, mauling the air, desperate to squeeze through.

Cannon holstered his weapon and bent down on one knee. He slipped his knife down to the next link and cursed the damage he was causing to the blade as he hacked through the wire.

***

"But what about Ali?" Ryan protested.

"He's obviously capable of looking after himself," Cahz said. "Have you got the handbrake on yet?"

Cahz was leaning against the bumper, holding the car at a stop. This was the second vehicle he and Ryan had broken into and lined up facing the fence. From his position at the front of the car, Cahz was looking directly at the fenced-out zombies. "They're getting very excited."

"There's got to be something we can do for him," Ryan complained.

"The best thing we can do is get rescued," Cahz said. "We get rescued and then we take a nice safe helicopter ride to go pick up your friend. Now hurry up. The natives are getting restless."

The zombies on the other side of the flimsy wire were shaking it with tremendous force. Cahz guessed the fence had been weakened by the years of weathering, but it looked like the undead in their frenzy might just be able to tear it down themselves.

"I've cut away about half the links," Cannon reported as he rejoined the others. "But I daren't do any more than that in case they break through."

"I was just thinking that," Cahz confessed.

Ryan got out of the driver's seat and wiped chunks of shattered safety glass from his backside. "Next time I'll remember to put in the passenger window."

"You not going to pump up those tyres?" Cannon asked.

"No point," Ryan said. "I doubt they'll take any pressure. They've been sitting on the rims for god knows how long. The rubber will be cracked and perished."

"So no chance of getting one of these started and driving out of here?" Cannon asked, a note of hopefulness in his voice.

"Sitting idle like this for years? The battery will be dead for a start. Hell, I was out of town for a week and had to dry the spark plugs on my old Nissan before she'd turn over," Ryan said. "That's even if they had fuel." He nodded at the forced open flap to the tank. "What we haven't siphoned will have evaporated dry by now."

"Okay, I get the point," Cannon snapped.

"You really know fuck all about cars," Ryan said.

Cannon puffed up his quite considerable chest. "Yeah, well, we'll see how smug you are next time you've got a diaper change. And besides, you've left your gun on the passenger seat."

"Shit," Ryan cursed, checking the small of his back as he looked at the discarded weapon.

"All right, you two," Cahz said. "We need to focus on this." He put a hand on each of his companion's shoulders. "On my signal, you two whip off the handbrakes and roll the cars at the fence.

I'll be by the fence thinning them out. By the time you guys catch up to me it should be clear enough to jimmy open that back door and get inside." Cahz pointed at the back entrance to the shop they were aiming for. "Once we're inside, Ryan leads the way out. We keep going until we pick up the railway line. It's four blocks west of here."

Ryan was slipping the gun into the back of his belt and nodded silently.

"Show me that gun," Cahz said.

Ryan pulled the gun out, barrel aimed at Cahz.

"Fuckin' hell!" Cahz battered the muzzle away. "Don't point it at me."

"You asked to see it," Ryan said.

"See it—not get shot by it." Cahz looked at the side of the weapon. "Just checking the safety's on; don't want you blowing your ass cheeks off."

Ryan frowned and tucked the gun away.

"Once we're on the line it should make our lives easier. It reduces the directions the W.D.s can come from." Cahz picked up the crowbar and passed it to Cannon. "I guess you'll be able to take that door off its hinges without this," he joked, "but to save time you'd best have it."

"Want me to carry anything?" Ryan asked.

"Just her." Cahz pointed at the baby in the makeshift papoose.

***

Cahz took a sip on the tube from his camel pack. The warm water quenched his thirst but did nothing to shift the sour taste in his mouth. He took a reassuring glance round at the others. Both men were in position, ready to push the first car, Ryan by the handbrake, Cannon at the rear.

Cahz cleared his throat.

"Three, two, one, go!"

Cahz started firing.

Over the shots he could hear Cannon and Ryan grunting as they battled to get the car moving. Seconds later the first car careered into the fence and ploughed through. The fence screeched as the wires buckled and snapped down the fault line. A whole section of mesh popped off from its posts and wrapped around the front of the vehicle. Those zombies pressed in against the wire were hauled off their feet and thrown back, but the mass of dead bodies were too thick for the car to make much headway. The car ground to a halt only a few feet past the fence, leaving a gap twice as wide for the dithering zombies to shamble through.

Cahz kept firing, felling as many as he could and hoping he could stem the flow of zombies trickling past the stalled car.

With a loud crash the second car tore through the other section of fence.

Cahz reloaded, but before he could fire again he heard the bark of Cannon's support weapon.

Looking round, he could see the second car had also failed to block the alleyway.

Cannon stood with the butt of his machine gun tight against his shoulder, taking well-aimed bursts at the encroaching zombies. With each burst, one, sometimes two, zombies would topple over, but Cahz knew the recoil made the weapon wildly inaccurate even at these short distances.

"Ryan!" he shouted. "Grab the crowbar! Get that door open!"

"What?!" Ryan shouted back, unable to hear Cahz over the gunshots and the screams of his backpack-swaddled daughter.

"The door!" Cahz screamed between shots.

Ryan ran as fast as he could with the child on his back. He skidded to a halt next to Cannon, one hand behind his back awkwardly trying to steady the load. The crowbar was sticking out of a sheath in Cannon's body armour like a ninja sword. Ryan grabbed it and whipped the crowbar free.

With the last few rounds in his second clip, Cahz floored the zombies between Ryan and the door.

Vaulting over the carpet of dead, Ryan leapt to the door and wedged the end of the crowbar into the narrow crack at the doorjamb.

Cahz loaded his third clip, careful to secure the empty back in its pouch. Although he'd been able to reload from Cannon's belt of ammunition back in the office, he knew there'd be no chance of a top up, exposed like this in the middle of a horde.

"Get that door!" Cahz ordered.

"I can't! The wood's rotten! It keeps splitting!" Ryan called back as he dug the crowbar in again.

"Move!" Cannon bellowed and he swung round, pointing his weapon at Ryan.

"Shit," Ryan gasped as he dived out of the doorway.

Cannon bounded towards the door as if it wasn't there. Just a couple of strides away a burst of fire erupted from his gun and he twisted to barge the door full force with his shoulder. Splinters of wood flew from the devastated door and Cannon disappeared through the freshly made opening.

"Go! Go! Go!" Cahz roared.

Ryan vanished into the building, the child on his back screaming.

Cahz bolted after him, making the doorway only seconds before the first zombie. In the dark corridor he could see Ryan's light shirt through the murk. Cannon was on all fours, still working to get to his feet after the crash through the door.

"Ryan! Go! Lead us out!"

Ryan looked surprised.

"I'll help Cannon. You take point." And with that, Cahz found Cannon's grab handle on the neck of his body armour, wrapped his fingers around it, and pulled. "Come on, soldier. On your feet."

"Yes sir!" Cannon snapped back out of reflex.

The light streaming through the busted door faded and spluttered. Cahz turned to see the silhouette of a zombie snatching for him.

Cahz caught the creature's hip with a swift side kick, sending it spinning to the floor. Right behind it came another cadaver, then another, and another, each soaking up more and more of the light.

Still on the ground, Cannon flipped round to sit on his butt. A staccato burst of light and the thunder of shots followed, hammering through the pursuing zombies.

Cahz grabbed his buddy by the bicep and dragged him up.

"Move!" he yelled as he stumbled into the darkness.

Within feet the last usable light from the narrow doorway was eaten up by the musty gloom. Cahz and Cannon lurched into the darkness. A myriad of squeaks echoed from the dispossessed rodents scurrying into the shadows.

Cahz called out, "Ryan?!"

The sound of Ryan's daughter crying could be heard somewhere up ahead.

"Through here," came Ryan's voice.

Cannon flicked on his torch. The slender beam of white light cut only a thin wedge from the darkness. A rat with matted brown fur scampered from the glow back to its nest of tattered linen. The light dimmed and went out.

"Piece of shit!" Cannon griped as he wound the mechanism. As he did the yellow light flickered on and grew brighter.

Cannon scanned the beam around the corridor. The once white tiled floor was awash with rat droppings and garbage. Most things had degraded to a brown pulp but there was still the odd recognisable item, much of which was out of place in the back of a store.

The beam cast over a child's bike. Cahz stepped over to look at the plastic trike, its bright yellow and reds still visible under a coating of crud. He rested a friendly hand on Cannon's shoulder and Cannon juddered.

"Whoa. You okay?" Cahz asked.

"Fine," Cannon snapped, flicking the light from the bike. "We've got to move. Where the fuck is Ryan?"

"Up here I think." Cahz pointed to the T-junction at the end of the corridor.

The sound of shuffling and moans from behind hastened Cahz's steps. As he drew level with the junction it was easy to tell which way Ryan had turned by the baby's crying. Ryan was standing rubbing the side of his head a couple of paces down the passageway.

"Which way?" Cahz asked.

"I don't know," Ryan confessed over the sobs coming from his backpack.

"Take a guess."

A grizzly moan and a burst of machinegun fire from behind forced Ryan's decision.

"This way." He pointed down the junction.

"Cannon, on point." Cahz said.

Cannon pushed past, his weapon still smoking. "Sure thang, boss," he said.

Cannon slung his machine gun and pulled out his pistol. With his arms crossed at the wrist, he marched into the darkness, his torch darting back and forth trying to push back the black.

"He doesn't sound like a soldier when he talks to you," Ryan whispered to Cahz.

"He never has," Cahz whispered back. "Maybe it's because he'd been out of it before his reactivation. It's never bothered me. He's always sound."

"Yeah, but what's this 'boss' thing?"

"Irony, I guess." Cahz shrugged. "All my crew use it. I think Private Bates started it. Like I say, I don't mind it. A lot of standards have slipped, especially among conscripts. But they're a good crew. A bit irreverent at times, but military protocol is not what it was."

"I thought you said you both served overseas?" Ryan said.

"We did separate tours, but he's never said where."

"And you've not been curious?"

"A lot of bad shit happened," Cahz replied in an even more hushed tone. "A lot of guys had a hard time getting back to the real world. Cannon was one of them. He'd been discharged long before the Rising. When they put him back in a uniform he wouldn't tell them anything about his previous service. Things were shot to fuck by that point so they couldn't check. They stuck him with private and left him with me."

"So you don't know what his story is then?"

"Never asked," Cahz answered. "We all got stories."

Ryan's nod was lost to the gloom.

The torch light from up ahead died then burst back on.

"Cannon? Everything okay?"

"Look," Cannon said.

He shone the light at the bottom of the door in front of them. When he switched the torch off, a faint glow of light could be seen.

"Okay," Cahz said, placing a hand on Ryan's shoulder. "If that's a way out it's a way in, too. Ryan, you open the door. Cannon will be left, me right." He double checked his carbine and side arm. "We break out fast. Dispatch Whisky Deltas only if you have to." He waited for agreement to manifest in his companion's eyes. "We get out and into the street as fast as we can. Got it?"

"Got it."

"Okay." Cahz counted a silent three, two, one, and shouted, "Go!"

CHAPTER SIXTEEN
NEIGHBOURHOOD

Behind his closed eyes Ali could hear a rasping—something moving close to him. Slowly he raised his eyelids. A shadow crept across the floor. Ali stiffened up and held his breath. Drawn to the movement, he looked up from the chair.

The shadow rushed forward. Ali leapt from the chair, his heart bursting from his chest. A twinge of pain sliced though his wounded leg and his balance snatched from him. He stumbled back until he thumped to a stop propped against the wall. Frantically he looked around the room, but was unable to see the zombie.

Then he registered the source of the movement. There was a sheet of weathered plastic wrapped around the balcony. It was the type of thick translucent sheeting used to temporarily waterproof building works. The ragged ends lashed out at the window, creating both the rasping sound and the dancing shadow.

"Getting jumpy," Ali said to himself as he caught his breath. And in spite of the false alarm he peeked down the hallway to check the front door was still closed. Satisfied that he was still safe, he threw his arms back at the shoulders and puffed his chest out in a stretch. He gave an expansive yawn that lifted him up onto his tiptoes before letting out a sharp sigh.

Ali walked over to the window, limping slightly from the

aggravated wound.

Judging by the light it was still early afternoon. He checked his watch, convinced he'd slept longer than he had. The big hand hadn't even moved half way round. Slender white clouds were racing high in the sky and on the horizon out towards the ocean; darker, more menacing ones rolled in towards the mainland. He walked out onto the balcony and in an act of hope he looked around.

Across the road the blaze had engulfed the far building and the zombies crushed against its walls had burnt to a crisp. The mass of undead funnelling in to get at Ali were shoving some of the weaker zombies into the burning flames.

Any fleeting thought that there was a benefit in the reduction in numbers was erased when Ali saw the space directly below the apartment. From his vantage point he couldn't see the tarmac, so tightly packed were the zombies.

He lent on the railing and peered across to the building he'd seen Ryan in. It wasn't yet alight, but Ali guessed it wouldn't be long before the fire took. His eyes caught the window he'd spotted his friend at. It was still open but there was no movement and he spotted nothing in any of the numerous windows.

Ali unsnagged the sheet of polythene and balled it up before dropping it onto the crowd below.

"I hope you're all right, my friend," he whispered to the wind before walking back to the dining area.

Pulling a fresh bottle of water from the plastic wrapped case, he unscrewed the cap off and took a refreshing gulp. Then a sharp crack caught the air and Ali's grip on the bottle broke. The flinch sent the plastic container skating across the kitchen counter. Another shot rang out, distant and muffled.

Ignoring the precious water glugging its way to freedom, Ali rushed to the window. He slammed the handle down and burst onto the balcony.

The cold moist air caught his hair, obscuring his view for a moment. Sweeping it to one side, Ali clasped his big hands round the balcony and leaned out. He scanned the street below, desperate to spot Ryan and the soldiers. More and more gunfire could be heard and it was obvious to Ali that these were no well-aimed shots. The bursts were frantic and erratic, the noise of combat, not the steady aimed shots he'd heard this morning.

He scanned the windows in the office block across the street, but there was no sign of anyone.

Must be round back, he thought.

Within a few minutes the sound of gunfire was gone.

Ali wrung the balcony railing tight in his grasp. He shook his head and sucked air through his teeth. All the time he listened to the wind and the moans, trying to pick out the slightest noise—a scream, a gunshot, anything to tell him they were still alive.

"Come on, Ryan," he whispered, knowing his friend would never hear his encouragement. "Come on."

Off in the far distance a shot barked out.

"Yeah!"

Ali punched wildly into the air.

The crowd below also responded with excitement, lifting their moans up a gear at the stimulation.

"I knew you'd make it," Ali told the damp air. "You mind telling them you're old friend Ali is here?"

He stepped back into the flat, closing the glass doors behind him. He rubbed his wind-chilled hands together and surveyed the sanctuary before him. Strewn around the room were the contents of the scavenged rucksack. There was more than enough in the kit to keep him comfortable for a number of days.

He righted the dropped bottle of water. Two thirds had spilt across the counter. The small lagoon had surged its way to the edge and was now running off the work surface in a series of thin rivulets. Ali opened the kitchen drawers and found a clean dishtowel, and with a long sweep he brushed the water into the empty sink.

Again he berated himself for his latent domesticity.

"Right. Let's get to work," he announced as he dried his hands.

CHAPTER SEVENTEEN
RAIL

The long stems of the wild grasses whipped against Cahz's shins as he ran down the street. Everywhere there was a crack or pothole, lanky green shoots had sprung up, wrapping round the rusted streetlights and corroding cars. He stumbled for a moment, footing lost to the wobble of a broken services hatch. The slab had cracked down a fault line fractured open by winters of ice.

"I need…" Ryan panted out from behind, "…to rest."

Cahz spat out a distasteful wad of mucus like an old time prospector chewing tobacco. "We're not far from the railway line, Ryan." He turned and grabbed the man by the bicep, pulling him on. "You can rest when we're safe."

Ryan stumbled forward. "Nowhere is safe."

"All right, somewhere they're not coming at us from every angle," Cahz barked out. "Now move!"

"I'm gonna hurl."

Cahz grabbed the young man by the shoulders and spun him round.

"Look at them." He pointed down the road.

Bent double trying to catch his breath, Ryan lifted his head to look. Clambering past the rusted cars and derelict buildings, an army of walking dead shuffled after them, a thousand pairs of dead eyes transfixed by the fleeing living. The cries of distress from Ryan's daughter did nothing to drown out the clamour. Like the howl of icy wind the monotonous sound hung steady in the air, a dull drone perpetually calling, the cries from their dead mouths and the scuffing of their dead feet. It all echoed off the walls and clutched at Ryan's pounding heart.

"Listen to them," Cahz repeated demandingly. "Listen to that. That's the sound of a million lost souls and they're coming for us. Now I stayed behind to save lives, not waste them." He grabbed Ryan under his left shoulder and violently pulled him upright. "Get your ass in gear."

"I can't," Ryan pleaded in gasps.

Cahz held his gaze. "Don't let Elspeth down." He let go of his grip and watched the young man's face for a sign that his goad had worked.

Finally Ryan took a deep breath and nodded.

As they turned to move a shot rang out.

"Cannon?" Cahz called.

Cannon appeared from a corner ahead.

"Embankment's this way," he bellowed. "We've found the railway."

Cahz and Ryan jogged past the freshly dispatched cadaver and up to the fence cordoning off the railroad track.

"How do we get in?" Ryan asked.

"I don't see a gap in the wire," Cahz said, looking up and down the track.

"Do we follow it up and look for a way in?" Cannon asked.

"Cut it," Cahz decided.

"But they'll just follow us in," Ryan argued.

Cannon was already sawing at the wire with his knife.

"Yeah, but if we get in and run up away from the opening they'll make a beeline for us. They'll miss the gap," Cahz said as he anxiously surveyed the road they'd come down.

"I'm only cutting a crawl space," Cannon said over his shoulder. "Enough for us to squeeze through. But those dumb fucks ain't smart enough to think of bending down."

The first zombie came round the corner on stiff, jerking legs. It shuffled like the lobotomised inmate of some insane asylum. Cahz fired and a dime-sized hole appeared in its forehead. Its head snapped back and its infected brains exploded out the rear of its cranium. The force of the impact threw the limp cadaver hurtling back. It landed hard in a mound of masonry with a crunch.

From behind him Cahz heard scrambling.

"Come on!" Cannon called as he followed Ryan through the gap.

There was a steep drop down to the gravel of the railroad. Cahz used the momentum of the slope to break into a run as he hit the level.

"Come on, run!" Cahz called as he barrelled past his companions.

Cannon grabbed Ryan's backpack strap and hauled him along.

The three jogged along the lines, each trying to find their own rhythm over the sleepers. The screams of the baby secured in the rucksack wailed like an emergency siren.

Cannon turned to Cahz. "We've got to shut her up, boss."

"How?" Cahz had been hoping his buddy's undisclosed parenting skills would have held the answer, but Cannon's statement scuppered that hope.

"She's not…" Ryan panted out, "…going to stop while we're…"

He tripped and fell sprawled out across the tracks. He gave a grunt of pain.

Cahz whipped round. "You all right?"

Bent double, Ryan gurgled.

"Are you all right?" Cahz asked for a second time.

"Ah, fuck," Ryan moaned. He slowly sat back on his haunches.

"Oh, nasty," Cannon let slip.

Ryan's face was pitted with gravel and blood. He brought a blooded hand down from his face and took a sobbing breath in.

"Get a move on!" Cahz grabbed Ryan's hand and hauled him on like a parent dragging a reluctant child.

"I'm bleeding here," Ryan said as he stumbled to his feet.

"It's just superficial," Cahz said.

"It stings to fuck."

"You're a big boy, Ryan. I'm sure you've skint your knee before," Cannon said.

"Fuck you, big guy!"

"You'll have far worse than a bloody nose if you don't shut up and move out," Cannon said.

Ryan picked up his pace to catch Cannon. "You threatening me, you prick?"

"Whoa!" Cahz interrupted. "Stow it. We don't have time to dick around like school kids." He pointed at Ryan. "Listen, you pick up the pace if you don't want to be supper for those dead fucks back there. As for you," Cahz turned to Cannon, "I know there's shit going on, but stifle it until we're safe."

Cannon clamped his mouth shut and drew a loud breath through his nostrils.

"Got it?" Cahz asked.

Cannons nostrils flared like an enraged bull.

"I mean it, Cannon!" Cahz barked.

The forlorn pine of the undead interrupted them. All three men looked round to see a zombie pressed up against the railing, trying fruitlessly to barge its way forward. Further down the line a second zombie answered its call. Within moments it too was pressed against the fence, groaning.

"Move!" Cahz shouted and renewed his jog.

The thick lumps of gravel crunched as the three men ran down the railway line.

"We need a distraction," Cahz said.

"Why?" Ryan asked. "They're not keeping pace with us and they're not getting on the line."

"That'll do," Cahz said and he sped up.

Ahead of them, sitting on the track, was an abandoned train. The elements had not been kind to the aging rolling stock. Its rear window was smashed open, the protruding buffers were rusted, the green paintwork was flaking, and a handful of small shrubs were erupting from its battered frame.

Ryan and Cannon caught up as Cahz was tugging open the carriage door.

"What you doing?" Cannon asked.

Cahz grunted and the door started to give. "Give me a hand here."

Cannon lent forward and wedged the fingers of one hand into the crack between the door and the frame. He licked his lips and counted, "One, two, three."

With a disapproving rumble the door shuddered open.

"You still haven't said what you're doing," Cannon said as Cahz disappeared into the abandoned railway carriage.

When Ryan and Cannon followed they found their leader dumping the contents of a litterbin onto a seat.

"Rip out some of those seat cushions," Cahz said as he rifled through the garbage.

"What the fuck for?" Ryan huffed.

"I saw this documentary once about wolves," Cahz explained. "Wolves aren't fast enough to catch deer, but they do." He started screwing up balls of paper and laying them out on the seat. "They lie in wait along a valley. The first wolf jumps up and chases the deer. When the first wolf tires, the second jumps up. And when it gets tired the third wolf takes over. By now the deer's exhausted and the fourth wolf can make easy meat of it."

Cahz stood up and looked around. He spotted an abandoned coat lying in the aisle. He grabbed it and ripped off a strip of material. He hurriedly continued ripping off strips of material until the entire garment was shredded. He then piled the ripped fabric neatly over the wads of paper on the seat.

"We're the deer," Cannon said softly.

"We can outpace those dead fucks, but there's hundreds of them up ahead. The ones following us will keep moaning their dead heads off, alerting W.D.s for miles around."

"No matter how fast we run, the ones behind will keep drawing them in," Cannon said.

"So how do we stop that?" Ryan asked.

"We set fire to the train," Cahz said, book of matches in hand.

"They're not on the line," Ryan said. "You're not going to torch any of them doing this."

"Use the fire to distract the ones following," Cannon said. "The noise of the fire might well draw them in."

"Ah-ha! I get you," Ryan clicked. "When we Molotov'ed them sometimes the sound of them cooking would draw more in. Curiosity killed the Zed."

"At the very least the smoke and the noise will disorient them," Cannon added.

Cahz struck a match and let it take. "And the noise of the fire will drown out their moans so the W.D.s ahead of us won't get worked into a frenzy from a distance. It means they won't be converging on us." With his hand cupped around the flame, Cahz eased it up to the kindling. "If they're not calling their buddies in, hopefully we'll have less to contend with."

Ryan slipped his backpack off and set it on the table. He rubbed at his sore shoulders and made a cooing noise to his distraught daughter. The palms of his hands stung. He turned them over to examine them. They were dirty and scuffed from his fall on the track. He untucked his shirt and brought the end up to his face. He gently dabbed it to his raw cheeks. The cloth came away mottled in fresh blood. Using the soiled fabric, he wiped the worst of the detritus from his hands.

"Since we're stopping, can you get out that first aid kit?" he asked.

"I'm lighting this and we're moving out," Cahz said.

He slipped the match into the kindling. The small flame fizzed and puckered as it was held against the tinder. He gave a gentle blow to encourage the fire.

"What do we do about her?" Cannon asked.

The baby was still crying.

"We'll need to stop and feed her if we want her to calm down," Ryan said.

"She'll call them in for miles, boss," Cannon warned.

"I know, but we'll just have to deal with that the best we can." Cahz gave one more nurturing puff of breath to the burgeoning fire.

"You're just defeating the purpose if we can't stop and give her something to eat," Ryan argued.

"He's right, boss," Cannon added.

"We'll find somewhere quiet we can hold up for a few minutes, but we need to get this distraction going so we can afford the time."

They watched the embers grow. Satisfied the licking flames had caught, Cahz stood up.

"Let's move."

And with that Cahz ran down the narrow gangway.

Ryan went to shoulder the papoose when Cannon grasped the pack.

The big man lent in close. Ryan could see the faint growth of stubble framing his curled lips. Ryan's eyes narrowed as he waited, senses peaked. Ryan was a muscular man; he could hold his own in a fight with most. But Cannon was a hulk with a torrent of seething aggression just beneath his veneer of military decorum. His pupils narrowed as the soldier started to speak.

"If you can avoid falling flat on your face again, wear the pack on your chest," he offered. "That way she can see her dad's face. It might help keep her calm."

Ryan's tense expression dropped. He was taken aback.

"Um, yeah, sure," he stuttered. "Good idea."

Ryan had expected a confrontation, so he was somewhat embarrassed now at misreading the situation. He slipped on the pack, taking the parental advice, so that his daughter was looking at him. The child's wide blue eyes met his. Her stare held a searing intensity.

From behind Ryan came the crackle of flames. As he turned, Cannon squeezed by him.

"Fire's set. Let's get a move on."

Ryan watched the flames take hold of the fabric on the seat and start to lick up to the luggage rack. Cannon placed a firm hand on his shoulder and said, "Let's go."

Cahz grabbed hold of the handle to the door at the other end of the aisle and stepped into the connecting space between the carriages. "Come on," he called, looking back at the stragglers as he pulled open the door to the adjacent carriage.

"Grrrrrr!"

He turned round to see a black dog growling at him. The beast's fur was matted and damp and from its mouth dripped white frothy drool.

Cahz reached for his gun. "Easy," he said softly, trying not to agitate the creature further.

Still snarling, the dog's lips drew back to display its yellowed canines.

"Easy boy," Cahz said in the most assuring voice he could command. His fingers found the flap to his holster and he tugged at the Velcro. The rip of the hooks and eyes pricked up the dog's ears and it pounced. The sound of snarling and screams filled the train.

Cannon sprinted to the end of the carriage to see Cahz tussling on the ground with the dog. The animal snarled and whined as it shook Cahz in its teeth.

Cannon pulled out his pistol but the black shape bobbed and twisted half on, half off of Cahz.

A shot threw the dog whimpering to the floor.

Cahz pushed himself back, his pistol still trained at the animal. The dog convulsed and let out a sobbing whine. Its claws scrabbled against the floor and the benches as it juddered randomly.

Cahz fired a volley of shots at the wounded animal. With a final yelp the dog slumped to the floor.

"You're bleeding!" Cannon exclaimed, seeing the crimson torrent flowing from Cahz's arm.

"It ain't that bad," Cahz said.

"Let's take a look at that," Cannon offered, kneeling down beside him.

"I said it's fine," Cahz snapped back.

Cannon fumbled for his first aid kit. "It'll take a minute."

"There's no time!"

A thick wet pool had seeped from the animal and was rapidly spreading down the passageway, threatening to link up with the pool of blood Cahz was forming.

Snapping out of his daze he looked back up at Cannon.

"Give us a hand up," he said, offering his good arm.

Cannon pulled him to his feet. "You all right?"

"Just a stupid dog bite," Cahz said. "Not like it's a W.D."

"Why'd it attack you like that?" Ryan asked.

Cannon nudged the dog's muzzle with his foot. A lump of white froth dripped into the lake of blood and started sailing off, pushed by the current. The limp dog's neck twisted at the push to expose the matted light fur under its chin.

"Rabies," Cannon said.

"Rabies?" Ryan echoed.

"Sure, it's rife these days," Cannon answered. "No one to keep it in check."

"Come on," Cahz said. "Let's move. Those flames are taking."

"But isn't Rabies fatal?" Ryan asked.

"So is burning to death," Cahz said. He started jogging down the carriage. "Get a move on."

As he sped off, a spotted trail of blood marked his passage.

"He's going to bleed to death," Ryan whispered.

"Stubborn idiot," Cannon added, and sped up after him.

Cannon and Ryan closely followed Cahz out of the abandoned train. As Cahz ran the seeping blood continued to drip from his sleeve.

Cannon upped his pace to draw level.

"We need to look at that arm and you know it," he said.

"We don't have time, Cannon."

"Then *make* time," Cannon said. "I don't want to carry you when you pass out."

Cahz stopped.

"Fine," he spat.

He popped open one of the pouches on his body armour and pulled up a med kit. "Fetch out a bandage from that," he said, passing the kit to Cannon. He gingerly rolled up the tattered sleeve of his jacket. The sandy coloured random pixels of his camouflage were soaked in bright red blood. As he drew back the material, his arm started shaking. It was a light tremor indicative of shock. From his wrist almost all the way up to his elbow were gaping punctures. Blood surged from of each of the wounds, obscuring much of the damage.

"How's it lookin' boss?" Cannon asked.

Cahz rolled his tongue around the inside of his mouth. It felt waxy, like it had a layer of scum over it.

"It's fine," he lied. "Now pass me that."

Cannon held onto the dressing, "Let me do that—"

"It's okay! I can do it!" Cahz snapped, the warm blood dripping off his fingers.

"It'll be—"

Cahz snatched the bandage from Cannon's hand. "I said I'd do it!"

"Everything all right up here?" Ryan panted as he caught up.

Cahz covered as much of the bites as possible with the gauze, the wet blood acting as an adhesive to help hold it in place.

"Yeah, it's sound," he said as he wrapped the bandage with his uninjured hand. "You keep going. I'll catch you up."

Ryan and Cannon didn't move.

Cannon offered over a tiny silver safety pin. "Need this?"

Cahz started to hold his hand out, then realised just how much it was shaking.

"Would you get it?" he asked Cannon. "Just the end is a bit awkward."

"Sure." Cannon slipped the pin into the fabric and closed it. "That good?"

Cahz nodded. "Let's move."

CHAPTER EIGHTEEN
RESIDENTS

The guttering from the apartment's roof was a few feet above him, only just out of reach. As much as Ali wanted to stay in the warm apartment he knew he couldn't afford to miss the chance of rescue. From Ryan's wild hand gestures his guess that the helicopter would be returning had been confirmed, but would it spot him out here on the balcony?

He doubted it. Instead he had resigned himself to a lengthy wait on the rooftop.

He dragged out a set of drawers from Frank's bedroom and pulled it onto the balcony. The breeze wasn't that strong, but hoisting himself onto the railing of the penthouse it felt like a hurricane. With the wind whistling in his ears, Ali used the guttering as a handhold to steady his balance before easing himself up. His breaths were short and shallow as he stood looking at the sloping red tiles of the roof.

He glanced down at the mobbed street below and immediately regretted it. He was only a few feet higher up, but the lack of a railing caused his heart to flutter.

He closed his eyes and mouthed a prayer before continuing.

He reached out and placed his hand flat on the cold tiles, searching for some purchase. A tile sheared and slid free, clattering as it trundled over the lower tiles. For a split second Ali considered moving out of its path before he froze, kept in place by the fear of falling. The tile slid into the moss-choked gutter and stopped.

Slowly Ali set free his captive breath. With measured, deliberate moves he lowered himself back to the security of the balcony.

He stood there for a moment trembling. He turned back and looked up at the gutter. It wasn't that hard a climb, but bereft of the adrenaline he'd had this morning it was an impossible ascent.

He marched back into the apartment and shut the doors to the balcony behind him. He pulled out the coffee jar, unpacked the camping stove, and set about making a fresh cup.

***

His nerves stilled, Ali decided on a new tact. He slipped the good strap of the rucksack over his arm and picked up the makeshift hook he'd used to snag the zombie hiker.

There was no roof access in this modern building, but there would be access to the roof space. Ali had decided to get into the crawl space and smash his way out onto the roof. All he needed to do was find the entrance hatch.

He opened the door to Frank's apartment and looked up at the ceiling. Exactly where he'd expected it was, he saw the half-metre square entry hatch. He picked up a kitchen chair by the wooden slatted back, set it under the access point, and stepped up onto it.

He pushed the wooden hatchway. It didn't budge.

Readjusting his position, Ali braced himself and pushed again. Still the hatch didn't move.

He dropped his arms a few inches and then slammed the palms of his hands into the wood. In its neglected frame, the hatch squeaked and lifted up by the tiniest of margins. Ali battered the hatch again and again in quick succession. The cover separated further from the frame with each heavy pound. Then with a groan it was free. He pushed it clear and slid it out of the way.

There was another groan but this time it came from bellow. Ali slowly turned and looked down. Two landings below the lone zombie was looking up at him. The expression on its vacant face could have been mistaken for disbelief. Its head craned up on its stiff neck and its mouth opened. A foul, flat-keyed wail bellowed from its dead lungs.

The droning horde on the first floor, which up until now had been intently concentrating on the door Ali had disappeared behind, turned their heads up in unison. Their dull monotonous chant raised a pitch with excitement.

"Ah, bollocks," Ali said.

He tossed the rucksack and the hook into the loft space. He placed a foot on the stairwell's railing and stretched upwards. The chair beneath slipped and clattered to the floor. With his right foot precariously on the handrail, Ali pushed himself up.

The slapping footfalls of the undead horde on the stairs mingled with the alarming chorus and Ali's own strenuous grunts. He wriggled up and wedged his elbows into the hatch frame. He spread his forearms out, feeling for something solid to gain a grip of. Finding the flat surface of wooden beams, he heaved himself up. He writhed and twisted trying to haul himself up, but he wasn't a fit man. The years of confinement in their warehouse sanctuary and starvation diet had robbed him of his strength.

The encroaching zombie saw Ali's head and shoulders disappear through the access hatch. But like a worm on a hook his torso and legs wriggled and squirmed.

The sweat dripped off Ali's brow and he panted with the exertion. He just didn't have the muscle to lever himself up and with every moment of struggle the strength drained from him.

Then his foot caught something.

The panic coursed through him. It could be only one thing. A hand grasped at Ali's ankle. Instinctively he lashed out, kicking in all directions. The hands grabbed his foot and drew it in for the inevitable bite.

Ali stomped his foot down, trying to kick the creature away. Miraculously his stamp found the zombie's shoulder. With his shove he knocked the zombie back and at the same time propelled himself those vital few inches further up. His blood saturated with fresh adrenaline, it was enough for him to scramble through the opening.

Ali paused for a moment to snatch a breath before turning and looking back through the hatch. The cadaver was directly underneath, its arms stretching up in a futile attempt to catch its prey.

Ali showed the zombie his middle finger.

"Fuck you, you fucking dead fuck!" he screamed at the corpse. It wasn't the most eloquent of taunts, but the rant felt cathartic.

Ali sat back for a minute to catch his breath. His shoulder ached; undoubtedly he'd strained muscles in the adrenaline-charged tussle. The stairwell below was becoming quite crowded. More and more zombies had found their way up the stairs and were stretching their arms up for him in what looked like some kind of supplicant salute.

"You are not eating me today, so go fuck off."

Ali made a shooing motion with his hand. It had no effect.

Then Ali's eyes were drawn to someone familiar. In the gathering crowd below stood Ray. He had lost his signature glasses and his skin was painted in his own fresh blood.

The corpse of his friend shuffled his way up the stairs, head cocked arms outstretched. It was a painful sight to see a friend consumed by the infection, to see them mindlessly searching for anyone to contaminate.

Ali picked up the hatch and put it back in place, blocking out the sight below.

The roof space went black. He sat for a moment letting his eyes adjust to the lack of light and listened to the muffled moans. Under the insidious call of the dead there was a soft cooing coming from somewhere in the loft. With a flutter of wings, a plump bird hopped out of the eaves, bobbing its head like it was dancing to a powerful beat.

Ali recalled people's distain towards pigeons. 'Rats with wings' he'd heard on numerous occasions. Sure they were opportunists, but so was he now.

His mind wandered back to a forlorn-looking bird that had been brought into the animal shelter where he'd worked. The underweight bird had hobbled, unable to stand, its right claw tangled in a mess of fishing line. He'd gently snipped the line free, but the claw had been too badly injured to be saved. It was a stark equation for an animal charity. Treat the wound and then release the bird knowing its chances of survival were low, or put it down and spend the money on a creature with a better chance. The cash-strapped centre had made the economical choice.

The sad fact is, Ali thought, *there are now more pigeons than people.*

As his eyes became accustomed to the dark, the small chinks of light breaking in through the gap between the roof and the building fabric were just enough to work by. He could open the hatch and let light in from the hallway below, but he preferred the psychological comfort of the closed hatch.

A barrier between him and his dead friend.

Crouching down in this tomb of rock, wool, and plaster sheeting, Ali got to work. He prized the insulating boards down from the eaves and then started smashing through to the tiles. It wasn't long before the first beam of daylight streamed through the punctured roof.

Spurred on by the daylight, Ali hacked at the roof with renewed strength. Within minutes there was a hole big enough for him to climb through. He stuck his head out of the fissure like a bizarre parody of a prairie dog. He looked around and got his bearings.

The pitch of the roof was quite steep and he didn't fancy his chances if he had to scramble up it. Across the street the fire had finally leapt to the adjacent buildings and pillars of smoke billowed skyward. Ali was thankful the wind was blowing the clouds away from him. But that same wind was foreboding. A sharp gust or misplaced foot and Ali feared he would slip from the roof and fall into the mob of zombies filling the street.

No, he would not simply sit astride the roof waiting for his rescue, he decided.

Ali picked up the metal rod again and started remodelling.

Within a few hours Ali had dislodged a good portion of the roof, producing a rubble-hewn veranda. He pitched the tent he'd retrieved from the zombie backpacker and set up the camp stove. He brewed himself another coffee, and half in the sleeping back sat back sipping the beverage, waiting for his rescue.

CHAPTER NINETEEN
TRIGGER

"Hold your fire!" Cahz cried. "Hold fire!" he called again, this time forcing Ryan's arm down. "Cease fire!"

The railway line fell silent.

Ryan's daughter was screaming, shocked by the crescendo of gunfire.

"Calm down," Cahz said. "We don't have much ammo left."

"I shat myself," Ryan protested, his gun still aimed at the undergrowth.

"It was just a fucking rabbit."

"Yeah." Ryan waved the gun in the general direction. "Well, when it came crashing through that bush, I didn't know that, did I?"

"You shouldn't have shot at it, let alone blast away like Yosemite Sam!" Cahz barked. "How many shots did you waste?"

"You didn't even hit the fucking thing," Cannon chipped in.

"Look, don't come down on me like that," Ryan protested. "It fuckin' jumped out at me. Okay, I bricked myself, but can you blame me?"

"All right," Cahz said in a more conciliatory tone. "All right, point taken. It's done now, anyway. We're running low on ammo, so in future you back off and let me or Cannon handle it."

"Look, I just reacted, man."

Cannon snorted, "You're reactions are shit."

"You're not helping, Cannon." Cahz shot his subordinate an angry look. He turned back to Ryan. "You use that as a last resort. I don't want any more fuck ups." He looked at both men. "From anyone. Now let's keep moving."

Ryan nodded and turned his attention to his daughter. He slipped a pinkie into her mouth and the child instantly started sucking.

Cahz turned to start walking when he saw Cannon scoop something up from the track.

"Spotted something?" Cahz asked.

Cannon flicked a small grey object across the track. "It's nothing, boss."

With that Cannon marched on.

Curiosity tugged at Cahz. He stepped a little way off the track to see what had caught his friend's attention. Almost lost among the gravel there lay a small hunk of grey plastic. Cahz picked it up and examined it as he walked. At first it looked cracked but when he took a closer look he could see what looked like crazy paving etched on it. He turned it over to see the familiar web of struts that formed the female part where the building bricks connected together.

Cahz held in his hand the patio to some child's diorama. Some time ago, before all the madness and carnage, this lump of moulded and coloured toy would have been lovingly assembled in to a house or garage or some other plastic-bricked representation of the world.

A smile came across Cahz's face as he considered how many children had played with this innocuous construction toy; how many hours of simple pleasure it had provided? Then, just as suddenly, he wondered how it had ended up on a railway track and where those little children were now.

As the smile fell from his lips, Cahz tossed the rubbish aside.

Ryan trotted up to him. "I only fired five shots," he said. He had the magazine in one hand the gun in the other and he was trying to show Cahz the remaining bullets. "We've still got plenty of ammo left. Right?"

"There isn't enough ammo left in the world," Cahz said in a dry voice and picked up his pace.

Up ahead Cannon was negotiating a tree that had fallen across the line. He could see the big soldier scanning left and right for any hidden danger. Satisfied there were no surprises he hopped over the trunk to the other side.

Cahz hopped over the obstruction, leaving Ryan a good distance behind.

"How you doing?" Cahz asked as he caught up with Cannon.

"Saw a horse once," Cannon said, looking back at Ryan negotiating the fallen tree. "Didn't try to shoot it though."

"When was that?" Cahz asked.

"A few years back now. We were on a tagging run. Remember them?"

"Sure do. Fucking waste of time, those," Cahz huffed.

He turned back to Ryan as he jumped down from the obstruction.

"You wouldn't believe the shit we've had to do," Cahz boasted. "At one point we were capturing W.D.s and collaring them with GPS trackers. They wanted to see where the fuckers went, how far they travelled what behaviour they would exhibit."

"Oh yeah?" Ryan asked. "Do any good?"

Cahz shrugged. "What do you think?" He turned back to Cannon. "You saw a horse?"

"Yeah, big brown thing with a white patch down its nose. We were flying over it in the chopper. I didn't see it until the noise of the engine spooked it. It threw its head up and ran away across a field."

"You never mentioned that," Cahz said.

"No point. It was gone before I could say anything." Cannon took a deep breath. "For a while I took it as a sign. I mean if a horse could survive on its own, then there was still hope."

"I suppose," Cahz said, not really sure where this was going.

There was a long pause before he realised Cannon had finished.

Cahz marched along the railway line, the gravel crunching under foot. A rotund black bird looked up at the party from its spot on the rusting track. Its black beady eyes focused on the trio and it cocked its head in the same way the zombies sometimes did. As they drew closer it opened its beak and cawed at them, angry at being disturbed. It hopped off its low perch, and too lazy or too cocky to fly away, it skipped off to the side of the track.

"I miss the birds," Cahz suddenly said.

"The birds?" Ryan asked.

"On ship you get the odd seagull, but they just bray at you." Cahz pulled a face as he recalled the distasteful sound. "Normally we've got the chopper thundering away but…"

He stopped speaking and looked up at the sky. Tall green trees overarched the track, their branches encroaching on the abandoned line. Every now and then, silhouetted against the grey sky, Cahz could make out the isolated shape of a nest.

"But out here now you can hear them twittering away." Cahz looked back at the path ahead. "I've missed that."

"There's a lot to miss," Cannon said in a cold voice.

"Yeah," Ryan added. "What do you miss?"

Cannon didn't answer. He kept marching ahead of everyone. "Ammunition," he said eventually. "Right now I miss having a full belt."

Cahz ripped open the Velcro tab over his ammo pouch. He knew exactly how much ammunition he had left, but he felt the need to check. With each pouch he opened he willed there to be a forgotten full magazine.

He said, "I've got one mag left since we refreshed them back at the office."

As his hand fell by his side it brushed against something hard and square edged. He slipped his hand into his pocket and pulled out a magazine.

"What's that?" Ryan asked, scampering over the gravel to get a closer look.

"It's Angel's spare clip." When he saw Ryan's blank expression he elaborated, "The sniper—the woman with the busted arm."

"Oh, her," Ryan said with a flash of recognition.

"I have no idea why I took it," Cahz said, examining the magazine. "Guess in the rush when she handed me the pistol clips I didn't think."

"Why? Are they no use then?" Ryan asked.

"Wrong calibre," Cannon said.

Cahz explained, "The pistol clips were fine. She uses the same pistol as us, but the rifle rounds are for the Drangunov. It takes seven point six twos."

"Oh," Ryan said, plainly lost.

"Cannon's SAW or my M4 both take the standard NATO five point five six," Cahz elaborated. "It means we can use each other's ammo."

"So what are you going to do with those then?" Ryan asked, looking at the magazine. "Just toss it?"

"Oh no," Cahz chuckled. "Last thing I want is to make it back alive only to piss off Angel."

Cannon laughed as he walked up ahead, "Sour-faced Commie."

"Why's she touchy about the ammo?" Ryan asked.

"She spends a lot of effort on these things."

Cahz held the magazine out in front of him and twisted it, examining it like an ancient relic.

In a sense it *was* an ancient relic. Since Eastern Europe had been overrun, nowhere made magazines like these any more.

"Every one of these bullets was made by her," he told Ryan. "She's anal about the grains."

"The what now?" Ryan asked.

"The amount of propellant that goes into each of these," Cahz said, still focused on the magazine.

"Gun powder," Cannon simplified. "If we need to, we can always decant the powder to start a fire or use as an accelerant."

"I once saw a special forces boy rip open half a dozen casings and pour the powder into an infected bite. He lit it with a match and his whole arm crackled like so much bacon in a frying pan. The guy screamed his tits off."

"Did it work?" Ryan asked.

"Fuck knows," Cahz admitted. "I got pulled into a mixed unit and set about filling sandbags. Twenty minutes after that we got overrun and the whole compound was napalmed. Never saw the guy again. Filling sandbags…" Cahz gave a huff. "I'm still mad at myself for following orders from that stupid weekend warrior. Should have been bugging out or at the least cracking the ammo boxes open."

He still held Angel's magazine in his hand. Around the lugs and the facing edges, the black anodising had become scuffed and worn, allowing the bare metal to poke through. This magazine had been used and reused time and time again. It suddenly struck Cahz that the magazine wasn't meant to help aid their escape, it was Angel's way of assuring his safe return. He was expected to return the magazine intact; it was a motivational reminder.

A round splash of water plopped into the dull metal clip.

Cahz looked up. The sky was choked with rolling dark grey clouds.

"Looks like rain," Cannon said sardonically.

Ryan looked up at the heavens and let the first drops of rain splash onto his face. "I never used to like the rain," he said, gazing at the clouds. "All those years surrounded by those rotting pus bags changed my mind, though. On the days it poured down it drowned out their moans and washed the air clean of their stench. On days like that you could almost pretend the world was normal."

"Take a look around. World's far from normal." Cannon kicked at a long shard of plastic cover from a florescent light strip and sent it flying. The brittle edges sheared off and went bouncing across the gravel.

"How far have we come?" Ryan asked.

Cahz slipped Angel's ammo back into his pocket. "Difficult to say for sure," he admitted. "The map's just a general one, covers a hundred square miles." He looked out past the fencing that bordered the railroad track. "Those houses are suburban. I've not seen an office block or an industrial unit for over a mile now. We're well out of the city."

Ryan was looking hopeful. "So we're almost there then?"

"I guess we've come a fourth of the way," Cahz estimated.

"What?! A fourth?! But we've been walking for hours."

Cahz held out his hand and watched as spits of rain found the palm of his glove. The brown leather instantly turned darker where the spots landed.

"Yeah, we've done maybe ten, twelve miles," he said.

"We're never going to make the coast by dark," Ryan said.

"I'm guessing you're right."

"We can make the coast easy," Cannon said. "Even doing four miles an hour we can make it no sweat."

"I don't share your optimism, Cannon." Cahz looked up at the rain-filled sky, letting the cold droplets refresh him. "I don't think it's worth the risk walking through infected territory in the dark with a civilian and baby in tow. It would be fine if all we had to do was follow this line, but we're going to have to come off. It runs at least ten miles inland."

"Then we've missed our ride out of here," Ryan said.

"No, it's not that dire. I want to get as far from the city as possible. The place was heaving with W.D.s." Cahz looked at Ryan. "You did an outstanding job of calling them in."

"Yeah, well, what were we supposed to do? Each spring thousands would find us and surround the place," Ryan argued. "We used to try and thin them out. Molotov cocktails in the summer, baseball bats when they were frozen solid in the winter. Made no difference; they just kept pouring in."

"I wasn't trying to put you down, Ryan," Cahz said. "World's been dead a long time. You and your friends were the only entertainment that remained for the dead. I'm not implying you could have done anything about it."

"You must have been drawing them in from hundreds of miles," Cannon said.

"One winter we totally wiped them out around the fence," Ryan said. "Wasn't a pus fuck for miles. Couple of weeks after the thaw they'd surrounded us again. How's that possible? I mean, they're not texting their buddies." Ryan pretended to hold a mobile phone between his hands and punched the imagery buttons with his thumbs as he spoke, "'jst 8 hmn c u soon.'" Shrugging, he asked, "I mean, how do they know?"

"It's the moan," Cahz explained. "It's like tom-tom drums in the jungle. One pus bag moans and his mate a hundred yards away hears it and he moans right back. Urbanised area like this, you could get an unbroken chain for miles."

"Hence setting fire to the train back there. Using it as a decoy," Ryan said.

"It seems to have worked."

Cahz looked over his shoulder. For a long time they could see the smoke from the fire they'd set reaching up into the sky. Now the distance and the rain-laden air had obliterated any sign of it.

"Looks like the rain's getting heavy and the kid could do with something to eat. Let's break off from the tracks and find a house to shelter in while we get our shit together. We can check our ammo reserves and do a radio check. Maybe scoff down that veggie pasta?"

The approval was obvious to see on Ryan's weary face. but Cannon wasn't as keen.

They came off the embankment and down to a dark wooden fence. The branches of unkempt bushes poked between the slats of wood.

"It's going to be impossible to get in there," Ryan said.

"That's a good thing," Cahz said as he gripped hold at the top of the fence. "If it's tricky for us to get in it'll be just as hard for W.D.s to follow." He pushed a toe hold between the slats and scrambled up. He threw a leg over and straddled the fence. "Looks good," he said. "Garden's overgrown but the house looks like its weathered well."

He offered a hand down for Ryan.

Within moments the three men were stalking through the gangly weeds that had invaded this once pristine lawn. They made their way past the rusted swing set and up to the back of the house.

Cahz drew his pistol. "Cannon, you check those windows. I'll check these."

"What do I do?" Ryan asked.

Cannon glared at him. "Stand still and shut the fuck up."

"Whatever you say, Cannon," Ryan said with a scoff. "Have you even got a real name?"

"What?" Cannon snapped.

"I mean *Cannon*," Ryan said. "It's a bit fucking macho for a big man with a big gun."

"It is Cannon," Cahz said.

"What's wrong with Cannon?" the hulking soldier demanded.

"I mean come on," Ryan shrugged. "You've got that big assed

gun. Is that why you get called Cannon?"

"I get called Cannon 'cause that's my fucking name," Cannon snapped back.

"Oh, come on," Ryan protested.

"David Joseph Cannon," Cannon said. "It's fucking French. Cannon was the surname given to a church rector."

Cahz chipped in, "It's like Cooper being the surname of the barrel maker or Smith—"

"Yeah, yeah, I get it," Ryan interrupted. "Okay, I'm an ass. You happy now?"

"Yes, you are an ass. Now will you shut the fuck up and stay still?"

Cahz peered into the dark interior of the kitchen. "Anything your side?" he asked.

Cannon shook his head. "I can't see any movement, but there's a ton of blind spots."

"I'm on left, you on right," Cahz said.

"What about me?" Ryan asked.

"You're staying outside," Cahz said. "This will go a lot smoother with just us."

Cannon added, "We're used to working together."

"You stay out here and cover out exit. Got that?"

"Yeah, sure," Ryan said.

"No *'yeah sure'*," Cahz gave Ryan a hard stare. "Cause if you come in there at the back of us we're likely to shoot you by mistake. So you stay here and don't come in until we tell you it's safe."

"Got it," Ryan said with a crisp tone.

Cahz tried the handle on the back door. It didn't budge. Drawing his knife from its sheath, he slipped the point between the window and the frame. Gently he pulled back but there was no give.

"Check your side," he instructed Cannon.

"Nothing boss," Cannon confirmed after trying the windows on his side.

"I didn't figure we'd get in that easy." Cahz took a couple of steps back and gestured for the other two to do the same. He aimed his carbine at the space between the lock and the door, a steady green dot marking the intended target.

Cahz fired. Splinters of wood burst out from above the lock, pale and fresh in comparison to the weathered paint.

"Go."

Cannon stepped up to the door and booted the handle. The door shuddered and edged forward. A second thunderous kick and the door flew open.

As it did, Cahz stepped inside.

The kitchen was musty and dry. The air was stale with the smell of mould.

The two soldiers scanned the room for danger, pistols at the ready. A trickle of blood mustered at Cahz's wrist before dripping off to the floor. His fear and adrenaline was more than enough to mask the clawing pain from his wound.

"Clear," Cahz said in a subdued voice.

"We've found dinner," Cannon said and he nodded to the kitchen floor.

One of the kitchen cupboards was open and a horde of tins neatly laid out on the tiled floor. There was even a can opener resting on top of a tin of meatballs.

A floorboard creaked from overhead. Both men looked at the ceiling. A soft muffled moan found its way to their ears.

Cahz signalled towards the kitchen door. Cannon slid an empty cereal box from his path and stepped up. He slowly turned the handle and pulled it open.

Cahz scanned the dim hallway, his gun sweeping the empty space, primed for action.

"Clear," he said in a voice just loud enough for Cannon to hear.

A dark winter coat lay in a heap piled up against the wall and a knocked over corner table had spilled a few household bills across his path, but aside from these few scattered objects the hall was deserted. There were two doors. The one on the right was open, the one on the left was closed.

Cahz could see the door closest to him led to a small toilet that occupied much of the understairs space. As he edged forward he could see the room was empty. The toilet was clogged with the decomposed remnants of rotten stool and wet wipes. He moved on, making a cursory check of the closed door on the right. He placed his gloved hand on the handle and checked it was secure. It no doubt led to the living room, but as all was quiet behind the firmly shut door.

Cahz decided to press on.

The moan was clearer now and there was a scratching and creaking from upstairs.

"Clear up or clear out?" Cannon whispered.

It was a good point, Cahz thought. They could easily leave and find another property, an empty property. But they could spend half the day trying to find somewhere like that.

"No time," Cahz whispered back. "Only sounds like one. Should be quick enough to neutralize it."

He stepped up to the front door.

Something crunched and jingled underfoot. He glanced down to see what he presumed were the former owner's house keys. He stepped past the abandoned keys and onto the first stair.

The carpeted step creaked under his weight, not the worrying sound of rotten wood, just the natural expected groan from an old staircase. But it was a louder noise than Cahz would have liked and it precipitated an upsurge of noise from the creature ahead.

Cahz swiftly climbed the stairs. The wallpaper had waist high dirty drag marks in random patches all the way up. Behind him he heard the heavy footfalls of his comrade.

At the top of the landing the source of the moans became apparent. Although there were three doors on this floor, two were open and the sound was definitely coming from behind the closed door. Pinned to the closed door at eye level was an envelope, its white paper yellowed, and even though the writing was obscured by a thin layer of dust, the name 'TONY' was still visible in bold black letters.

"Cover the door," Cahz whispered.

Cannon nodded and took up position.

Cahz ducked down the hallway and peeked into the first room. The unkempt double bed and the ransacked dresser made the room look like a crime scene, but other than the mess it was empty. He moved on to give the second room a brief examination. Even with the cartoon character adorned curtains closed, there was enough light to see the child's bedroom was also empty.

"Looks clear," Cahz informed his partner.

"It's definitely coming from in there," Cannon confirmed.

"You kick the door open. I'll blow its brains out."

Cannon nodded.

Cahz mouthed a countdown, the culmination of which was Cannon's sharp kick.

The force of the kick shattered the feeble lock and threw the door flying. A blizzard of paper whipped up into the air, carried by the gust from the swinging door. But before the door could open fully it smacked against something and reverberated back.

Cahz raced through the opening. The small bathroom was littered with sheets of paper and the white enamel surfaces were smeared with brown smudges. He turned into the blind spot behind the door just as a pair of dead hands grabbed for him.

The woman's long black hair obscured most of her face, but one pale dead eye had locked its gaze onto his. Her head cocked slightly to the side and her raw lips parted, revealing glistening teeth in a black mouth. With a hiss of putrid breath she lunged.

Cahz was well prepared for this encounter and as the zombie lurched forward he fired.

With most of her brains splattered against the shower curtain, the zombie toppled to the floor. She smashed off the edge of the bathtub, spilling more of her contaminated juices before crumpling in a heap on the bathroom floor.

Cahz drew a sleeve across his lips, the bitter tang in the air a sharp reminder of the rancid taste in his mouth.

"Clear," he said.

The creature lay there spent and unmoving. Her ragged hair lay clear of her face, vacant dead eyes staring off into the distance.

Cahz heard a splash as a droplet of ickier fell onto a sheet of paper on the floor. Strangely, pages of plain white paper littered the room. He knelt down and picked one up. There was a crude doodle on the sheet, a knot of orange and green and blue. He picked up a second from the dozens. There was again a profusion of lines snaking their way around the sheet in every imaginable colour. As Cahz looked closely, all of the pages had some adornment of splodges and scribbles.

"You okay in there, boss?" Cannon asked.

"The note on the door," Cahz said in a shaky tone. "Read it."

"What?"

Cahz marched out of the bathroom and snatched the letter down. He ripped it open and whipped out the contents.

"What's it say?" Cannon asked, baffled by its sudden significance to Cahz.

"Tony, I'm so sorry. I know you told us to stay inside but you've been gone so long. I know I shouldn't have, but I was worried about you. Don't open the bathroom door." Cahz looked back at the scattered paper on the floor. He continued reading, "I've been bitten. I know what will happen next so

I'm going to lock myself in. I've left out sandwiches and juice but I'm dreading the next few hours. I love you, Tony. Take good care of Jacob for me. Tell him every day his mummy loves him."

"That's tragic," Cannon let slip.

"Wait," Cahz interrupted, his finger scanning the note. "You told us to stay inside."

"She should have listened," Cannon said.

"No, '*us*'." Cahz dropped the letter and leveled his pistol. "Us! She wasn't alone."

"Fuck," Cannon snapped.

Both men scanned the hallway for signs of movement. The house had taken on an eerie silent quality. Since the zombie in the bathroom had been dispatched the only sound was the rasp of their own breath.

"I'm going to check the bedrooms again," Cahz said. "Keep my back,"

"Yes, sir," Cannon replied in a crisp military tone.

Cahz strode purposely into the master bedroom. The décor was a mix of dark woods and cream fabrics. The bed clothes were thrown back and the linen crumpled.

Cahz checked each side of the bed. Nothing but wayward pillows and discarded clothes. He lent over and checked the side of the open dresser but it was clear.

With a hard swallow he got down on the floor to check under the bed. His heart raced. He knew how vulnerable a position going prone was. All his years of army training had taught him to get down and flat, stay low stay alive. But the tactics for surviving in this new theatre was to stay mobile.

His breathing still heavy, Cahz scanned the murky space under the bed. There was something there, something drawing the light away.

"Fuck it," Cahz whispered, getting to his feet.

He backed up and closed the door as he left the room.

"I couldn't see anything," he reported. "But there's no point securing the room when a closed door will do."

Cannon nodded his agreement as Cahz entered the child's room.

Again the cupboards and drawers were wide open. Clothing and toys scattered around the room. But the room was less cluttered with furniture than the adult equivalent next door. In only a few seconds it was obvious the room was empty.

"Downstairs. We've yet to check the living room," Cahz said as he passed his colleague.

"Maybe she's the only one?" Cannon said hopefully.

Cahz was ahead of him on the staircase, his gun sweeping, ready to snap off a shot at any second. "Maybe, but you know better than to work on maybe's," he said without looking back.

The stairs protested with loud creaks and groans as the two soldiers worked their way down. They knew that the noise they made would mask the sounds of a zombie creeping in the rooms below and even though the element of surprise was long gone they kept their voices low.

As Cahz reached the living room door he took up position on the right side.

"Take up the left. After me you cover left."

"Yes sir."

"Three, two, one."

Cahz whipped the door open and dived round the corner. Behind him he could sense Cannon doing the same thing, mirroring his actions.

Cahz swept his aim around the living space. The room had the usual array of expected furniture: sofa, TV set, DVD player with the disc drawer open. There was a photo frame-laden mantelpiece with an electric fire nestling beneath it. The room looked like the aftermath of a burglary just like the bedrooms upstairs, but there was something wrong.

The room hadn't been looted. The valuable items were still here. The place was just a mess. The missing cushions from the sofa, toys cast among the scattered DVD cases and empty food wrappers. At his feet lay an empty blackcurrant cordial bottle.

"Ah, Christ," Cannon gasped.

Cahz turned round to see what caused Cannon's exclamation. The other half of the room had been used as a dining area and he could see the edge of a large table, but Cannon's massive shoulders blocked the rest of the view.

Cannon slipped his weapon back into its holster and turned round. He took a deep breath and wiped his chin. "There was someone else in the house."

Cahz brushed past him. The dining room table was covered in sheets of the same white paper he'd seen in the bathroom. Crayons and felt tip pens lay higgledy-piggledy on the tabletop. There were a couple of empty glasses stained red from the remains of the blackcurrant drink.

Cahz's gaze fell and he spotted something under the table. Curled up in a ball, embracing a brown and white fluffy toy rabbit, was a half naked child. A blue pacifier was firmly stuck in his mouth. Wearing only underpants and socks, he lay on a bed of cushions surrounded by a nest of die cast cars and garish plastic toys. The boy's curly brown hair looked matted and unwashed. His grey dead skin stretched over the prominent ribs. A pair of blue, white and black camouflage cotton socks were on his feet, the soles blacked. A sob broke out from behind him.

"Cannon?" Cahz called as the big soldier stormed out of the room.

He turned back to the child. Coloured streaks of felt-tip pen covered his hands and mouth. In that tiny grasp he still clutched an orange crayon and beside him the last piece of art he'd failed to post under the bathroom door.

Cahz picked up the scribbled artwork and felt his heart sinking deeper in his chest. Breaking away from the pitiful sight, he followed his colleague out of the house.

"You all right?" Ryan was asking.

"Cannon," Cahz called absently, stuffing the drawing in his pocket.

Cannon stumbled into the garden, weeping, the rain bouncing off his thick padded body armour.

"Is everything all right?" Ryan asked.

Cahz stayed silent and walked past him.

"Can we go into the house?" Ryan asked. "Is it safe?"

Cannon ripped off the fastening on his chinstrap and hurled his helmet at the ground. He brought his hands up to his face and collapsed to his knees, his shoulders heaving under the weight of the sobs.

"Cannon?" Ryan's voice was weak and uneasy. The baby strapped to his front was awake and sucking furiously on her father's pinkie.

"Get in under shelter," Cahz instructed Ryan as he emerged from the house. "But don't leave the kitchen."

"Why? What is it?"

"Get inside and feed the baby. Just don't leave the kitchen," Cahz reiterated more forcefully.

"Why?"

Cahz whipped round, tears streaming from his eyes. "You don't want to know."

Ryan's expression dropped to see the emotion in Cahz's face. He nodded and made his way into the house.

Cahz stepped up beside Cannon and took a deep breath.

Cannon sat there in the overgrown grass of the neglected garden. He sniffed back a tearful snivel and tried to talk, but the pain grabbed his throat and the sobs burst back.

Cahz sat down in the wet grass. The moisture soaked instantly into his fatigues and drew the heat away.

"I must have shot a hundred W.D.s today," Cahz said softly. "You forget who they were."

"I left them," Cannon blurted out.

"You left who?"

"My little boy and my wife," Cannon said.

"I don't understand, buddy," Cahz said.

"We were always arguing," Cannon wept. "About everything. About when I'd come home, about money, about getting a job. I was fucked up when I got back to the real world. You know the score; the stuff we went through and they expected us to go back to our wives and families and jobs. I stormed out one night, her screaming at me and my boy in tears. I never went back." He looked over at Cahz with doleful eyes. "I swear I always meant to. I wanted to go back home. Once I'd spent that night away I just didn't know how I could go back." He waved a hand at the deserted and overrun garden. "Then all this shit happened. By the time I got home they were gone."

"You never said," Cahz whispered.

"No note. Nothing. House was empty." Cannon pointed an accusing finger back at the house. "I don't know if my boy died waiting for his daddy to come save him! I don't know if he died alone, cold and helpless cause I wasn't there!"

Cannon was sobbing uncontrollably. Cahz put an arm around his shoulder.

"I wasn't there." Cannon gasped for air between the tears. The deep heaves of his shoulders grew softer. A few bellowing snorts of air pushed out from his nostrils.

Cahz ran his tongue round his foul-tasting palate. He decided it was time to confess about the mouthful of contaminated vitriol fluid he'd swallowed this morning. He took his arm from around Cannon's shoulder and clasped his hands on his lap.

Cahz took a breath and began, "Look, Cannon, I think…"

"I can't do this," Cannon butted in with an oddly cold voice. He snapped open the Velcro on his holster and pulled out his pistol. He pushed the muzzle into his mouth and pulled the trigger.

The crack of the pistol filled the forsaken garden.

"Fuck!" Cahz jumped back fuelled by pure reflex.

Cannon's body toppled over and lay sprawled on the ground.

Cahz sat motionless and shocked. A light spray of blood coated his right cheek.

Ryan came running out of the kitchen to stand frozen in the garden.

The body lay twisted back on itself, blood steadily pumping from the massive exit wound in the back of Cannon's head.

Cahz could feel his head nodding from side to side as if his subconscious were screaming out *No!*

"Jesus Christ," Ryan mustered.

Cahz put a hand to his cheek, partially covering his mouth to try to stop the shake and stifle his disbelief. When he pulled it away his fingers were coated in bright red smears.

He took a trembling breath and tried to compose himself.

"Come on," he said, standing up. "Let's get moving."

***

Cahz was cold. The foul taste still clung to his tongue. He shivered and opened his eyes. For a moment he didn't know where he was and then he recognized the house.

Ryan was sitting propped up against a kitchen unit, his child cradled in his arms.

"How you feeling?" he asked the groggy Cahz.

"What happened?" Cahz asked, still dazed.

"You stood up and passed out," Ryan said. "I dragged you in here."

"How long?"

Ryan shrugged his shoulders. "I guess thirty minutes." He held out a bare wrist. "I don't have a watch."

Cahz started to sit up.

"Not so fast, tiger," Ryan said. "I put another bandage on top of the one over your bite. That's what you're supposed to do, right? I mean it was Ray who knew about the first aid stuff; he'd done a course at work or something."

Cahz looked down at his injured arm. The second bandage bulged and looked ugly, but it was still white and clean with no signs of the blood soaking through.

"Um, yeah." Cahz thought back to his battlefield training. "If the blood is saturating the bandage you shouldn't remove it; just put a fresh one on top."

"You should drink something," Ryan said. "I'm guessing you've lost more blood than you thought."

"Yeah," Cahz agreed, still feeling groggy.

Slowly he eased himself to his feet, his head swimming.

"You've cleaned up that graze," he said, nodding to Ryan's face.

He trudged over to the kitchen sink. There was a row of three open and empty tins on the counter. Out of instinct Cahz turned the tap on. There was a shudder and a hiss of air but no water.

"Used some of the water from the camel pack." Ryan looked up at the sink. "You'll not get anything from there."

Cahz looked up from the dry sink and out of the window.

Cannon was still lying in the backyard. The rain had soaked his uniform and washed the blood clean into the grass.

Cahz stared at the body. His breathing was heavy and laboured. He looked at his dead friend, the only constant in his life these past five years. The big, quiet, reliable soldier. A physical giant. A tower of muscle and stoic reserve.

Cahz was dumbfounded.

"Why'd he do it?" Ryan asked, breaking the long silence.

"Cause he couldn't live with himself, I guess."

Cahz turned and sat down next to Ryan.

Ryan offered up an open tin of cold beans.

"The cans are still okay," Ryan offered in way of assurance. "I've scoffed some already."

Cahz accepted the can robotically. Ryan held up a spoon and plopped it into the can.

Cahz stared down at the juicy beans swimming in the thick orange sauce. He didn't feel much like eating.

"Why now?" Ryan asked.

"There's a dead child in there." Cahz nodded over to the kitchen door. "I never knew he was a dad. I never knew anything about him. I just figured he'd tell me if he wanted." He wiped his nose with his good arm. "We all had shit to deal with. We all lost someone."

Ryan nodded.

"I never knew how close he was," Cahz went on, staring absently at his beans. "It just happened so fast I didn't have time to stop him."

"Who can blame him?" Ryan said. "I've seen a lot of suicides. We had four the first summer. Then there are the people who got themselves killed on purpose. You know the kind who would take ridiculous risks."

Cahz nodded.

"There were these two guys, blond floppy hair young blokes. Looked alike, think they were at college together," Ryan explained. "We called them the Hanson brothers—you know, like the band." When Cahz didn't respond Ryan continued, "They were convinced they could go get help. In the end it wasn't worth trying to talk them out of it. We helped them leave just so they wouldn't do anything stupid that affected us—you know, burst the gate open or some such."

Cahz set the untouched can of beans on the floor.

"We need to keep moving," he said.

"Where to?"

"Somewhere we can secure," Cahz said. "Somewhere a chopper can land."

"Rebecca," Ryan said.

"What?"

"That's what I'm going to call her."

Ryan looked down at the baby. The girl was awake, but placid no doubt after a feed. There was a little speck of mashed-up cracker at the corner of her mouth. Her wide eyes caught Cahz's.

"Rebecca," he ran the name round. "Rebecca. It's a nice name. Any significance?"

"I'd thought of Hope or Miracle," Ryan said, frowning. "You know, 'cause she wasn't infected. But…"

"Yeah, a bit much," Cahz agreed, sensing Ryan's disapproval of the names.

"Then I remembered Sam had mentioned she liked it," Ryan explained. "I thought that was a bit more appropriate. I mean she's going to have it for the rest of her life."

Cahz levered himself up on the kitchen counter and made for the back door.

Ryan gently lifted the newly named child into the papoose.

"Wait for me," he said.

Cahz paused. "Wait here a minute."

Ryan watched out of the rain-splashed window as Cahz walked up to the corpse of his dead comrade.

"You stupid big bastard," Cahz cursed as he sat down next to the body. He reached over and started tugging at the straps on his body armour.

"Why'd you do it?" Cahz asked the dead man. "You could have talked to me."

Although the fastenings came away easily, the unresponsive corpse made removing the equipment hard going. Cahz gently slapped Cannons cheek as if he was trying to wake him. The skin was already cold, drained of heat as well as life.

"After all the shit we've been though and you leave me in the middle of this."

Cahz undid the neck protection and left it to one side.

He stood up and switched positions to stand over Cannon's corpse. With a hand on each shoulder he pulled the body armour free. There was a squelch as the material slid over the raw exit wound. The limp body slumped back into the grass.

"Remember the first day we met?" Cahz asked, patting down the pockets on Cannon's fatigues. "No you don't, 'cause your brains are splattered all over this lawn. I'll remind you: I was scared shitless. There was me, the Captain and a couple of other grunts who'd made it out of Nelson. And all those fuckin' yahoo civvies. And there you were, being ignored and avoided. You didn't seem to care; you just kept your mouth shut and tagged along."

Cahz stood up, the rain splashing across his face.

"I ignored you—had no idea you were ex-military. I mean, who would have? You saved my life that first night, man. I wish you'd given me the chance to repay you."

Chapter Twenty
Shroud

"Put this on," Cahz said, handing Ryan the body armour and helmet.

Ryan looked at the bloodstains on the neck and shoulders.

"I'll pass," he said.

"You'll put it on," Cahz said, shoving it at Ryan.

"Watch it!" Ryan blurted, shielding Rebecca from Cahz's aggression.

"Just put it on."

"It's covered in—"

"I'm doing my best to keep you alive. Now put it on. It'll protect you from being bitten." Cahz thrust the armour into Ryan's shoulder.

Ryan took a step back, knocked off balance by the shove.

"All right," he gave in, laying the baby down to take the armour. "You going to show me how to use the big gun then?"

"No," Cahz said.

"Why not?"

"Just because. You are not using it."

"Why don't you use the machine gun and I use your rifle?"

"Where do I start?" Cahz shrugged.

"Why not?"

Cahz wore a blank, weary expression. "For a start, the SAW is a squad support weapon. We are not a squad. We're two men and a fuckin' baby."

"Well, it still fires bullets," Ryan said.

"Second, my 'rifle' is a carbine and yes, they both fire fuckin' bullets, but they both need training to use. It's not like the nun chucks on your pissy Wii."

"Well, that SAW thing is still better than this crappy pistol."

"And just how the fuck will you be able to fire that with a baby strapped to your chest?"

"Aw, come on! The firepower will be useful."

"Ryan!" Cahz snapped. "This is not a discussion. You are keeping the pistol. And you will fire it only in self-defense and as a last resort."

"It's not like I haven't shot a gun before."

"Yeah, and you wasted a mag on Peter Rabbit. The SAW weighs a friggin' ton and you're shattered just carrying the baby and a crowbar."

Ryan opened his mouth to object, but Cahz cut him off.

"Look, I have spent untold hours honing my skill as a marksman." Cahz's voice was clipped and stern. "We don't have the ammo to dick about like you did on the tracks back there. You pumped off half a dozen shots with a semi. God knows what you'll waste with that on full auto. We leave Cannon's SAW and pistol here. They're just dead weight. I've replenished my mags and between my M4 and the two pistols we've got over a hundred rounds. That's enough to keep us safe until we get picked up—If we're careful. Now let's move out."

Ryan's lips were tightly shut, his eyes still looking at the long hunk of black metal that had been Cannon's SAW.

"What if we don't get picked up?" he asked, still focused on the machinegun.

"It's not an option," Cahz said, opening the door to the hallway.

"What if we don't?" Ryan asked again more forcefully.

Cahz spun round and locked on Ryan's eyes. He jabbed a finger in the direction of the back yard. He shouted, "Then we end up like him out there!"

The baby burst into tears from the barking noise.

"Or worse," Cahz spat.

Ryan was about to say something when they both heard a thump.

"What was that?"

The thud sounded again, this time accompanied by a long, chilling moan.

They opened the door to the hallway. Through the frosted glass of the front door, Cahz could see the shadow of someone pushed up against the window.

He marched up to the front door and pointed his weapon at the silhouetted head. Casually he pulled the trigger. The shadow disappeared.

Picking up the set of keys he'd kicked earlier by accident, he unlocked the door. He walked out of the house, nonchalantly stepping over the dead body.

"Are you coming?" he called back over the noise of the crying child.

"Shit," Ryan grumbled.

He pulled a plastic bag from a holder by the fridge and loaded a selection of the unopened tins and the can opener into it.

"Yeah, I'm coming," he said as he slipped the papoose into position and trotted after Cahz.

The paving slabs in the driveway were a dark grey from the rain. A trail of black liquid was being washed off the dead zombie down towards the gutters. The suburban street was grey and eerily quiet. The only noise was the patter of the thick raindrops and the gurgle of the water as it passed over the leaf-blocked drains.

Cahz pulled out a piece of paper from his pocket and lit it with one of the matches from the MRE. The white edges turned brown then black before it caught. The flames licked up, obliterating the orange and blue scribbles. With the rain failing to extinguish the fire, he tossed the burning artwork back into the house.

"Why'd you do that?" Ryan asked as he watched the hall carpet ignite.

Cahz didn't answer. He just walked off down the rain-drenched street.

The fire was spreading quickly by the time Ryan turned and chased after him.

"What's the plan then?" he asked.

"Keep walking," Cahz said without slowing his pace. "We've got about four hours before it goes dark."

"Keep walking, eh?" Ryan questioned.

"Keep walking," Cahz said back, his eyes on the path ahead.

***

The two men walked on in silence. They weaved their way down the shattered streets of what was once a desirable housing development. The executive cars that would have seen a wax and polish every Sunday afternoon now sat on flat tires, quietly rusting away. The once perfectly tended lawns were choked with weeds and ornamental bushes gone feral.

The odd zombie that stumbled into their path was quickly dispatched by the irate Cahz. The venomous soldier would simply march up to the wailing creature and fire a shot into its skull from point-blank range.

Ryan's feet felt raw and blistered, his legs were burning from the exertion, and his lungs were scorched with the effort of breathing against the weight on his chest. The forced march was ripping at every muscle in his body. But he dared not complain.

Ahead of them, atop a rise, was what would once have been the home of a company executive, large and imposing, an expansive garden with a tall fence. The building though had caught fire at some point. The roof was gone and the windows were boarded up. The entrance gates lay twisted and useless in the driveway.

As they marched past a zombie lurched out at them. It was naked other than a pair of army style boots and its skin was blackened from grime and dirt. Cahz automatically strode up to the creature so he could put a shot in its brain, but all of a sudden the zombie snapped to a halt. It strained but it couldn't move any closer.

Cahz stopped and lowered his gun.

"What is it?" Ryan asked.

As he caught up, Ryan could see a burnt-out corpse on the driveway of the gutted house. Snaking up the paving stones was a chain attached to the husk.

Ryan put the heavy bag of provisions down on the ground. His fingers were red where the thin straps bit into his joints. He looked more closely at the zombie that struggled to get them. Around its neck, there too was a thick chain. The metal links bit deep and raw into the dead flesh. The blood encrusted links trailed off to a padlock secured to a fixture in the solid fencing.

"Guard dogs?" Ryan asked.

"Hell of a bite," Cahz muttered.

He turned his back and marched off, leaving the zombie to strain against its chains. Ryan looked at the pitiful creature chained in the front yard of the burnt out house. Now that he looked he could see the weeds were trampled flat within its range.

"Why would you do that?" Ryan asked no one.

Then it struck him that the house had its windows boarded up. The sort of thing a homeowner would do after a fire or to protect it if it were being left uninhabited. Ryan looked more closely at the soot smudged plywood. Under the smoke damage he could make out writing: 'LOOTERS WILL BE SHOT!' with a skull and cross bones underneath.

Then a second warning on a different window: 'INFECTED WILL BE SHOT!', again with the skull and cross bones motif.

Ryan was about to leave when he noticed a less prominent sign. On the driveway there was something scrawled in orange spray paint. He skirted past the tethered guard zombie and towards the house for a better view.

Written on the paving stones was the simple line, 'DICKS WILL BE TORCHED!'

"Hurry up!" Cahz called in the distance.

Ryan turned from reading the epitaph, picked up his bag and hurried downhill to catch up.

"Did you see that?" he puffed.

"See what?" Cahz asked in tone that showed he didn't really care.

"Back there," Ryan said. "That house was burnt down deliberately."

"So what?"

Ryan started to explain, "There was some graffiti. It—"

"I don't give a shit, Ryan," Cahz said.

"Oh," Ryan said, thwarted by the uncaring reply.

He stood for a moment, stunned by the soldier's ambivalence. The plastic straps of the carrier bag were becoming thin and taut, stretched out by the weight of the cans. Ryan rested the cumbersome bag on the ground and let the circulation flow back round his fingers. Cahz wasn't waiting for him. The angry soldier continued marching off into the rain. Ryan slipped his fingers into the wet plastic handles and lifted the bag back up. Reluctantly he started walking again, the hard lips of the cans bouncing off the side of his leg as he moved.

***

"What now?" Ryan asked, looking out at the lake.

Cahz was standing astride two lichen-mottled concrete bollards to get a more elevated view. Ryan recalled seeing a similar stance in a picture book at school: the Colossus of Rhodes guarding an ancient harbour, the stone giant facing out to the dangerous Mediterranean Sea.

Before Cahz lay an expanse of water not marked on the puny map he held. He looked out at the murky waters. The steady rain was beating into the surface, making the stagnant pool ripple. Here and there little rusted islands emerged from the depths, the tops of partially submerged cars. Water-loving weeds had congregated around the banks of the pool, some even finding anchorage on the wrecks.

"I think this used to be a car park," Ryan said, scratching his chin. "Yeah," he said, more confidently. "That big building was a super store. I guess the water can't be more than three or four feet deep."

A fresh moan chased after them from down the road.

"Well, what do we do?" Ryan asked. "Do we wade through or go around?"

Cahz hopped down from his perch, the loose ammo jingling in his pockets. "Fuck knows what's waiting under that water," he said with a stern voice. He turned ninety degrees and started skirting the lake edge.

"This is going to take ages to get around," Ryan called after him.

"Best make a start then," Cahz said without looking back.

Ryan looked up at the sky. The rain splashed down on his face, it soaked through his hair and trickled down his neck to be wicked up by his shirt. He wasn't sure if the rain clouds had become heavier or if it actually had become darker. One thing he knew, it was impossible to get any wetter. His jeans were a saturated dark blue and stuck to his thighs. With every step forward he had to carry his own weight, the weight of his child and the resistance from the clinging clothing. Each pace he took forward was slower and shorter than the last. Step by step he was losing pace with Cahz.

A fresh gust of wind gave Ryan a cold clout. He shivered. His whole rib cage felt like it was contracting in on him as he shuddered.

Cahz was up ahead, just sidestepping a weed-draped shopping trolley.

Ryan opened the rucksack strapped to his chest. The child inside was still dry and warm and best of all, sleeping. He pulled the zipper up over the child's head, leaving a gap at the side for ventilation.

"Better get moving or I'll freeze to death," Ryan said to the sleeping child as he strode off after Cahz.

He trudged forward on the moss-covered road, the spongy plants squelching with every step.

"Cahz!" he shouted.

"Keep up," Cahz absently called back.

"No, Cahz, look at this." Ryan had spotted something on the other side of the lake.

Cahz turned round. "What is it?"

"Look over there." Ryan pointed to the slope on the far side.

"It's an embankment up to a flyover," Cahz observed. "So what?"

"Look at the trees."

Cahz stood, his carbine resting on its sling, his arms resting on the carbine.

After a moment he called back, "What trees?"

"That's it exactly," Ryan said, pointing. "You can see the stumps."

"So," Cahz said indignantly. "Someone cut them down. Firewood or lumber. It's not important. We need to keep moving."

He turned and started walking again.

"It's recent though," Ryan said, still staring at the other side. "The undergrowth would have obscured the stumps if it weren't." He looked round at Cahz. The soldier was marching away, ignoring him. He said, louder, "That means there must be other people alive out here!"

"That means there *were* other people alive," Cahz said without stopping. "Past tense."

"We can't be sure of that," Ryan said, trotting to catch up. "Shouldn't we search for them or something?"

Abruptly Cahz stopped and turned round. "Do we look like a fucking search and rescue team? We get ourselves out of this shit before we worry about anybody else."

Ryan flung his arms out. "I'm just saying—"

"Well don't!" Cahz snapped.

"Shouldn't we do something?" Ryan pressed.

Cahz turned round and started walking again.

"It was doing something that got us in the shit we're in," he mumbled.

***

"Thanks for waiting," Ryan said in a sarcastic tone as he caught up.

For the better part of a mile, Cahz had been relentlessly pulling ahead of him. Every now and then Cahz would call out to demand Ryan stop lagging behind. But Cahz would never wait for him to catch up; at best he would turn around and march backwards for a few metres to check his ward was still following. When Ryan started to catch up, Cahz would turn and march off, forcing the exhausted refugee to keep up the pace.

Ryan put the heavy bag of tins on the ground and rubbed his fingers, trying to bring the circulation back to the purple tips. He gave a shudder as the heat generated from moving evaporated in the cold rain.

"I'm not waiting for you," Cahz said. "I was checking if the radio was working."

"Oh well, thanks a bundle then," Ryan said, hooking his thumbs into the straps of the papoose.

"India Tango One calling. India Tango One to anyone receiving. Please come in, over." Cahz stood still, almost holding his breath, listening for an answer.

"Still nothing," he said breaking the silence. He pushed back the cuff of his glove and checked the time. "Nineteen hundred hours."

"Shouldn't the chopper hear us? Or your ship?" Ryan asked. He had the straps of the rucksack pulled tight, like a comedian about to snap a pair of braces as he took the strain off his shoulders.

"Ship is well out of range. These sets only have a two or three mile range." Cahz slipped the radio back in its pouch and fastened it secure.

"So the chopper could be like five miles away and he'd never pick us up?"

"Yep," came Cahz's glib reply.

He walked off.

Ryan wiped the rain from his face and called after him, "You seem a tad casual about that."

Cahz didn't bother to turn round to speak. "We've got flares and signal smoke we can use to get his attention. And even if he's too far out of range to hear us, he might still get the static buzz and know there's someone close."

"Wait," Ryan said in a puzzled tone. "What time did you say it was?"

"Nineteen hundred hours."

"That's seven o'clock," Ryan said. He jogged up to Cahz. "You said the chopper would be back at six o'clock."

"I said the earliest to expect it back was six," Cahz corrected. "I didn't say it would be."

Ryan threw his arms out in frustration. "Oh that's great. It could have been and gone."

"I've been doing radio checks every fifteen minutes since six—and anyway we'd have probably heard it," Cahz said, still marching.

"Oh, great. *Probably*," Ryan raised his voice in exaggeration. "We'd *probably* have heard it."

Cahz came to a sudden halt. "Listen, Ryan. If we spot it, great; if we don't we keep going." Cahz's voice was strained. "It's as simple as that. There's no point wasting energy on shit I can't control."

A short distance away a zombie gave an excited moan.

"You hear that," Ryan said. "You going to ignore that too?"

Cahz didn't answer as he strode off.

Ryan turned round to look behind them. The street was choked with weeds and debris but no sign of the undead. The rasping call came again, closer and louder than before, but still Ryan couldn't see the zombie. From somewhere further off a response call echoed.

Cahz seemed unperturbed by the distant moans. Their winding route through the housing estate meant that Ryan's view was only ever clear for a few hundred yards before a twist in the road obscured it.

"I'm sure we're being followed," Ryan said, looking behind them into the sheets of rain.

"Yeah, I'm sure we are, too," Cahz said without breaking stride.

"It's going to get dark soon." Ryan put some effort into his stride and caught up with Cahz. "I thought the plan was find somewhere to hold up before it got dark."

"Plan went to shit a while back."

"Whoa! Hold it right there!" Ryan grabbed Cahz by the shoulder, dragging him to a reluctant stop. He kept his grip on Cahz's body armour. "Yes, the plan's gone to shit, but so has the whole fucking world! But it's the shit we have to deal with. Now I know you're in a bad place right now, but you'd better get it together or I'm going to leave you."

Cahz laughed. "*You're* going to leave *me*?!"

"Yes, mister fucking hard ass soldier," Ryan replied. "You've got the big gun and the big attitude, but I've been stuck out here for years! What about you? When was the last time you were out here without your men and your guns and your helicopter?" He let go of the body armour and gave Cahz a light push on the shoulder. "You go on on your own if you like. I'm finding somewhere to spend the night." He looked down at the girl huddled in the rucksack strapped to his chest. "I need a rest and she needs a change."

He slung the bag of cans over his shoulder with a clatter, then turned and walked away.

Cahz watched as Ryan made his way up a side street.

"Just fuck off then!" Cahz shouted. "You're not safe behind the walls of your precious warehouse now! You'll be dead in an hour without me hauling your ass along!"

Ryan shouted back, "I'm used to this shitty world, Cahz! How about you?!"

"I wouldn't be in this world of shit if it wasn't for you!"

Ryan stopped.

Cahz shouted to the back of Ryan's head, "And Cannon would still be alive!"

Ryan turned around calmly. "Don't pin that on me. I never landed you in this. And I never—"

"Yes you did! Yes you fucking did!" Cahz screamed back. "If you hadn't turned up this morning and fucked up everyone's day!"

"What were we supposed to do?! Jump up and down shouting yoo-hoo?! We were starving to death in there!"

"Yes, you could have," Cahz argued. His face was bright red and dripping with rain. "You could have jumped up and down! You could have run around butt naked!" He tapped two fingers to the side of his helmet. "Didn't you think? Didn't you think to light a fire or use a signal mirror any number of things rather than barge your way through and turn up asking for a rescue?"

"You'd never have spotted us. I'd rather not have left the warehouse, but what choice did we have? We'd have all starved to death within the month."

"Yeah, and you've fared so much better this way. Half of you never even made it to the chopper. Elspeth is dead. Cannon blew his brains out."

Cahz took a threatening step forward. His thumb hooked under the armpit of the body armour, he pushed the vest out. "Look at this!" he shouted, presenting the sodden fabric to Ryan. "Look at this! This is my best friend's brains. Splattered across me and the best part of that fucking garden back there! He died because he stayed behind to help you and your fucking ass wipe friends!"

"And who's this helping? *You*? Eh? *Who*?" Ryan started to walk off again.

"And now you're going to wander off on your fucking own!" Cahz barked through a hoarse voice.

"Yes, Cahz, I am." Ryan turned round and pointed a finger at the soldier. "And do you know why?"

Cahz scowled, saying nothing.

Ryan took an agitated pace towards him, the muscles in his arm taut from the effort of reining back his aggression. "Because with an attitude like that, you'll get me killed quicker than the dead. Look, I'm sorry for Cannon. I truly am. But you've lost it. You don't care anymore."

Cahz started to speak but Ryan cut over him.

"You don't care if either one of us survives. You've flipped and you just want to pick a fight. You want to take out that anger and frustration, and I can appreciate that. I get it. You're set on marching along and wasting pus bags. But if you don't snap out of it, your anger is going to get us both killed."

Cahz's face flushed red. "Fuck off. You're talking crap!"

"No, you fuck off!" Ryan shouted. "Why the hell have you shot every one of those pus bags since we left the house? Why?"

Cahz didn't answer. He stood trembling with anger, his nostrils flaring, his lips clamped shut.

"I'll tell you why. Because you're mad. You're pissed off Cannon topped himself. Why didn't you just club the dumb fucks?" Ryan demanded. "Why?"

"I… I…" Cahz stammered.

"You tell me not to fire unless it's absolutely necessary." Ryan's head bobbed with each word. "But you're wasting ammo left, right and centre."

Cahz's head shook with a strange tremor, like a geriatric with a neurological condition.

"Pull it together or you'll get your ass bit off." Ryan turned to leave. "I've seen it too often."

He turned and walked off up a pathway between two houses. A frothy stream of muddy brown water sloshed its way down the slight incline towards Cahz. Ryan continued marching on, the runoff leaving indistinct footprints in the accumulating sediment.

Cahz snapped the carbine up to the firing position.

"Don't walk away from me!"

He had the back of Ryan's head framed in the sight.

Ryan stopped but didn't turn around.

"Stop and about face!" Cahz barked. "That's an order!"

"I'm not one of your soldiers," Ryan said calmly. "I'm not under your command, Cahz."

He turned around. His eyes widened as he saw the weapon trained on him.

Slowly he raised his hands to show his surrender.

"What are you going to do, Cahz?" Ryan said softly. "You're all nice and democratic all morning; now you're going to shoot a civilian with a baby? For what?" Ryan cocked his head slightly. "For what?"

Cahz's teeth were clenched together, his muscles rigid with strain. The muzzle of the weapon was trembling as he barely kept his anger in check.

"You know what?" Ryan shook his head gently as he spoke. "Why don't you just pull the trigger? Waste me like I'm one of those things and then do my daughter." Ryan paused, staring down Cahz. "You'd be doing me a favour. I don't have the luxury of topping myself like Cannon did. I have to look after her." Slowly he brought his hands down from the surrender position and unzipped the rucksack.

He unveiled the crying child.

"I can't give up on her, on Sam, or Elspeth. I have to keep going, not for myself, but for her."

Ryan lifted the girl out and cradled her in his arms. The child was flushed bright red, screaming at the discomfort of the cold and the hunger.

Cahz looked down at his carbine. The black metal frame had fat drops of rain bouncing off its body. The same cold raindrops sprayed Cahz's face, soaking his skin before dribbling off like the miniature river coming down the alley.

"When you decided to stay behind, is this where you thought you'd be?" Ryan asked. Droplets of water dripped from his chin as he spoke.

Cahz felt the pounding of his heart and the rush of breath. The bad taste still coated his mouth. He brought up some phlegm and spat it on the wet ground. The spit was instantly swept away by the fast current of the runoff.

He took a deep breath and lowered the weapon.

"Do you even know where you're going?" he asked, his voice flat, his eyes still on the barrel of his weapon.

"We'll work it out, man," Ryan said. "We'll work it out." He lowered his daughter back into the shelter of the papoose and pointed off up the path. "I think there's a school this way; fences and a big flat playing field."

Cahz took a snort of breath in through his nose and followed where Ryan was gesturing.

"Sounds like the best plan," he said, his chest still heaving.

***

The dark rain clouds eradicated the last light of day and a hazy gloom reduced visibility still further.

Ryan's thoroughly soaked jeans clung to his legs, chafing him with every step.

"How far have we got to go?" Cahz asked.

The pair were walking side by side. Cahz's desire to distance himself had softened.

"Huh? Is that you whining?" Ryan laughed.

"No. I want to know if we'll make it before it goes dark," Cahz said.

"It's just down this road," Ryan answered.

"You said that ten minutes ago."

"I know, I know," Ryan said defensively. "Look, I don't know this area that well. I only ever drove down here back in the day. It's much further when you're walking." He scratched his chin. "Well, it's not any further, it's just taken longer than I expected. You know what I mean?"

"Yeah, I do. Me and Cannon walked over a hundred miles to get to safety when the whole thing kicked off," Cahz said. "Some days you'd walk for hours, then you'd look at the map and you couldn't see any progress."

"You and Cannon been friends since the kick-off?" Ryan asked.

"Yeah, basically," Cahz said. "A handful of us regulars managed to get out of Nelson."

"Nelson?"

"Yeah, a pissant little town. Nothing there, but we'd been sent to set up checkpoints to test for infected. They were quarantining whole parts of the country, trying to stop the spread at that point. Well, the shit hit the fan, like it did everywhere. When we lost contact, our captain took the decision that we should bug out and head for a naval base on the coast. We took a royal fucking getting out of there and on the way out we acquired a bit of a following."

"Pus bags?" Ryan asked.

Cahz sniggered. "Yeah, those as well, but I'm talking about civvies. Refugees spotted the uniforms and demanded we protect them. So the six of us that were left ended up escorting fifty-odd refugees all the way to the coast."

"Was Cannon in your squad?"

Cahz looked across at Ryan. After a moment he faced forward again and said, "Cannon was one of the civvies. He'd been out of uniform a few years by then, but he still had the skills. We'd have lost a lot more people if Cannon hadn't been with us. After that we kind of stuck together. It's good to have a man like Cannon you can trust…"

Cahz physically stopped.

"What is it?" Ryan looked around nervously.

"I thought I could rely on him. I thought I knew him." Cahz was breathing heavily. "I never thought he'd…"

Ryan waited for him to restart his sentence.

"Look, Ryan, there's something I need to tell you," Cahz said, his voice flat and serious.

"Yeah?"

Cahz spat a bitter mouthful of phlegm onto the ground. "I think I've been infected."

"What?" Ryan was stunned. "When—I mean how?"

"Back in the plaza this morning," Cahz said.

Ryan looked at either side of Cahz's face. "Where? How?"

"Shot a W.D. point-blank and got a mouthful of junk," Cahz

admitted.

Ryan screwed up his face at the thought. "But surely you'd have…" He paused. "I mean…"

"I know most people succumb in a few hours, but then most people get bit or scratched. I ingested it. I've been feeling steadily worse all day."

"But that's the loss of blood from the dog bite." Ryan looked down at the blooded bandage on Cahz's arm.

"It's more than that. I'm sure of it."

"I've never known anyone who's swallowed that stuff." Ryan looked at the bloody arm and back up at Cahz. "I don't even know if you can get it by eating it?"

"I don't know either. I know you get it if it gets in your blood."

"Surely you've have died by now and come back?" Ryan perked up. "It can't have gotten into your blood or you'd be one of them by now."

Cahz shook his head. "Ryan, I know what you're trying to do. There's no point—"

"Say it's just the dog bite, right," Ryan said eagerly. "It was a mangy thing and you've lost a lot of blood. It makes more sense it was the dog bite. All you have to do is hang in there. We'll get picked up and you'll get your rabies shots and everything's okay."

"What if it's not?"

"Then…" Ryan thought for a second. "Then I'll do what you did to Elspeth."

Cahz gave a silent nod.

"School's just down here," Ryan said, changing the subject.

"Thank fuck. I'm soaked." Cahz looked up at the black sky. "It will be good to get under shelter and dry out."

They rounded a corner to see a squat-looking old brick school. Its tall, flat iron fencing skirting the main road marked the end of its large grass covered playing fields.

"Looks perfect," Cahz said as he quickened his pace to the gates.

"Why the fuck are schools surrounded by this stuff? We never had this shit when I was a kid," Ryan said, shaking a rusted post. "It's like Guantanamo Bay."

"It's to keep the pedos out," Cahz said as he stepped onto a litterbin and scrambled over.

Ryan sniggered.

From the other side of the fence Cahz stretched his hands up. "Pass Rebecca over first," he said.

Ryan unfastened the makeshift papoose and handed the child

over.

A familiar moan drifted across the derelict street.

Standing on top of the refuse bin Ryan turned round and looked back the way they'd come. Even through the grainy cloak of darkness he could make out shadows moving. He stood there like a sentry on his elevated lookout. As he squinted his eyes against the rain-veiled gloom, the shadows grew closer. The fleeting glimpses started to coalesce and out of the rain lumbered the silhouette of a zombie, the dark figure ambling past the wrecked cars and drawing closer. Emerging from the downpour a second wretched creature shuffled resolutely towards him, then a third and a fourth. More and more until a dozen shambling cadavers appeared.

"Jesus Christ, Cahz. Look at them."

Not even the torrential rain could mask the cries now. Cahz looked through the railings to the platoon of drenched corpses shuffling their way towards them.

"Quickly, Ryan," Cahz said.

"Yeah."

He passed the strained plastic bag full of cans over to Cahz. Ryan grabbed the railing and vaulted over the top.

"Get inside and out of sight," Cahz said. "If we stay out here we're just going to rile them up."

Ryan and Cahz ran through the weeds and long grass to the school's entrance. Though the large glass fronted door all they could see was the pitch darkness of the hallway inside.

"Locked," Cahz said, rattling the door handle.

"Try another door?" Ryan looked left and right trying to spot a second way in.

"Fuck that."

With both hands Cahz swung his carbine round and battered the glass with its butt. The safety glass crunched with the impact but didn't break.

"To hell with this," he said as he swung the weapon into firing position and opened up on the pane.

Rebecca started bawling at the shock from the gunshot.

"Cahz!" Ryan protested as he tried to shield the child's ears.

"Come on," Cahz said, stepping over the broken glass.

Carefully treading through the doorway, Ryan followed close behind.

"You got that torch?" Cahz asked, his weapon pointing at the gloomy corridor ahead.

"Somewhere… Ah! Here."

He hooked the handles of the plastic bag over his wrist and with the whir of the dynamo the dim yellow light started to dispel the insidious darkness.

Before them was a short corridor that led to a set of double doors.

With his carbine hard against his shoulder Cahz, cautiously moved forward.

"Follow my aim," he whispered to Ryan.

The inadequate wind-up torch cast a pulsating glow of dirty yellow light over the desolate school. Impeded by the awkward position of the improvised papoose and the bag of cans dangling from his arm, the light dimmed and grew with Ryan's ungainly cranking. With clumsy jerks Ryan frantically tried to illuminate Cahz's sweeps.

It was a conflicting situation, the two men moving stealthily and with purpose while all the time the child strapped to Ryan's chest wailed.

They reached the end of the corridor past the small reception area and restrooms unmolested.

Cahz stretched out with his left hand and opened the swing doors, his weapon still trained. The door swung to with a loud creak. He stepped through, using his foot as a doorstop for Ryan.

The light died as Ryan negotiated the door. When the puny light came back on, the corridor was just as empty.

"What now?" Ryan whispered.

"We check…" Cahz stopped whispering and spoke at a normal volume. "We check the classrooms. And there's no point whispering with Rebecca crying."

"It's not her fault, man. She's only a little baby. Every time you fire off with that thing you scare the shit out of her." Ryan sniffed the air. "Literally."

"I'm sorry I upset her, but I'm not going to fuck around. I know this can't be any fun for her."

"At least give me a warning in future," Ryan said in a conciliatory tone. "I could cover her ears or something."

"Let's just find a room we can get comfortable in," Cahz said. "And I'll give you a hand changing her."

"What if there's pus bags in here?"

"If there were I'm sure they'd have come to greet us, or at the very least started whooping for joy. Now let's get dried off as best we can and see about signaling the chopper."

CHAPTER TWENTY-ONE
SAFETY

"Found these in the canteen," Ryan announced as he came into the classroom. He tossed a bundle of dishtowels in Cahz's direction.

Cahz was already naked, sitting on the only adult-sized chair in the room, warming his hands by the fire.

"Thanks," he said, catching the cloths.

"Ingenious," Ryan said nodding at the makeshift clothesline.

Cahz had knotted together a line of skipping ropes and was drying his fatigues over the fire.

"Adapt, improvise and overcome," Cahz quoted as he rubbed his wet hair with the small towel. "They're going to stink of smoke, but no one ever died of a smell."

Ryan pulled up a miniature plastic chair and sat down on it. His knees were up by his chin as he squirmed, trying to get comfortable.

"This is no good," he said, admitting defeat and sitting cross-legged on the floor.

"Did you take a look outside?"

"Yeah, but it was too dark to see anything," Ryan said. "I could hear them moaning and rattling the fence, but there can't be more than a handful of them."

"What's that?" Cahz asked, looking at the tin in Ryan's hand.

"Canned milk," Ryan said. He pierced the lid with the tin opener. "I thought Rebecca might like it since we've run out of crackers."

"How you going to feed it to her?"

"Spoon it in, I guess," Ryan said, brandishing the utensil. "Got one from the kitchen."

"Listen, Ryan…" Cahz stopped rubbing his hair. "About earlier..." He looked down into the fire and summoned up the courage to speak. "I'm sorry." He looked into Ryan's eyes. "I'm sorry for the shit I pulled on you. I was out of order."

"You lose anyone close before Cannon?" Ryan asked.

"Sure. Friends, family, girlfriend."

Ryan shook his head. "No, I mean up close. I mean right in front of you?"

Cahz folded the wet dishcloth and put it to one side. "I've seen countless people get devoured or put down—"

"That's not where I was heading. Have you seen anyone you cared for die in front of your own eyes?"

Cahz looked back down at the fire and nodded gently.

"When Sam died everything collapsed for me," Ryan said, looking at the baby as he opened the tin of milk. "I held her in my arms as she went. I felt the tension leave her body. I heard her last breath. I felt her hot blood on my fingers. I mean, like you, my friends and family died when all this shit kicked off, but that's different. I know they must be dead but I wasn't there with them. I mean, I know my dad is dead; I had to put him down, but I didn't see him die. I just saw him as one of them. It's a hard thing seeing someone you love die. I dealt with it by going on a bender. I drank every last drop of alcohol that was left in that warehouse. I didn't want to think about it, to feel it. I saw you in that same place this afternoon." Ryan flicked the moisture from his cheek. "You don't need to apologize. I'm just glad you snapped out of it quicker than me."

"Thanks," Cahz said.

Ryan fed a spoonful to Rebecca and the two men sat quietly by the crackling fire. The wind and the rain outside drummed at the windows.

"You ever thought of doing it?" Ryan asked.

"Doing what?"

"What Cannon did."

Cahz pursed his lips in thought. "No, not really."

"I have," Ryan said. "Nothing serious. It became kind of normal. There were a lot that first year. I remember I walked in on one. He had the noose and the chair all ready and I walked in as he was just climbing onto the chair. And do you know what I did?"

"No," Cahz whispered.

"I apologized," Ryan laughed. "I said sorry, looked at my shoes and walked out. Like I'd walked into the men's room and saw him taking a dump. I said sorry and walked out, embarrassed that I'd disturbed him. How fucked up is that?"

"You didn't try to stop him?"

Ryan shook his head. "Nope. I've seen so many, but never right in front of me. You know you'd wake up one morning to find someone's taken an overdose, or break into someplace to find a body with a blood-splattered suicide note. It became normal." Ryan waved the spoon towards the window. "You know, normal like not in the normal world normal but in the fucked-up world normal." He laughed. "Did that make any fucking sense?"

"A little," Cahz said.

"We had this one woman—Petra she called herself. I don't think that was her real name, by the way. She went on and on about it. Talked all the time about how she was close to killing herself, but she never did. Then we had that first one. An older guy slit his wrists and... Elspeth cleaned that up like she did after Sam." He shifted uneasily and placed a hand on his stomach as if he were suffering from indigestion. "Well, once he'd done it, that was the taboo broken. We had four that first summer." Ryan shrugged. "I guess what I'm saying is, who can blame them."

Cahz took a deep breath. "I used to wonder if you went anywhere when you died; Heaven and Hell Sunday school kind of thoughts. Then all this fucked up world—as you put it—happened, and it didn't seem possible anymore."

Ryan smiled at Cahz's use of his description and gave a snort of understanding.

"It doesn't seem that God is listening. Cannon killed himself and that's supposed to be a sin, but he isn't walking around out there." Cahz sighed. "That mass suicide at Masada doesn't seem as crazy now."

"No," Ryan said. "No, it doesn't."

The two men sat staring into the fire, trapped by their own thoughts.

Abruptly Cahz broke the silence. "Give it over here."

"What?" Ryan replied, puzzled.

"The milk. You're dribbling it. Pass it over here and I'll feed Rebecca. It'll give you a chance to get your wet clothes off."

Cahz scooped up Rebecca from Ryan's arms. Ryan handed over

the open tin of milk and a spoon he'd liberated.

"Should we heat this up first?" Cahz asked, looking at the milk.

"I haven't a clue," Ryan admitted, struggling out of his wet shirt. He stopped, the shirtsleeves still covering his arms, his torso bare. "Elspeth did all that," he said, looking into the fire of burning school books.

Cahz poured a spoonful for the child. "I don't know about any of that shit about sterilizing bottles. It's not going to harm her giving it to her cold?"

Ryan shrugged. "I guess not. She's been taking it cold and she ate the cracker all right. We'd better get rescued soon, if only because we're shit parents."

At that he pulled off the wet shirt and hung it on the clothesline.

"You want a can of soup heated up?" Ryan asked as he peeled his jeans off.

"Sure," Cahz said. "Pierce a couple of holes in the lid and stick it on the fire."

A dribble of milk ran down Rebecca's chin. Cahz gently wiped it away with a dish cloth.

"She seems to be taking this," Cahz said, pouring another spoon.

"Good." Ryan nodded. "So how do we signal this chopper?"

"Three possible answers to that," Cahz explained. "I've got a radio. It's only short range, but if the chopper passes close enough I should be able to raise them. If the radio doesn't work, I've got a flare."

"And the third option?"

Cahz smiled. "Star jumps."

"We'll want to put some clothes back on for that one, mate," Ryan joked. "I wouldn't land if there were two blokes in the nude waving their tackle at me!"

The two men laughed at the absurd image.

"God, I'm sore," Ryan groaned as he shifted to a more comfortable position.

"Guess you didn't get out much," Cahz said.

"Only in winter, when the dumb fucks froze," Ryan answered. "We'd forage maybe a few miles at most. Never got as far out as here."

Cahz nodded.

"Ah, man, even my tits are sore," Ryan said, rubbing his chest. "It's wearing that rucksack with Rebecca. It's been chaffing me nasty." He stretched out his shoulders one after the other. "What's the rest of the world like? I mean, away from all this?"

"Mostly like this," Cahz said. "There are a few military bases that have survived infection. Mainly shitty little rocks like the Diego Garcia, the Aleutians—those sort of ass-of-nowhere places with an airstrip on it. There's even a floating shanty town off Hawaii. The biggest infection-free zone is Antarctica. Got twenty thousand people living down there on the ice at McMurdo."

"Is that it?" Ryan asked despondently.

"There's a big plan to take back New Zealand. They've got a base on Stewart Island to support the Draw and Destroy campaign."

Ryan extruded the wet socks from his feet. "New Zealand," he whispered as he slung the soggy tubes out to dry.

"They fly in these huge concrete prefab defenses." Cahz fed a spoonful to Rebecca like an aircraft. "They build a central compound and a segregated kill zone."

"So they're just sitting and sniping at them?"

"Oh no, the kill zone is all measured out. They sit in their compounds playing loud rock music and launching flares. When the kill zone is full, they napalm the lot." Cahz nodded at the smoke coming off the fire. "That must really stink."

"We used to burn them at the fence when they got too many," Ryan said. "The stench would stick in the back of your sinuses for days."

"But the whole point of these kill zones is they've been specially sized so they can count how many W.D.s are incinerated," Cahz went on. "The concept is, if they can barbeque a million then they've got most of them."

"Sounds like a good idea," Ryan said.

"They want to take the island with the infrastructure intact. The plan is to secure the South Island and start rebuilding our industrial capacity, but there's no easy fix. The insertion teams who set up the compounds have a high mortality rate. You get sent to the South Island if you've pissed off someone high up. And anyway, those towns and cities have been rotting away just like this one. Don't know exactly how much they're planning on salvaging."

"Still, there's a future," Ryan said, looking down at Rebecca.

Cahz smiled and nodded.

***

Ryan woke with a start. Cahz had knocked over his gun; the hard metal object landed clattering on the classroom floor.

"This is India Tango One, are you receiving me?"

Still naked, Cahz ran over to the classroom window. Ryan sprang to his feet, throwing off the blanket he'd found in the first aid room.

"The chopper?" he asked, his voice quick and excited.

"Come in, over," Cahz called into the receiver.

He pulled the makeshift blackout curtain from the window and looked out. He turned the handle and pushed the window open ajar.

"I can't see any navigation lights," Cahz said, running back to his kit, "but it's still raining out there."

He undid one of the flaps on his body armour and pulled out a red flashlight-shaped object. With nary a stitch on, Cahz ran out of the classroom.

Ryan rushed up to the window. Outside, it was pitch black, the flickering light of the fire turning the window into a mirror.

With his ears cocked to the crack Cahz had opened, he listened as he stared back at his reflected face. The rain was drumming down outside and the moan of the dead wafted in the moist air.

With the crackle of the fire behind him, Ryan concentrated on the sounds outside.

And then, just like this morning, the sound of an engine drifted across the sky.

"Hell!" Ryan turned and ran to catch up with Cahz. He was out of the classroom when he remembered Rebecca asleep next to the fire. He paused for a moment debating whether or not he should wake her and take her with him or leave her there.

"I'll be back in minute," he assured the sleeping child.

With a quick about turn he was charging out of the school after Cahz. As he gingerly navigated past the broken glass at the door, Cahz launched the flare. The rocket streaked up into the black sky, a tail of flame trailing behind.

"Will it light in this rain?" Ryan called out above the noise of the moaning. He stood in the rain stark naked except for the first aid blanket tied round his neck like a cape. He craned his neck up, watching as the flare burst into a ball of brilliant orange light. The underside of the rain clouds turned orange from the brilliance of the glow. The fizzling signal wafted to and fro as it slowly parachuted down.

"They've got to see that, Cahz," Ryan said, transfixed by the light.

"Back inside," Cahz said softly.

Ryan was still watching the flare drift down. "What?"

"Get inside now!" Cahz grabbed Ryan's arm and pulled.

"Why?" Ryan demanded, being pulled off balance. His gaze dropped and he saw why Cahz was so agitated.

The playground was illuminated in the shimmering orange glow.

But beyond the playground, pressed up against the school fence, were hundreds of zombies. Every square inch had an undead face staring back at him.

The dozen or so zombies that had trailed them here had been reinforced by a legion of undead. But worse still, there were the handful of zombies trudging across the field towards the school.

"Oh fuck," Ryan whispered and he turned and fled.

As he barreled back into the classroom Cahz slammed into him. The nude soldier had his gun in one hand his armoured vest in the other.

"They're in the field!" Ryan's voice exploded.

"I saw," Cahz said. "Bring desks and chairs—anything you can. There must be a break in the fence."

"Can't we just barricade ourselves in here?"

"Hold this." Cahz thrust his carbine at him. "Would love to," he said as he squeezed into his body armour, "but we need space for the chopper to land."

"Right," Ryan said, looking around. "Where are you going?"

Cahz snatched the weapon back from Ryan and ran off down the corridor. "I'm going to stem the tide," he called as he turned the corner.

Ryan called after him, "Dressed like that? You'll catch your death—"

***

Ignoring the broken glass, Cahz ran out into the playground. The flare was still casting the peculiar daybreak glow over everything.

Looking around, the nearest zombie was a good ten metres away. The woman's hair was matted and wild. The sequined vest top she wore was still clean enough to sparkle slightly under the light. The skin on her bare arms looked warmer, more alive under the artificial light, but the fingers missing from her outstretched hands and the gaping maw left Cahz in no doubt that she was walking dead.

He aimed and fired.

The dead partygoer was floored.

There were a dozen or so zombies in the playground now making a beeline for Cahz, but none were dangerously close.

There was the sound of breaking glass behind him. Cahz turned to see a desk half out the already shattered window and Ryan shoving at it from inside.

Cahz looked up. The shamooli flare was halfway down. It

wouldn't be long before it landed, and although it would continue to burn on the ground for a time, it wouldn't throw out as much light.

With the carbine snug against his shoulder again, he marched off over the playing field to engage the shambling cadavers. Calmly and efficiently he walked up to within a few metres of the closest zombie and put a bullet between its eyes.

It was now that he wished Ryan had confronted him earlier. On the march over here, Cahz had succumbed to his anger and foolishly shot all the zombies he'd encountered. He knew he could have clubbed them when he'd come across them individually. Now he didn't have the time to waste; he had to dispatch these cadavers as efficiently as possible before they had a chance to push through in force. He wished he'd conserved his ammunition.

Pressing in against the rusted fence, unperturbed by the rain, a thousand dead eyes watched the half-naked soldier executing their brethren. Already there were far too many to deal with. He had to find and plug that gap.

In the gloom and the rain Cahz couldn't see the break in the fence, but the stream of zombies were all coming from one direction, leading him back to the source. From behind him the angle of the light flattened and his shadow stretched out over the tall grass.

"Fuck," he cursed as the illumination from the flare dimmed.

Ahead of him, zombies were squeezing between a pair of broken slats in the fence. It wasn't a large gap, just enough for the zombies to exploit.

Close enough to see the breach, Cahz stood his ground. The rain was bouncing off his skin; slick droplets trickled down his back. He held the M4 carbine in position and aimed at the approaching dead.

"Come get some!" he shouted.

Unaffected by the taunt, the undead marched on at their steady, lumbering pace, moving as fast as they could muster. Taunt or no taunt, all they knew was that warm, succulent flesh was only a few strides away and that was all the motivation they required.

Cahz nuzzled into the sighting line and picked his first target.

The machine gun barked. Quickly, effectively, Cahz dispatched the approaching cadavers until all the invading zombies lay motionless.

From the gap in the fence, a fresh zombie pushed from the crowd behind onto the playing field. It stumbled from its ejection like a new born fawn getting used to its unsteady legs. Eventually finding its footing in the slippery mud, it scanned the terrain ahead, its mouth open in a gormless pose. When it saw nothing of interest it turned its head and caught sight of Cahz. With a gurgling cry, it stretched its arms out and threw its stiff legs forward.

Cahz popped a round in its skull, ending the flicker of existence it had perversely maintained.

The next zombie to poke through the fence had its head blown clean off. Its lifeless body collapsed and partially blocked the breach.

"Ryan!" Cahz shouted.

A distant voice cut through the moans, "Just… coming."

Another zombie forced its way through the slats. Cahz aimed, then it went dark. The last of the orange glow from the flare burned out.

Cahz hastily pulled the trigger, the lightning flash from his muzzle burning the negative image of the balding zombie's pate into his eyes.

"Fuck."

He stood only feet away from the breach, not knowing whether he had gotten a clean shot off. In an instant he felt utterly vulnerable. In the dark he was deprived of his primary sense and the noise of the droning zombies made it impossible to hear from which direction he was being approached.

He hesitated.

Stay or retreat?

He knew if he left he would have to clear the landing zone all over again. He unconsciously felt for the magazine in his pouch. Would he have enough ammo to clear the field a second time? But if he stayed and fought on in the dark, his chances of survival would be slim.

Without thinking, he already had his hand on the last flare.

He dropped his carbine into its sling and pulled the flare out. In the burst of ignition light, he saw the zombie lunge. Eyes wide open, Cahz reacted with military-trained reflexes. He leveled his weapon at the cadaver without registering what weapon he had.

The flare rocketed forward, catching the bald zombie on the shoulder. The exhaust plume scorched Cahz across the arm, making him yelp in pain.

Knocked off balance by the impact, the zombie slipped in the wet grass and fell at Cahz's feet. The creature twisted and writhed in the mud, trying to crawl. The signal flare hurtled off and rattled against the fence, its chemical rocket illuminating the scene in golden flashes.

Invigorated by the commotion, the lights, the sounds, and the movement, the undead spectators slapped the metal struts of the fence and hollered as best they could through their rigid throats. The whole fence reverberated with the sound of the pounding.

Cahz leapt backwards and swept his carbine up into the firing position. Falling back on his pre-Z training, he put a double tap into the zombie's head. The fear, surprise and sheer volume of adrenaline conspired to rob him of his aim. The first shot narrowly missed, but the second silenced the undead creature.

As he looked up to check for more zombies, the signal flare lit up with a loud crack. The parachute deployed ineffectively, snagging the rocket on the fencing, but the bright radiance of the orange burn caught Cahz square on. He winced and turned away, screwing his eyes up as he did. His vision was filled with the bright green afterburn.

"Ryan!" he shouted.

"Cahz," came Ryan's reply from close at hand.

Cahz pressed the balls of his palms to his eyes. "I can't see! Shoot the pus bags!"

"What with?"

"Where's your pistol?"

Ryan's reply was snappy: "With my clothes in the school! I'm carrying a friggin' desk!"

"Here!" Cahz held out the M4 in the direction of Ryan's voice.

There was a tug on the weapon.

"How do I use this?"

Cahz had his eyes screwed shut against the pain. "Safety's on above the trigger. Flip it off then point and press!"

"Okay."

Ryan took the weapon from Cahz's grasp. There was the soft click of metal as he flipped the catch, then the scream of fire.

"Shit!" Ryan cried as the chatter of bullets filled the air.

"On semi!" Cahz screamed. "Put it on Semi!"

"How?!"

Cahz opened his eyes. The green blob of after burn still consumed his vision. Another chatter of machinegun fire ruptured the noise of moans.

"Stop wasting bullets!"

"They're too close!" Ryan screamed.

There was a third burst of shots and a click.

"It's stopped working!"

"You're out of ammo, goddamn it!" Cahz said. "Give it here!"

The next moment he felt the hard body of the weapon being pushed into his open hand. He flipped the magazine free, took a fresh one from his body armour and slotted the new one into place, a drill Cahz was trained to do sighted or unsighted.

He brought the carbine into firing position. The blur was starting to clear, but huge floating green blobs still obscured his vision. He blinked hard, trying to squeeze the internal lava lamp from his head.

"Cahz, give me the gun—they're getting close!" Ryan squealed.

Cahz opened his eyes. The amorphous blobs skittered across his view, but behind them, bathed in the orange light of the flare, he could see three immobilized zombies and a fourth attempting to crawl towards them. Emerging from the breach came half a dozen more.

Flipping the catch to semi-automatic, Cahz shot the crawling zombie in the head, then went straight back to clearing the breach.

"Block that up. I'll cover you," he said.

He fired repeatedly into the mass of bodies. Within moments he'd wiped out all the zombies who had made it through, but they were still squeezing their way in.

"Ahhh!" came a cry from behind.

"Ryan!" Cahz called without taking his eyes off the gap.

"I'm okay," Ryan panted.

"Where's our barricade?"

Cahz started shooting at the crowd around the gap, hoping their immobile bodies would add to the impasse.

"Coming." Ryan backed up alongside, Cahz dragging the desk as he did. "Can you help with this?"

"No," Cahz snapped. "I'm shooting dead fucks!"

With that, he popped another zombie through the skull as if to accentuate the point.

"How am I going to do this then?" Ryan asked.

Cahz took his eyes off the fence for a moment to examine the desk. Ryan had struggled with the large heavy teacher's desk rather than the lighter flimsier classroom ones.

"If you push it up to about half a metre you can tip it onto its end, then shove it up against the hole."

"There's no way you can push this through the grass. We'll have to pull it or lift it," Ryan pointed out.

"Then pull it!"

"No way," Ryan protested. "I'd have my ass up against the fence before I got it close enough."

"Okay, quit your whining and grab an end," Cahz said. "Ready?"

"Yes."

Cahz fired a prolonged burst into the crowd, expending the mag.

"Go!"

The two men lifted the desk, one on either side, and ran at the fence like it was a battering ram against a portcullis.

"Tip it!" Cahz shouted as they drew close.

He dropped the leading edge and used the momentum of the charge to throw the desk on its end. The upright desk rattled against the fence as it clattered to a stop.

Cahz and Ryan leapt back from the dozens of arms wedged through the railing trying to grasp them.

"You okay?" Cahz asked, ejecting the spent magazine.

"Yeah," Ryan replied. "Do you think that'll hold them?"

"No idea. Go back to the school. Grab a pile of tables and chairs and try to shore this up."

"What will you be doing?" Ryan asked in an accusing tone.

"I'm going to make a quick circuit of the fence while there's still some light."

With that, Cahz jogged off.

"What about the chopper?" Ryan called after him.

Cahz called over his shoulder, "Do you hear it?"

Ryan tried to pick up the sound of the engine, but it was lost to the rain and the tireless moaning.

CHAPTER TWENTY-TWO
DWELLING

Ali was bored and miserable. He sat in the tent, wrapped in a sleeping bag. It was pitch black and raining. The alcove he had wrecked out of the roof left him exposed to the lashing rain, with water running off the tiles into the gaping hole. It trickled down and dripped into the Rockwool insulation. No doubt it would have seeped down the plasterboard and started ruining the apartments below.

Not that his alterations would affect the resale value, Ali mused.

Even though the tent had a sewn-in waterproof groundsheet, he was still wet. He sat in the mummy-style sleeping bag like a caterpillar from some Lewis Carol nightmare, his face and bushy beard poking through. His thick eyebrows were furrowed, his eyes squinting against the rain, but he dared not zip up the tent.

What if the chopper returned? Would he hear it above the noise of the driving rain? How long would he have to signal it? Ali couldn't take the chance.

So he sat, the rain dripping from the tip of his nose.

The inside label of the sleeping bag had boasted a water resistant outer skin. But the amount of spray coming in the open tent flap was testing that reliance to the limit. Ali knew it wouldn't be long before the fabric passed its saturation point and he'd be even colder and wetter and more miserable.

There was a gas-powered lamp in the hiker's pack, the type that took the same canister as the stove. He had toyed with the idea of bringing a book to read, something to occupy his mind and help the time pass. In the end none of Frank's martial arts manuals or action adventure novels took his fancy. Besides, he might need the lantern to signal with later and he had no idea how much gas was left.

The small tower of Franks DVDs took the brunt of a gust of wind and toppled over. The plastic cases scattered among the eaves and insulation. Ali didn't bother to try to retrieve them. They would never light in weather like this, and besides, they were intended to produce a column of smoke. In the pitch dark and rain they were pointless.

There was a tremendous crash from across the street, like the rumble of dying thunder. Ali jerked his head up to look for the source of the noise. A veil of glowing embers wafted into the rain from a bank of shattered windows.

The buildings across the street had all caught alight and with frightening speed devoured the abandoned properties. The fire's furious consumption of the available fuel and the lack of any fire suppression had meant the buildings were gutted in a matter of hours. The steady rain had done little to quench the flames, but it had reduced the combustibility of the zombies in the street.

Ali knew from personal experience how flammable the undead were. Countless concoctions of sugar, flour, washing liquid and gasoline were tried as the survivors tinkered to produce the ultimate petrol bomb. In the beginning, the newly resurrected had burnt for hours, the flames intense enough to ignite the fat. Those early blazing culls had been powerful enough to reduce the bone to ash. As the corpses had decayed and rotted, it seemed that they lost the fat around their bones, becoming more gaunt and skeletal. The older the cadaver, the less well they burnt. But they still burnt. With their dry rag clothing and wispy kindling hair, even the old sinewy ghouls had been ample fuel for the flames before their dowsing in the rain.

In the street below, those zombies unfortunate enough to be next to buildings had perished in the blaze. As they fell others were pushed towards the pyre. Ali didn't know if zombies had no fear of fire or whether their desire for food overrode what self-preservation they had, but since he'd been watching hundreds of undead had been cremated.

But as the rain grew heavier only those undead crammed against the burning buildings took light. For a while, wrapped up warm in his tent, it had been like sitting before a massive campfire. He had watched the inferno, hypnotized by the light and movement as the flames danced. Even the crackling and pops as the buildings were consumed were comforting, the noise drowning out the clamour of the dead.

An hour ago the whole street was awash with the orange glow of flame. But the scolding blaze had abated. Now only embers glowed and the occasional crash as the scorched infrastructure collapsed. Now, above the sounds of the dying buildings, through the pitter-patter of the rain and gurgle of the rivulets, Ali could again hear the dead calling. It had been hours since he'd made a sound up here and even longer since a zombie had seen him. Yet they still held sentry, waiting for their chance to devour him.

The drone grew louder, rising against the rain, a monotonous dull whine.

Ali wanted to cry out, "Shut up!"

But he knew it would have the opposite effect, only aggravating them further.

Then it struck him: the noise held a steady rhythm, not the normal cacophony of disorder.

An engine?

He unzipped his sleeping bag and stood at the entrance to the tent. The full force of the rain lashed against his face. His long beard fluttered like a forgotten flag on a battlefield.

The sound was most definitely an engine. Ali burled round and found the gas lantern in the tent. He switched it on and turned the valve to full. A bright white light shone from the ribbed prism glass of the lamp and illuminated his island-like campsite.

Without thinking, he held the light aloft and waved it like a clichéd shipwreck survivor. In a sense that's exactly how he felt—marooned on this rooftop surrounded by a sea of dead flesh.

He raised a hand to his mouth and was about shout for help when he realized the noise of the rotor blades would drown out even his loudest cry.

Ali stood waving and waiting for the chopper to come into sight. The seconds stretched into minutes, and although the sound of the helicopter continued to grow, it was still maddeningly out of sight.

"Come on," Ali said anxiously.

Masked by the driving rain, he could now see the pulsing flashes of its tail lights. Tantalizingly near yet impossibly distant, the chopper's running lights beckoned.

Ali suddenly became acutely worried that the chopper wouldn't see him or his small insignificant light in a storm. With the embers of dying fires still drawing the eye, maybe he'd be missed. Still with the lantern aloft, he turned back to look in the tent. He scanned the contents there, the stove, the rucksack, sleeping bag. Nothing was of any obvious use. As the panic of missing his ride climbed out of the pit of his stomach, he couldn't remember what was in the rucksack.

He bent down, intent on spilling the contents on the ground, when it found him. A bright beam of light engulfed the rooftop, illuminating every streak of rain as it fell.

Ali turned round and the glare of the light forced him to screw his eyes shut. He placed his free hand in front of his eyes to shield them.

The force of the downdraft from the rotors tore at the tent and made Ali gulp down lungfuls of wet breath. Needles of rain stung his face, but Ali was jubilant. A triumphant smile filled his face and puffed out his cheeks. He waved the lantern, no longer signaling but rejoicing.

"I'm saved!" Ali beamed. "I'm saved!"

A crackle of static burst over the noise of the blades.

"Is your position secure?" the artificially amplified voice bellowed.

"Yes! Yes!" Ali shouted.

"I can't hear you," the disembodied voice replied. "Wave your torch up and down for yes, left and right for no."

Ail waved the lantern up and down.

"Good," the voice came. "Are the others with you?"

Ali signaled no.

"Have you seen other survivors since this morning?" the pilot asked.

Ali dutifully signaled yes, remembering the futile conversation with Ryan across the street.

"Are they alive?" came the next question.

In all honesty Ali couldn't be sure. They may have burned in the building, they may have been killed trying to escape.

Ali moved the light round in a wide circle.

"I'll take that as *I don't know*," the voice replied.

The helicopter banked slightly before the pilot could compensate for the gust of wind.

"Is there a flat roof nearby?" the pilot asked once he'd stabilized the flight.

Ali looked around. None of the buildings on this side of the street had flat roofs. The larger office block across the way no doubt had, but they had been destroyed by the fire.

Reluctantly Ali signaled back no.

"Is there somewhere flat I can land?"

Again Ali signaled no.

"I don't have a winch, man. So I can't pick you up without landing."

"What?" Ali said, even too quietly to hear himself.

"I'll come back for you," the voice promised. "I need to go back and refuel."

Ali was standing still, the lantern by his side, the rain lashing off his dumbstruck face.

"I won't make it back tomorrow, what with the turnaround time," explained the helicopter pilot. "I'll come back for you the day after. Can you hold out till then?"

Frozen by his disappointment, Ali just stared at the chopper.

"Did you hear me? Can you hold out for two days?"

Robotically, Ali waved the light up and down for yes.

"Good. I'll bring a winch operator and we'll get you out of here. Hang tight buddy," the pilot chirped.

The searchlight flicked off and the helicopter rose into the rainy sky.

"Two days," Ali whispered despondently.

He stood like a stone gargoyle, the harsh white light of the lamp, his blank expression and unruly beard making him look all the more haunted and gruesome than the cadavers below.

"Two days," he said again.

The blinking taillight was quickly lost to the rain-laden clouds and the moans from the excited dead below climbed above the noise of the receding chopper.

Ali stood frozen, unmoving against the rain.

"Two days," he whispered.

CHAPTER TWENTY-THREE
BREACH

Ryan was tidying away the contents of the first aid kit when Cahz came padding into the schoolroom.

"Perimeter secure?" he quipped at the half naked soldier.

Cahz nodded. There were splashes of dark brown mud up his bare legs, but he looked pale even in the yellow flame.

"You okay?" Ryan asked.

"Feeling light headed," Cahz said, perching on the edge of a desk.

"Sit down." Ryan moved the first aid kit to one side to make space for him.

"Can't. We need to set a signal fire." Cahz looked down at the crisp white dressing on Ryan's toe. "What happened?"

"I ripped a blister open on that fuckin' desk," Ryan cursed.

"Right. Come on then, we need to set a fire." Cahz pushed himself up.

"You look like shit."

Cahz let out a short sigh. "Feel like shit, too. I think it's the infect—"

"No way, man!" Ryan broke in. "It's the blood loss from the dog bite. That's all it is and you know it. We'll get you back to that ship of yours and you'll be fixed up just fine."

Cahz pushed himself up from the edge of the desk. "Regardless of what it is, I used both the flares out there. We need to build a signal fire or none of us are going to that ship."

"Okay," Ryan said.

He stretched up and pulled down his grubby jeans. They were still damp to the touch but at least now they had been warmed by the fire.

"Cahz," Ryan said. "Stick your pants on, at least."

Cahz nodded and snatched down some of his clothes from the line.

"How do we do this?" Ryan asked as he gingerly pulled his trainers on.

"Grab everything we can that will burn." Cahz wriggled into his still damp fatigues. "Lay it out in a cross at the edge of the playing field. Set it alight and wait."

"How do we keep it dry enough to get it lit?"

Cahz looked puzzled for a moment before leaning back on the desk. The metal legs scraped across the floor at the pressure. He looked down at the table. He ran a hand over the smooth varnished top and gave it a firm pat like it was a family pet.

***

Outside, the rain was still pouring down and the undead cried out for the flesh they could see through the railings.

"How many more of these do we need?" Ryan puffed, his arms full of textbooks.

"That'll do," Cahz said as he spread out his own bundle of books.

Although it was pitch black, he knew the zombies had a bead on them. The fence rattled and creaked as they pushed against it, trying to break through. And even though the wind and rain did much to muffle the sound, their deathly moans were all too clear. Inside the school, with the crackling fire, neither Ryan nor Cahz had any idea of the sheer numbers of zombies accumulating beyond the fence, their moans softened by the elements and the illusion of safety.

Although Cahz couldn't see the enemy in the enveloping darkness, he sensed their vast numbers.

He pulled out the book of matches from their MRE and looked into the darkness.

"Shouldn't we wait until we hear the chopper?" Ryan asked.

Cahz paused for a moment, thinking it through, and looked at the half empty book of matches.

"Visibility is low. By the time we light it, he could have flown past."

Cahz struck the match and held it to a corner of the paper. The flame spluttered and hissed before popping out, leaving a warm ember and a thread of smoke. Cahz tried again and before the scorched paper could ignite, the match had fizzled out.

"Too damn wet!" Cahz snapped.

He shifted round on his haunches to try and block the worst of the rain.

"Aw." Cahz winced as something hard and sharp dug into his thigh.

"You okay?" Ryan asked.

Cahz dipped his hand into his thigh pocket and pulled out the curved magazine. It was the spare Angel had passed to him this morning. He felt the cold metal magazine in his hand and remembered the woman's stern warning to return the empties. It seemed like a lifetime since he'd seen her, since becoming exiled in this forsaken land.

Cahz teased the top round and flipped out it out. He pulled out his knife and plucked out the bullet that sat snugly in the case. It was too dark to see the cordite underneath, but Cahz knew it was there.

Cupping a hand round the open page of the schoolbook, he poured the powder into the crease of the spine. He ripped a page from an adjacent book and screwed it into a ball.

Cautiously, he lit the second to last match and introduced it to the small heap. The ammunition flared into life and a thick flame lapped up the side of the scrunched-up paper. He balled up more paper and nurtured the growing blaze.

"Keep fuelling this fire. Don't let it go out."

Ryan looked concerned. "Where are you going?"

"To get more shit to burn," Cahz called back as he ran to the school building.

Copying Cahz, Ryan added a steady supply of balled up paper. The blaze spread quickly, its light and heat growing in intensity. As the flames took hold, the darkness was pushed further and further.

Ryan looked up at the rain clouds, praying to see the flash of the helicopter lights. There was nothing. Dejected, he lowered his eyes. As he did he saw the horde of undead at the fence. Their cyanotic faces snarling, their palsied arms forced between the slats, their fingers stretched out, grasping for their prey. Ryan stared, mesmerized by the forest of dead arms. For as far as the light extended, all he could see were hundreds of arms waving and clawing, desperate to seize him and devour his flesh.

Cahz's voice broke Ryan from his daze. "Lend a hand," he said from behind a massive bookcase teetering precariously across his shoulders.

"Sure," Ryan said, glad for the distraction.

He grabbed the swaying end of the bookcase and helped Cahz extract himself from under it. Cahz turned as if to leave, but instead of running off he delivered a brutal side kick to the shelving. The wood cracked and snapped under his powerful and accurately placed kicks.

"Add some of these bits," Cahz said, tossing over a broken shelf. "The wood will burn longer."

Ryan swept up an armful of lumber and went back to diligently stoking the flames.

Cahz delivered a brutal kick to the last intact length of shelving. "Listen, I'm off to get some more. You keep at the fire."

"How's Rebecca?" Ryan asked as he angled the wood over the fire.

"I don't know," Cahz confessed.

"Oh for god's sake, Cahz. Why didn't you check in on her and make sure she's still safe?"

"She's sound asleep," Cahz argued. "She'll be fine."

Ryan looked up at Cahz, his face framed by the glow of the fire.

"You didn't know that. You've just told me you haven't checked in on her. Look, just check in on her on the way past."

"Okay," Cahz replied, and jogged off.

Ryan watched the soldier as he ran into the school.

"For fuck's sake, it's like it's too much to ask," he moaned as he grabbed a handful of smashed shelving.

As he stood back up, Ryan froze. The zombie marched straight at him, battering into the table that separated them. Carried forward by its momentum and unable to brace itself on stiff limbs, the dumb creature toppled over.

Ryan dropped the splinters and went for his pistol.

But it wasn't there. His mind flashed to the gun sitting with the body armour and the bag of cans.

"Cahz?!" Ryan called, but there was no reply.

He turned to run for the school and then he heard it. Through the rain and the moans came the sweeping sound of helicopter blades.

By the time he'd ran to retrieve his gun, Ryan knew their rescue would have passed them by.

"Cahz!" he hollered at the school.

He turned and lunged at the fallen zombie. The decaying creature was struggling to its feet when a pair of warm hands grabbed it.

Fuelled by rage, Ryan picked up the animated corpse and threw it back over the tables. Ignoring where it landed, Ryan started tipping over the desks acting as an umbrella. The fire hissed and spat as the raindrops evaporated in its heat. But already the pyre was beginning to wane. The section Ryan had lit first was close to consuming the last scraps of paper.

As he reached the last table the zombie was upon him. Ryan snatched up the table and thrust it between them like a shield. Its dead arms tried to curl round the desktop to claw at Ryan, but they couldn't reach. The walking dead stood in the flames, its skin too leathery to catch, its tattered clothing too wet to ignite. But as it shuffled among the flames it was kicking the fuel away, extinguishing the flames. Ryan shoved back with all the rage in his heart and the zombie went flying across the field. He raised the desk above his head and charged at the cadaver, screaming like a berserker.

Standing over the zombie, he hurtled the table down at its head. The blow from the flimsy school furniture wasn't enough to destroy the squirming cadaver, so Ryan stomped his foot down hard. The writhing creature couldn't move out of the way and Ryan's sole stamped straight down across its jaw and neck.

Underneath that leathery skin, bones snapped and grey matter turned to mash. The zombie lay still.

Ryan stood above the corpse like a conquering gladiator, his chest heaving from the exertion. An agitated moan caught his ear and he turned to see a second zombie plodding towards him. And in the sky behind it, Ryan could see the blink of navigation lights.

"Yes!" Ryan let slip in relief, the light rain splashing down, bouncing off his face.

More movement caught his eye. Across the playing field, a swarm of undead were pushing past the dislodged desk, pouring in faster than before.

The barricade had failed utterly. Lubricated by the sodden grass and mud, the desk Ryan had used to block the gap had been forced back by the combined strength of a thousand undead. Now that legion were raging through the breach.

Ryan looked back at the school for a sign of his companion.

"Cahz!" he screamed as loud as he could.

There was no reply. Ryan turned to see the undead shuffling closer.

The signal fire made their faces look even more monstrous as the flickering orange light twisted and warped their slack-jawed expressions.

Ryan turned and ran for the school.

***

Cahz battered open the double doors from the gym and stumbled into the main corridor. He held two long, unwieldy wooden benches sandwiched under his arm to fuel the signal fire. The corridor was lit by the dim reflected light from the fire in the schoolroom where Rebecca slept.

Ryan stood motionless by the open doorway, silhouetted by the golden flicker of fire light, his shoulders hunched over, looking thoroughly drenched, a pool of water forming at his feet.

"I've checked in on her already," Cahz said, struggling with the gym equipment.

Ryan didn't react; he simply stood there staring into the schoolroom.

"Give me a hand here," Cahz said as the two benches started to slip.

The benches scissored in opposite directions. Cahz tried to calm the swinging with his free hand, but the stress was too much and they clattered to the floor.

"Don't just stand there," he said as he bent down to stack them.

As he gathered them up he caught sight of Ryan moving into the room.

Cahz started lifting the load. "I know you've got a sore foot, Ryan, but for fuck's sake hurry it up."

With the bench back in place, Cahz stumbled forward again. As he drew up to the door he shouted inside.

"Grab an end for fuck's sake—"

Cahz froze.

By the light of the fire in the classroom, he could see it wasn't Ryan he'd been speaking to. A thick-set zombie, its skin crisp and burnt, stared from lidless eyes at the slumbering baby. The child twitched in her sleep and the creature let out a baneful moan.

"Ah shit!" Cahz shouted.

The benches hit the floor with a clatter and Cahz pulled his carbine up to fire. The zombie seemed oblivious to the noise and threw itself at the child. It was on the child before Cahz could fire. The two merged and he lost his clear target. With no time before the creature bit down, Cahz pulled the trigger.

The zombie toppled over onto the floor. The child screamed.

Cahz vaulted over the toppled benches and kicked the neutralized zombie away from the child. He bent down and scooped up the crying baby. Her cheeks were puffed out red as she screamed in discomfort. Cahz gently placed his hand on the child's forehead, his breath forced to a fearful stop. The baby was tiny, his cupped hand covering her whole head. The skin was burning hot, flushed with blood from screaming. He drew his hand over the child's hair, ruffling her short silky curls as he felt for any wet patches.

With a puff of relief, Cahz let out his stifled breath. There was no bite, no spray of contagion. Again the baby had escaped infection.

"There, there," Cahz said, bouncing the baby. "There, there."

"Cahz!" Ryan cried out as he ran into the room.

"Ryan?" Cahz squeaked back in a surprised, high-pitched tone.

Ryan stopped just short of the incapacitated zombie. "The choppers back!" he gasped before he had time to take in the scene. He saw the inert zombie sprawled across the floor and caught the look of panic in Cahz's eyes. "What the fuck happened?" he asked as he practically pulled Rebecca to his chest.

"It's all okay," Cahz said in a calming tone. "I took the W.D. out before he got to her. She's fine—just a little freaked."

Ryan held the child out at arm's length and examined her. In a childish voice he comforted the girl.

"You said the choppers here?" Cahz asked.

Ryan nodded. "Yeah, but they've broken through the fence. The field is full of pus-bags."

"Christ!" Cahz sprang over the body and out towards the main door.

***

Cahz sprinted out of the front door with such speed that he ran straight past the first zombie. The retarded cadaver swung round to grab at him, but Cahz was too swift. In the exigency to grab its prey, the zombie lost its balance and fell over.

Ryan was right; the playing field was swamped with undead, and maybe a mile away in the rain-laden sky there shone the lights of an aircraft.

"This is India Tango One, are you receiving?" Cahz shouted into his mic. "Are you receiving?"

The cross of burning desks was still alight, but the flames were lacklustre, dampened by the rain.

But there was still enough light to plainly see the dozens of zombies shambling towards him. Cahz fired his weapon, dispatching the approaching vanguard of undead.

"India Tango One calling. We need immediate extraction. Do you copy?"

The zombie Cahz had run past picked itself up. It stretched out its bone thin arms and lumbered after its kill.

Cahz looked up at the black night sky. He could see the flashes of light from the chopper illuminating the undersides of the clouds. Taking in a deep breath he hit the toggle to send, "Idris, you son of bitch, look down!"

The zombie edged up behind Cahz. It let its jaw drop and tried to let out an excited moan, but no sound emerged from its infection encrusted mouth. Maybe the fall or the rain or some other factor prevented it from moaning. It didn't matter to the undead creature; it would still sink its teeth into the living flesh and gorge on its warm meat.

Snarling, its teeth at the ready, the zombie stepped in for the attack.

A shot rang out from behind him and Cahz whipped round just in time to see a zombie collapse at his feet. Ryan had emerged from the school building, the papoose strapped to his chest, pistol in hand.

Cahz looked at Ryan, the muzzle still pointed at his face, and then down at the crumpled zombie.

"Your aim is improving," Cahz said, then turned round and looked back up at the sky. "Idris, this is Cahz. Come on, buddy, we really need a lift."

As Ryan drew up Cahz could hear the baby zipped up inside the bag, her howls of displeasure marginally stifled by the fabric.

"What do we do?!" Ryan shouted above the child's screams and the lashing rain.

A swathe of zombies where shambling towards them, converging on their position.

"Get closer to the breach," Cahz said. "We've got to seal that back up before we run out of ammo."

"What about the chopper?"

Cahz gave Ryan a solemn look. "If you can think of a way of signaling him, I'm all ears."

"The school!" Ryan yelped. "Torch the school!"

Cahz slapped him on the shoulder. "It's worth a try. Get to it. I'll try to secure the area."

Cahz edged forward, shooting as he did. Within seconds his carbine gave a dreaded click. He flicked the catch and let the empty fall to the ground. He pulled a fresh magazine from its pouch and slapped it home. There was no time to retrieve the empty and since there was no more ammunition, there was no point.

"This is India Tango One, situation is critical." Cahz held firm as a fresh wave of zombies shuffled towards him, "I repeat, situation is critical. Request immediate evac. Please respond, over."

The zombies were just seconds from grabbing him, but Cahz waited, desperately wanting to hear his radio crackle into life.

A dead hand pawed in front of his face. He batted the dead flesh away with his carbine and shot the zombie, muzzle pressed against its nose. The headless cadaver slumped to the ground, clearing Cahz's aim for the next targets.

The first dozen rounds cleared the immediate ground around him, then he pushed on, closing on his enemy. Out here in the drizzle with the rising moans of a thousand undead, it was easy to get overwhelmed. The faint fire light behind was illuminating just enough to see by.

Squeezing the trigger, the hammer fall ended in silence. Another magazine depleted. Cahz let the empty slip free and grabbed the last of his rounds. Unceremoniously he loaded the weapon and aimed it at the horde.

"This is never going to work," he said as he lowered the M4.

Between him and the breach there were still a good couple of dozen undead. Even if he took one with each round, by the time he'd done that another hundred would be through the gap.

Cahz lowered his gun and charged into the mob of decaying flesh.

He screamed a guttural, primordial cry that rivaled the moans of the amassed dead. He thumped into countless zombies, knocking the soggy lumps of dead flesh flying with his momentum. He was almost at the gap when his footing slipped on the muddy grass and he skidded head first towards the opening.

The thick wet mud sprayed his face and flooded into his mouth. He coughed out the choking slurry as he scrambled to catch his footing. Before he could get up, a lump weight fell across his shoulder. Cahz tried to push himself up, but more eager zombies were piling on top. His fingers dug into the earth, his teeth gritted. He forced his muscles to push. Summoning every ounce of strength in his flesh, he burst out of the scrum, throwing cadavers off in all directions.

Clambering on all fours, digging for traction in the chewed-up earth, Cahz threw himself at the upturned desk. Reaching what had now become a breakwater in the path of the undead, he slammed his back up hard against it. It was only a few feet from its original position blocking the hole, but Cahz knew this would be a Herculean task to get it back in place.

Stamping his heels into the quagmire, he pushed his weight into the desk. The abused piece of school furniture slid a few inches then came to a jarring halt.

Before Cahz could change his purchase a dead hand grabbed at him. At the end of the gnarled and decaying arm a petite little zombie hauled itself. Cahz stared into the vacant eyes of a dead child. No more than seven or eight when she'd turned, the little girl wore a shredded school uniform. Her black lips curled back, revealing missing teeth from her demonic grin.

Cahz whipped out his pistol and shoved it straight into the child's open mouth.

"Chew on this," Cahz heard himself quip as he pulled the trigger.

The zombie's head exploded, throwing shrapnel-like chunks of skull into the darkness.

Pistol still in hand, Cahz braced his shoulders to the wooden surface and dug in. As he pushed again and again, the desk started to slide. It slithered a few inches in the mud before stopping firm. Another zombie came round the side and made a grab for him. Cahz kicked out at the undead's kneecap. The bone snapped like rotten wood and the zombie fell to the ground. As it hit the mud Cahz dispatched it with a round to the head.

Cahz's eye was drawn back to the school as a lick of flame shot up inside one of the classrooms. The yellow beam of light shone like a beacon from the window.

"Come on, Idris! You've got to see that!" Cahz barked, face upturned to the rain.

Round the edge of the desk a pair of cadavers came at him. The first one he floored in an instant, the second he had to grapple with before his shot found its brain.

"Come on, you dead fuck motherfuckers!" Cahz shouted as he threw his strength behind the desk again.

A wave of half a dozen cadavers lumbered into arm's length of him. He repeatedly fired his pistol, trying to keep the zombies at bay. Through the mob of undead he could see a second then a third classroom in quick succession burst into flames.

A necrotic hand wrapped around his gun arm, pulling his aim off true. He wrestled the gun free and fired wildly at point-blank range.

"India Tango One, we are setting signal fires at our location," Cahz radioed as the pack of cadavers fell upon him. He strained to get out the last of his message, "West of your position."

The drone of the helicopter engine sounded closer now, even

above the rain and moans.

With the hope of rescue masking his fear, Cahz ignored the dead hands grasping for him. He changed his angle of attack on the desk and pushed hard.

Over and over, he thrust his whole body at the desk, each time taking it a little further into the gap.

A fresh zombie grabbed his arm and pounced. Cahz pulled the trigger, but the gun was spent. He tossed the empty pistol aside and pulled himself back away from the zombie's jaws. A second zombie seized him from behind, throwing him off kilter.

Cahz stumbled back, vigorously trying to shake off the ravenous dead. In only a few short steps he had a congregation of zombies all snatching at him.

Feeling for the M4 on its sling, Cahz twisted and turned, desperately to escape the attackers. His fingers found the handle of the weapon. He tried to level it, but the dead were pressed too tightly around him now. He could feel teeth gnawing into his armour and he knew it wouldn't be long before they found his flesh.

Gasping against the choking stench of rot, Cahz tried unsuccessfully to break loose. Unable to get a clear shot, he started firing wildly, popping off shot after shot in a frantic attempt to loosen their hold. As the shots rang out, he bucked and twisted trying to break free, but for every zombie he dislodged another took its place.

Cahz tripped in the melee and fell to the mud, a dozen voracious cadavers falling with him. As he hit the ground and took a face full of putrid slurry there was an electrical hiss through his earpiece.

***

The school was ablaze, fingers of flame stretching long into the night sky.

And in the glow of the fires Ryan saw the knot of zombies on the ground a short distance from the defunct barricade. Although the gap in the fence was only wide enough to let one zombie in at a time, the mass of undead clambering to get in was terrifying. Every second, like some macabre spawning, a zombie would spew through the gap and stumble onto the playing field.

Ryan ran up to the seething heap of bodies. Under the pile Cahz was screaming.

"I'm coming!" Ryan hollered as he grabbed a cadaver.

The force of Ryan's pull ripped the rotten shirt off the zombie's back, exposing the putrid flesh underneath. Unperturbed, Ryan leveled his pistol and shot the assailant through the head. He snatched a zombie out, rammed his gun into its head, and pulled the trigger.

Ryan dug deeper into the pile of squirming, rotting meat, blasting away with his pistol as he did. Time and time he hauled out a zombie and blew its brains out, rummaging through the mess trying to find his partner.

A gloved hand punched out from the corpses. Ryan grabbed hold and pulled.

Cahz emerged from the clawing, biting boil of cadavers, dragging a squirming corpse with him. The raging creature was firmly tangled in the soldier's armour. Ryan stuck the muzzle of his gun in its face and fired. Cahz battered and kicked furiously to dislodge the more determined undead.

"Fuckin' busy!" Ryan shouted as he fired.

"Hold them off!" Cahz shouted. He called into his radio, "India Tango One, I know you're there, Idris. Come on! We're in deep shit, buddy!"

Ryan's gun barked and flashed as he shot at the dead. Even as inexperienced with a firearm as he was, it was proving impossible to miss at such short range.

"What are you doing?" Ryan demanded to know.

"I heard a crackle!" Cahz shouted over the gunshots and moans. "I heard a crackle over the radio."

"What's that mean?" Ryan asked. "Has he seen us?"

"It means he's transmitting."

"He heard you?"

"I don't know—look," Cahz pointed at the sky. "He's not moving fast—he's searching for us."

Ryan looked down at the backpack strapped to his chest. From inside Rebecca was screaming in terror.

"It's going to be okay, honey. It's going to be okay," Ryan promised the child, tears of his own tumbling down his face.

"We have to close that gap," Cahz said, pushing his back up to the desk.

Ryan moved to help him push. "How? There's thousands of them out there now."

"You cover me. I'll push the desk back in place." Cahz let his M4 drop in its sling.

"You're a better shot. I'll push."

Cahz looked up at Ryan. "I'm out of ammo."

"Here." Ryan passed over his gun and braced himself against the desk. Cahz took the pistol and stood clear. "Here." Ryan held out a magazine. "That's my last one."

Standing sentry over Ryan, Cahz took up his firing stance and started shooting. The knot of zombies around the breach were obliterated in seconds. Cahz turned to the fence and exhausted the remainder of the magazine trying to thin them out.

It was futile. The weight of zombies was so massive that the ones he shot refused to fall, pinned to the fence by the pressure from behind.

"Idris!" Cahz barked into the mic as he loaded the pistol for the last time. "Come on, Idris. We're right next to the burning school. Look out your window!"

Beside him, Ryan was huffing and grunting as he forced the desk into the mass of zombies. He had almost plugged the gap, but a mound of dead were wedged between the desk and the opening, effectively jamming it.

Cahz holstered the pistol and set about clearing the space. He picked out the first inert cadaver and tossed it to one side. But as he cleared the ground another zombie pushed its way through the gap. He grabbed the scrawny bag of infected skin and bones and lobbed it back over the fence. As he turned to get back to his task another zombie pushed its head through the gap.

Cahz tore the pistol from its holster and pointed it at the gnashing zombie. He held his fire. He looked down at the loaded pistol in his hand. For all it was worth, it was useless to him. The fifteen rounds it held would never be enough.

"Ryan," he said.

Ryan looked up from his exertions.

Cahz tossed the weapon to the young man. "You've got a full clip left," he said before turning to the gap.

He delved into one of his pouches and pulled out a hard, slightly curved metal object. There was a knot of wires and duct tape strapped to the rear of the device. Cahz checked the modifications, reassuring himself that he could still use it without the jury-rigged timer.

He wasn't fearful. A strange calm had gripped him. He knew he had to clear the ground so Ryan could seal it.

He sucked in a deep breath, girding himself for one more tremendous effort.

As he barged into the mass of cold bodies, he could hear in crystal clarity their hungry moans, Ryan's grunting, the crackle of flames, the pitter-patter from a myriad of raindrops. And somewhere in those rain-swollen clouds, the sound of rotor blades chopping through the moist air.

Cahz felt the mud underfoot squelch as he powered forward. The solid metal body of his carbine bounced, suspended from its sling. The butt of the M4 was hooked under his forearm, the muzzle pointing at the sodden ground. With every awkward strength-sapping step in the slimy quagmire, he felt the barrel slap against his leg.

Cahz grabbed a corpse that stood blocking the desk and hurled it out of the way. As he did a zombie grabbed for him through the fence. He ignored its grasping hands and dragged a second corpse free.

The edge of the desk bashed against his shoulder as Ryan pushed it in. A few extra inches and the space would be blocked.

Another dead hand reached out and grabbed him. They were still pushing through the gap.

Cahz had to stop them. His legs ached all the way up to his backside, yet he had to muster every last iota of strength. Fighting against the resistance of the grasping hands, he pushed off against the desk and into the breach.

Spread eagled, Cahz barred the zombie's entrance to the playing fields. All around him were the men, women and children who had found no rest in their demise, wretched creatures tortured by a malodorous and corrupt immortality, possessed by an insatiable hunger for living flesh—his flesh.

A multitude of dead hands clutched at his body; a crowd of rancid faces snarled and gnashed their shattered teeth with excitement. Their rain-soaked corpses were illuminated by flashes of light as they lunged in at him. The putrid breath of decay that escaped their rotting lungs as they moaned assaulted his nostrils and matched the rank taste festering in his mouth.

The dead hands tightened their grip and there was the sharp pain of a bite on his shoulder.

Cahz screamed, but the sound was lost to the downwash from above.

The constant heavy beating of rotor blades and the drone of a turbine encased him in noise. He closed his eyes and listened to the din from the helicopter's engine. He pulled his arms in and flicked the detonator on the claymore.

EPILOGUE

Ali slowly surfaced from his sleep. He swallowed deep in his parched throat, trying to move the sticky mucus from his mouth.

"Time to get up, Ali," he said to himself as he tentatively peeked out from behind his eyelids. He placed a hand against his brow to fend off the worst of the light.

He unzipped the sleeping bag and tussled with its embrace to get his feet free. As he kicked it loose he glanced around.

The sky was clear and bright. A few puffy white clouds floated in the azure blue, but it looked like it would be a fine day.

He heaved himself upright, his body giving a disparaging array of clicks and pops as he stretched out.

He looked down at his bare feet. His toenails were getting long and needing a trim. As he looked at his hairy toes he wiggled them, feeling the plastic groundsheet stick and cling to his soles.

He had been sleeping in his vest and threadbare underpants and he knew the garments, like himself, could do with a wash. He knew his long black beard was wild and unruly, his hair just as untamed. He knew he looked a sight.

The light wind whistling through the eaves made the rooftop strangely silent.

As he pulled his thick and well-worn shirt on, Ali listened for the moans of the zombies. He focused carefully and there it was, like an unending incantation. The incessant droning of a thousand coarse voices were conveyed in the air only as background noise to him. Like the constant drone of traffic outside the old apartment where he used to live. When the world was alive.

The drone of the dead were what he was used to ignoring now.

His head pounded. He knew he should be drinking more water, but had no idea when he would get some. The storm had passed and the puddles of rainwater long since dried up. His stomach growled, eager for some breakfast. But the food in the backpack had run out a couple of days ago.

Stiffly he walked to the edge of the roof. With each step his rigid joints eased off. It was even harder for him to get going in the morning these days. He would shuffle around this confined space until his ligaments and muscles had eased off.

He stepped up to the edge of the roof. Before him lay the dead city. Hundreds of abandoned buildings, thousands of rusting cars and what seemed to be millions of dead inhabitants.

He looked down at the seething mass of undead flesh below. The street was packed with cadavers, all calling their baleful lament.

Ali sniffed back hard, then hocked up the phlegm from the back of his throat and spat it at the baying swarm.

The undead milled around, jostling with each other for position, arms outstretched as if in worship.

Ali cleared his lungs with a sharp cough and pulled the crotch of his underwear to one side. A torrent of thick yellow urine streamed off over the lip of the smashed rooftop. As the urine fell the long way to the ground, the wind caught it and dispersed it into a thin mist. The piss drizzled down onto the upturned faces of the reverent zombies filling the street.

"That why you moan so much, eh?!" Ali shouted out at the mass of undead. "'Cause I still piss on you?!"

THE END

PLAGUE OF
THE DEAD
Z.A. RECHT

DYING TO LIVE
a novel of life among the undead
BY KIM PAFFENROTH

DOWN the
ROAD
ON THE LAST DAY
Bowie Ibarra

ISBN: 978-0-9765559-6-4

Twilight of the Dead

BY TRAVIS ADKINS

Five years after the dead first walked, a small pocket of humanity survives in the fortified town of Eastpointe.

When a stranger arrives claiming to know the location of a cure for the zombie plague, the town will risk everything to possess it.

But does the cure even exist?

And what price must be paid?

"If you love zombies, this is a must-read."
—Nickolas Cook, *Hellnotes*

"Adkins has a knack for raw storytelling that shocks and entertains. Great stuff!"

—Jonathan Maberry, Multiple Bram Stoker Award-winning author of *Zombie CSU* and *Patient Zero*

AFTER TWILIGHT
WALKING WITH THE DEAD

by Travis Adkins

At the start of the apocalypse, a small resort town on the coast of Rhode Island fortified itself to withstand the millions of flesh-eating zombies conquering the world. With its high walls and self-contained power plant, Eastpointe was a safe haven for the lucky few who managed to arrive.

Trained specifically to outmaneuver the undead, Black Berets performed scavenging missions in outlying towns in order to stock Eastpointe with materials vital for long-term survival. But the town leaders took the Black Berets for granted, on a whim sending them out into the cannibalistic wilderness. Most did not survive.

Now the most cunning, most brutal, most efficient Black Beret will return to Eastpointe after narrowly surviving the doomed mission and unleash his anger upon the town in one bloody night of retribution.

After twilight,
when the morning comes and the sun rises,
will anyone be left alive?

ISBN: 978-1934861035

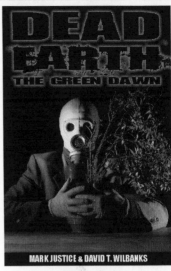

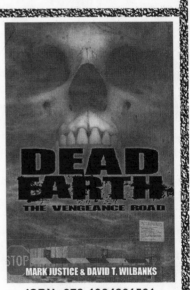

Made in the USA
Lexington, KY
11 April 2012